Your Place or Mine?

A feel-good, laugh-out-loud
romantic comedy

Jo Lyons

Gekko Press

For my sister Philippa
Thank you for shining so brightly in our lives.

TO Elaine

Happy Reading

♡

Jo Lyons

Chapter 1

Kitty McAllister had always dreamed of one day being offered a well-paid job to work with a famous TV presenter in an exotic location; just not one who happened to be so familiar with the entrance to her reproductive system.

She was looking forward to working with her ex-fiancé, Adam Johnson, in the same way she'd look forward to her house being burgled. He had humiliated her, all but jilting her at the altar and yet here she was, about to face him again after three whole years. The thought of having to direct him on set every single day for the next month was far from ideal, and she was on fire with embarrassment as she waited near the check-in desk for the rest of the crew to arrive. Her phone buzzed as she checked her bag once more to make sure all the work visas, car hire and hotel confirmations were where they should be. It was six-thirty in the morning and her friend and business partner, Perrie, was video calling.

'Just checking you're okay,' she said.

Kitty forced a bright smile. 'Oh, you know. It's not every day your executive producer bails on you without notice. I still can't believe Jake has let us down like this.'

'I know,' said Perrie, her voice catching. 'And why did he book his brother for the talent? I mean, Christ Almighty, I'd have preferred anybody but him. I'm so sorry you've been put in this situation, Kitty. I really am. I have no idea what's going on. He's not picking up.'

Kitty nodded sadly. After all their years of working together, it was so unlike their business partner, Jake, to let either of them down.

'What will it be like, seeing Adam again after all this time?' Perrie said, breaking into her thoughts.

Yes. What will it be like? Harrowing? Excruciatingly painful? Humiliating?

'It'll be fine,' lied Kitty. 'I'll just remember to leave my personal baggage at the door. I'll make sure that he knows that this is strictly business.'

'That's such a relief. Unfortunately, we have too much at stake to risk him walking away. For some reason our company finances have not added up this month, so we're having to do this shoot on a super tight budget and the last thing we want to do is antagonise or upset him and risk losing this contract.'

Kitty nodded in agreement. 'Don't worry. I'll try not to remind him of what a terrible person he is. Or how he shattered my heart into a million pieces and never looked back. Not once. Or how he ruined the last three years of my life.'

Perrie, eyes ballooning, gave her an unconvincing smile. 'I know what will cheer you up. This little lady would like to say good morning to her mummy. Wouldn't you? Yes, you would. Who's a little cutie? Who? Yes, you are. Who loves Aunty Perrie? Yes, you do.'

Kitty watched as Perrie, and an excited Alma, her ginger Cockapoo, slobbered over each other. Even though she was less than a year old she had the biggest, saddest-looking eyes Kitty had ever seen. Wise, troubled eyes. Deep wells of sorrow. It had been love at first sight. Kitty felt instantly lifted to see Alma's wet nose sniffing the screen inquisitively.

'That sleep suit looks so cute on her. The blue really makes her eyes pop.'

'Yes, she can wear absolutely anything and look adorable. Unlike her mother. Kitty, what are you wearing? You're going to Spain, not off to dig for clams.' Perrie, eyebrow poised, continued her instructions. 'Don't forget, Kitty. You're in charge. Adam has to do what you tell him. Not the other way round, okay? You've done this a thousand times before. You've won a string of awards. Do not let him unravel you.'

'I know, I know. And I won't, I promise. Even though he is a despicable human being, I'll make sure not to upset him. I'll be nothing but professional.'

'Good, because I've heard he's a total nightmare these days,' said Perrie. 'A real diva on set and never sticks to the script. That's not the worst of it. They say he's got a terrible habit of sacking –'

She could almost hear the screeching of tyres as Perrie stopped talking. With her nerves wound tight to snapping, Kitty, keen to get off topic, ran through a few last-minute instructions on how Alma likes to wind down for bath time, what she likes to watch on TV and the detailed specifics of her bowel movement information.

'And don't forget, she can't sleep without Mr Stinky. Whatever you do, don't try and wash it or she'll never settle.'

Perrie snuggled Alma. 'We are going to have so much fun, aren't we? Yes, we are. Yes, we are. She won't notice if I give it a little wash, it's filthy.'

'Well, don't say I didn't warn you. She likes routine. Everything must be organised and on time. She hates to be taken out of her comfort zone.'

'I wonder where she gets that from.'

'Thanks again for looking after her. I really appreciate it. I'm going to miss you guys.'

The two women exchanged a poignant look.

'Good luck, honey. You've got this!'

Kitty felt calmed to know Perrie had her back.

'And remember, do not let Adam wield his penis anywhere near you or the crew. The last thing we need right now are any added complications.'

Kitty rolled her eyes, *as if that would ever happen.*

'We'll be in constant contact with you every step of the way. Now kisses for Mummy. Bye-bye Mummy,' said Perrie waving Alma's paw before they both disappeared.

While she waited for the crew to arrive, Kitty got to work on the all-important process of stalking Adam on social media and raked through the catalogue of shows he had presented during his fifteen-year career in TV. It wouldn't hurt to go into the shoot battle-ready. Adam Johnson was one of the country's favourite presenters and headed for national treasure status.

Within seconds she was watching videos of him on his Instagram: Adam drinking a collagen protein shake with links to the sponsors and a caption from him saying his skin and nails had never looked so good, Adam eating a breakfast of organic, poached eggs on mashed, sustainably farmed avocado on locally sourced, rye sourdough asking his fans if there was any other way to start the day, Adam on his moped weaving recklessly in and out of London traffic #lateforhairappointment, Adam striking a variety of poses in a collection of tight-fitting shorts, loafers and shirts for a well-known designer brand.

'*What happened to you?*' thought a baffled Kitty, her mind flicking to images of the Adam who would lie in bed with her all day rather than go to glitzy award shows. The Adam who would make time in his hectic schedule to pop in to see her aging parents and take them for lunch while she was away. The Adam who made her sparkle and shine with every touch, every look, every kindness. She blinked away the memories. She had been completely and utterly consumed with love for him and he had promised her that he'd feel the same way for ever.

Seeing him so willing to sell himself out, she was having trouble recognising the man she once knew, but it was crucial she kept his traitorous actions to the forefront of her mind and not allow herself to feel anything but bitterness towards him. She clicked on his story labelled fitness very much hoping to see him making a fool of himself posing at the gym. She was surprised to discover that chasing sunrises was his thing. Very much his thing. Endless videos showed Adam cycling along misty roads and hiking up mountains in search of the perfect sunrise where he'd be silhouetted against the sun in a variety of yoga poses or seemingly caught unawares stretching his lean torso, often with a protruding crotch.

Talk about shoving it in your face, thought Kitty. Adam was well known on TV for his powerful sexual nature. Kitty thought that perhaps Adam was having an early mid-life crisis. To the innocent follower, Adam would appear a solitary soul, a deep thinker and a man in tune with his surroundings, whereas she had been in this business too many years to be fooled. There was no way any of this was real. She had much personal experience of TV presenters and how outrageously unprofessional and false they could be. Especially once you'd been in a loving relationship with them and they'd left you reeling, heart-broken and quite unable to maintain a healthy relationship with anything other than an adorable, sad-eyed puppy.

Her career in television production had spanned ten years, two BAFTA nominations and a string of accolades and she'd made a good living from it, but the mental checklist of things she disliked about this *new* Adam Johnson was growing by the second and sapping her confidence to pull this off.

A noise caused Kitty to spin round.

'Sorry,' yelled a nervous-looking man of around his mid-twenties, running up behind an out-of-control trolley. 'It got away from me. I'm just so excited about all of this. I can't think straight. I'm working with Adam Johnson. Adam frickin Johnson!'

'You must be Wilf, the sound technician.' She took in his easy-on-the-eye youthful looks, his shy, polite manner and decided on the spot to take him under her wing. *It would be good to have a solid ally on the crew,* thought Kitty.

'Don't be starstruck,' she told him. 'Your job will be difficult enough, especially as we have a presenter who loves the sound of his own voice and might never let the house hunters get a word in.'

'I don't think we'll have any problems there, babes. Adam Johnson is the best there is,' interrupted a honeyed voice.

They turned to see Shiraz, the camera operator, push her trolley alongside. 'Which, by the way, is the only reason I'm here. I was supposed to be on another job, but Adam and I have such great chemistry, I couldn't refuse.'

She watched Shiraz lick her lips, which must have been excessively dry despite the thick coating of frosted pink lip gloss, because she was licking them many, many times as her eyes darted about the terminal. Kitty put her at around 35 years old, a few years older than herself.

7

'You've worked with him before?' Wilf asked excitedly.

Shiraz waved an elaborately manicured hand at him. 'Not in actual person, no. But I can always tell if we'll have chemistry. I've worked with many famous TV presenters but there's something about Adam…'

Shiraz seemed to disappear off into a slight trance.

'Yes, what is it about him that's so…'

Apparently, Wilf was joining her. Adam had managed to win them over and he wasn't even here yet.

'Wilf,' said Kitty. 'Meet Shiraz, our camera operator. Looks like you'll both have a lot in common.'

'I'll sit with Adam on the flight to make sure we bond,' Shiraz said, snapping back to face Kitty.

'Yes. He can sit in the middle of us,' Wilf agreed eagerly. 'We'll all bond together.'

Ten minutes later, a disappointed silence fell across the trio. This whole thing was a bloody nightmare, and Kitty was only just beginning to appreciate the extent of it. She grinned weakly at their blank faces as swarms of people jostled around and flight announcements were made. Adam was late and seeing as they only had fifteen minutes before the gate closed, he was cutting it dangerously close. Feelings of panic were beginning to flutter in her stomach.

'He's definitely coming, isn't he?' asked Shiraz.

'Yes. He'll expect air traffic control to wait for him. TV presenters think the show is all about *them*, so he'll want to sweep in late to make sure we all know that he's the most important person in the team. An inflated ego goes with the territory unfortunately.'

She hadn't meant to sound facetious, but nerves were getting the better of her and before she had the chance to finish explaining the nuances of the corporate food chain, she was interrupted.

'You forgot to mention the trumpets and the standing ovation when I board the plane.'

They turned to see Adam Johnson, cappuccino in hand, legs power stance apart, head cocked mockingly to the side. Her ex-fiancé was one of the most ridiculously good-looking men she had ever laid eyes on and seeing him this close up was enough to knock the breath out of her entire body.

'Jake should have warned me that you'd be here,' Adam said in a reproving tone as he wafted nearer to them on a cloud of expensive-smelling cologne.

Kitty hugged the large notebook, over-spilling with sheets of paper, closer to her rib cage. She was dismayed to find that Adam not only had the power to rattle her, even after three years apart, but he was also clearly not pleased to see her.

He pointed to her chest. 'Still obsessing about keeping to schedule, I see?'

All she could do was nod dumbly.

Where was the pithy retort? Where?

9

After a few beats, he swept his gaze from hers to the bustling terminal. Nothing could detract from his enormous sex appeal as he drew everyone's attention like a magnet. It was obvious why the Network had been in favour. He was tall with striking features and piercing dark eyes. He had a rebellious vibe to him with his slightly overgrown, glossy dark hair and an aura that was incredibly charismatic. He looked confident and tanned as though he'd been presenting property shows abroad all his life. He turned his focus to the rest of the film crew who were staring admiringly at him, as he raked a hand casually through his silky locks. The man had obviously turned into a walking cliché since she'd known him last.

Celebrity presenters often had this effect on people and Kitty had no idea why. If anything, celebrity presenters were among the least functioning humans she knew. High on caffeine and self-importance. Arrogant and smarmy. Or maybe that only applied to presenters who had jilted her at the altar. Kitty shook off the negative thoughts, immediately regretting having stirred up such antagonism early doors, but before she could assert herself properly, she was interrupted by Shiraz elbowing her out of the way.

'I'm Shiraz, babes,' she said in a sleek voice, directing her exotic eyeline straight at Adam. 'I'm silky and smooth and sometimes a little fruity.'

Shiraz let out a distinctive, nasally laugh and switched her eyelashes to bat on a slow setting. The high-pitched rattle sounded like a desperate mating call, and yet it seemed to work like a charm. Adam reciprocated her flirting with an appreciative wink.

It was as though Kitty had become invisible. 'We're running very late. Let's do introductions after we –'

'I'll be your camera woman and in charge of ensuring you look devilishly handsome,' Shiraz went on, suggestively swishing her glorious mane of thick, black hair over her shoulder and thrusting out her pointy chest.

'Okay. Fine. Wilf, our sound recordist,' Kitty said, redirecting Adam's attention. 'This is your first job out of apprenticeship, isn't that right? There, we're all introduced. Let's go.'

'Mr Johnson.' Wilf blushed, unable to look him in the eye. 'Mr Johnson, I'm a huge fan of your work. A huge fan. I especially loved the way you handled the Middle Eastern crisis...'

'And who have you been training with?' Adam said, cutting him off.

'I've been over at,' Wilf cleared his throat. 'Sporadic Films?'

'I'm sure we can continue this riveting exchange while we walk,' Kitty said, grabbing her trolley as the last call for their flight was announced.

'Ah yes. Excellent crew over there. Top notch,' nodded Adam, scratching his chin thoughtfully as he made eye contact with Kitty. 'Very respectful.'

Wilf unjustifiably ecstatic at the praise, looked about wide-eyed as if to make sure they had all heard correctly.

'Sorry to interrupt the bromance but Middle East?' Kitty asked astounded. 'When did you cover the conflict in the Middle East?'

Surely, she would have spotted that on his Instagram during her stalkfest?

Before Adam could reply, Wilf puffed out his chest and stepped in to boast.

'Adam split up an Iranian couple who were fighting over whether to add more coriander to a show-stopper main course on *'You're a Lousy Cook'*. It got really out of hand and when her burka caught fire, Adam had to step in and throw a jug of water over the pair of them.'

Kitty bit her lip and lowered her head. The balance of power had been restored.

'It was her niqab.' Adam looked pointedly at Kitty, his cheeks colouring. 'I could have covered the crisis in the Middle East if I'd wanted to. I do other things you know.'

'Like sharing photos of foam art on Instagram,' Kitty said, pointing to his coffee. 'And your many hashtags… oh, and Cow's Pose at sunrise? Now, that's what I'd call a real crisis. Such an obvious cry for help. Now, can we get on this plane, please?'

Kitty feared she might still be slightly drunk from the previous evening.

Adam seemed to grow an extra inch as he loomed over her. 'Seriously? You think you're in any position to judge me? I used to be a senior investigative journalist. Nothing gets past me,' he said, before elaborately sniffing the air around her. 'Is that… is that stale wine?'

This tit for tat was very typical of the Adam she once knew. Why couldn't they have exchanged awkward pleasantries like normal estranged and embittered couples?

'No!' Kitty said in alarm before remembering that Adam could famously sniff out the truth like a snuffle pig.

He arched an eyebrow and leaned towards her, invading her space.

'Well, yes,' she hissed at him quietly before he could make a thing of it. If she hadn't been dreading facing him so much, she would have had camomile tea. Well, no, she wouldn't because she couldn't stand it, but he was very much to blame for her downing a whole bottle of wine last night.

He threw a cold look her way, the atmosphere becoming immediately tense. She caught sight of Shiraz frowning at her.

'You're right,' she said, fighting a sudden hysterical urge to run for her life and never come back. The effect he was having on her made her feel dazed and a little out of control. 'Not Cow's Pose. I meant Downward Dog.'

Everyone looked at Kitty while she took a moment to reflect on what she'd said and the tone in which she'd said it.

Oh my god. I can't do this, she panicked. She could feel herself unravelling. She was going to ruin everything. One look at Adam confirmed her suspicions.

'Tell Jake this isn't going to work for me. I quit,' Adam shrilled unattractively, his face puce.

Shitting hell.

Chapter 2

Everyone seemed to freeze. She had always been able to bring the worst out in him and quickly figured that he was not accustomed to a few home truths about his ridiculous and juvenile behaviour online. He was a man in his mid-thirties not some Gen Z fresh from university with a degree in teeth whitening and turning heads.

Snapping to attention, she slapped on her game face. She had promised Perrie that she would make Adam feel every bit the star, and here she was falling out with him before they even got to the check-in desk.

She glanced at an open-mouthed Shiraz clutching the trolley piled high with cases and camera equipment. They had less than five minutes to check in.

'Adam, you're so hilarious. Such a kidder,' she honked, encouraging Wilf and Shiraz to do the same. Honk, honk, honk. They looked devastated. Honk, honk, honk. 'Jake will find this so funny.'

Adam crinkled his eyes, assessing the situation. Her heart was thumping triple time as he took forever to reply.

Please, please ignore everything I've just said. Please.

'Fine,' said Adam tightly. 'I'll do it.'

Kitty let out a huge sigh of relief.

'Why didn't Jake mention you'd be part of the crew?' Adam asked sharply, looking about. 'Can't you bear to be parted from each other?' He screwed his eyes at Kitty. 'Where is he?'

Caught off guard, Kitty stopped to consider her reply. She had no idea what to say. Jake had well and truly dropped her and Perrie in it, and she was yet to find out why. But one thing she knew for certain was that Adam would only have agreed to this job on the condition that his brother Jake was directing the shoot.

'Still keeping secrets, I see,' Adam said in a disappointed tone. 'Some things never change. He assured me he'd be here.'

Secrets? Kitty had no idea what he could mean.

'Well, yes. He's erm... well, he's what you would call...' Kitty consulted her clipboard, as though the answer would be hidden somewhere in the small print. '... not coming.'

Adam looked thunderous.

'But he'll follow us in a few days,' she lied quickly. 'He'll meet us in Malaga.'

Adam cocked his head to the side as he held her gaze. 'Really?'

No, not really. The opposite of really. Kitty nodded vaguely.

'I'm surprised he trusts you,' Adam said, ignoring the bored huffing of Shiraz.

'Of course he trusts me,' Kitty shot back. She might have known Adam would try to undermine her authority from the off. 'I've

15

directed award-winning shoots all over the world. Now, follow me everyone. We're very late.'

'My belongings have already been fast-tracked. I'm in First,' he said with a shrug designed to give the impression that somehow this was not his idea and that he'd much rather be travelling with the crew in cattle-class.

Normally this would have incensed Kitty, seeing as it was her budget he was blowing, but Jake must have authorised it. And if she was to gain the allegiance of Shiraz and Wilf, then she'd have to have Adam on side first. Just like in military combat, you needed to take out the leader and the opposition would crumble. She would recover from this disastrous start and win him over.

'Of course you are. How very lovely for you, Adam. I'm thrilled. Absolutely thrilled. Such a shame the private jet wasn't available.'

Adam didn't appear to be falling for her charms. On route, Kitty found out that not only had Adam already checked in online, but there was a champagne and truffle-infused scrambled egg breakfast waiting for him in the Highflyers Business Class lounge. She watched as he strolled away towards the fast-track security baggage area where a few travellers mobbed him for selfies and autographs. Security treated him like royalty and the women officers elbowed each other out of the way to be the one to frisk him down.

Kitty took in the forlorn expressions of Wilf and Shiraz. They were destined to have their hearts broken by Adam. The least she could do was soften the blow.

'Come on you two. I'll treat you to breakfast.'

Once they'd sat down, Kitty and Wilf were interrupted every few minutes by Shiraz cooing over photos and thrusting her phone into their faces.

'Look what Adam's posted. He's on his second champagne cocktail. That breakfast is so aspirational. He's right. There's no other way to start the day.' Shiraz glanced quizzically up from her swiping. 'What's a frond of samphire? He's saying it's a succulent halophyte.'

'It simply means,' said Kitty, taking the phone from Shiraz and laying it face down on the table, 'that he's an arrogant prick who likes to show off and make everyone feel inferior.' When Shiraz's face fell a thousand feet, she tried to backtrack. 'Sorry, I didn't mean that. It's a salty, grassy, weed type of thing.'

Eaten by pricks.

Kitty took a moment to have a word with herself. When it came to Adam, she simply could not bring herself to say one kind thing. Perrie was right, if she couldn't manage the toxic levels of bitterness swooshing through her veins, she would put the whole trip in jeopardy.

'Let's go over the schedule for arrivals. Wilf, you and I will drive a car each and take one passenger and half the kit between us.'

'I should travel with Adam,' Shiraz said in a determined tone. 'For professional purposes.'

Kitty had seen this many times before. She noted the faraway look in Shiraz's eyes. The fantasy of her and Adam travelling together from the airport, sharing private jokes in the back seat, giggling over a shared interest in memes of cute kittens and a proposal of marriage before they'd even arrived at the hotel. Sparkles were coming out of her ears. Kitty would have to burst this bubble now before things got out of hand, otherwise she could foresee nothing but disaster ahead.

'Sorry, Shiraz. You travel with me. Wilf you take Adam.'

Wilf's face lit up like a Christmas tree. 'Sure, yeah. Cool. Whatever. Cool. Great. Sure.'

Shitting hell, thought Kitty. *Bad enough having one member of the crew with a crush, how would she manage two of them?*

Shiraz got up from the table. 'I'm off to find a kale smoothie. Adam says it's the best thing to drink before you travel. It hydrates the skin and replaces lost acolytes.'

I'll bet it does.

'It's electrolytes,' said Kitty helpfully to a retreating Shiraz who turned to give her a sulky look before stomping off.

'Wait for me!' yelled Wilf galloping after her.

Kitty stared after them. Had she just alienated the crew before they'd even taken off?

Kitty worked hard during the flight to get Shiraz back on side and ended up promising her a membership pass for the spa and beauty salon in their hotel. Against her better judgement, Kitty would have to try to blag one for free as Perrie would never authorise that type of spending.

'It was so kind of Adam to send that bottle of fizz through to us,' gushed a squiffy Shiraz, ignoring Kitty's warnings that just because they were on a plane, units of alcohol still counted. And because they were designated drivers, Adam's generosity had resulted in a downcast Wilf who'd spent the flight watching Shiraz prance up and down the aisle, as cabin crew thwarted her every attempt to sneak into First Class.

On landing, due to Shiraz being unable to help them in any meaningful way, because she had dropped and cracked the first piece of kit she'd tried to handle and had dissolved into peals of laughter, Kitty and Wilf loaded up the cars. Kitty instructed Shiraz to wait in one of the hire cars and check on Adam's socials to see his whereabouts.

'He's still doing autographs with the passengers and signing their luggage,' Shiraz called from inside of the car. 'Don't worry, I've love heart emojied all of his posts.'

'Can you DM him please and tell him to hurry up?' Kitty called back as she lugged the last piece of kit over to the car and heaved it up onto the roof rack. 'We have a very tight schedule to stick to.'

'I'd hate to put us behind schedule. Whatever would we do?' Adam said, breaking unexpectedly into a smile. He strolled towards her. 'It's just like old times, isn't it? You bossing me about. Me pretending to listen. Now, let me put these magnificent muscles to use.'

He rolled up his sleeves to reveal toned, muscular forearms. Kitty, immediately suspicious, pretended not to notice. While it was important that she keep him onside, it was much more important that he knew exactly who was boss.

'Other car,' she said, watching him sling several expensive suitcases into the boot. 'You're in with Wilf.'

It was as though he hadn't heard her. He slammed the boot shut, jumped into the driver's seat and started up the engine.

'Hop in,' he said to Kitty. 'I'll drive. I know the way. I've been here a million times.' He shouted over to Wilf. 'Don't be nervous. Just watch which way you go round the roundabouts but stay close to me, so we don't lose you. Okay, buddy?'

Wilf nodded enthusiastically. Kitty was not loving the way Adam had suddenly taken charge nor had she thought to check whether Wilf had driven abroad before. She had assumed he'd be okay with it. She'd also assumed that Adam would be blotto what with all the free bubbly.

'You've been drinking,' Kitty accused, opening the driver's door. 'You're better off going with Wilf.' Her nerves were in shreds at the thought of having to sit next to him.

'I have not,' he said indignantly before breaking into a wide grin. 'Ah... you've been following me on Instagram.'

Kitty felt her cheeks burn.

'Well don't believe everything you see or hear,' he said, his voice dripping with sarcasm. 'You've always been so judgemental.'

Kitty squirmed.

She had been swept up in the social media and believed every word. Shame on her. Satisfied that he was being genuine, she raced round to the passenger side and got in, feeling an unexpected sense of relief. Maybe real-life Adam was actually a much better version than social media Adam. And maybe this whole production was not going to be the shitemare she was anticipating.

Adam waved at Wilf, signalling that he was about to set off and Kitty could see an unimpressed-looking Shiraz scowling beside him in the passenger seat. She'd have to deal with that later.

'Ready?' Adam asked.

Kitty nodded and relaxed into her seat. At least she would be able to have a mature and sensible conversation with him about how they would conceivably work together for the next five weeks, if only to avoid spats like the one at the airport where she says something harmless, and he melodramatically threatens to quit and ruin her professional reputation.

'It'll give us the chance to go over the –'

'RACE YOU TO THE HOTEL, ADAM!' bellowed an excited Wilf, revving his engine. 'LAST ONE BACK GETS THE ROUND IN!'

Kitty threw Adam a horrified glance. Men could be so juvenile. She shook her head. 'Do not under any circumstances indulge him.'

He gave her a look that made her feel instantly silly for even thinking it, but no sooner had she clicked her seat belt in, her head was thrown sharply back against the headrest as they jolted off at breakneck speed, tyres squealing, engine growling loudly. The roaring sound of music filled the car, drowning out her shrieks as Adam, laughing maniacally, hurtled recklessly through the traffic.

In order to prevent a panic attack *and* a simultaneous murder taking place, she gripped tightly on to the seatbelt and imagined it was his throat.

I am not bitter, she chanted silently as Adam wove in and out, overtaking cars as though he was defending his Grand Prix title. *I do not hate this childish, imbecilic wanker sitting beside me. I will rise above it. I will be professional.*

It was some moments before the trepidation subsided and Kitty was able to form enough consecutive thoughts into a basic plan of action, as the glorious scenery whizzed past. They had simply gotten off on the wrong foot. Successful leadership was, after all, a state of mind.

Simply a state of mind.

After arguing bitterly over every twist and turn in the road as to which was the best way to get to the hotel, Kitty was mentally frazzled. She would be the first person to admit that she was a terrible backseat driver and Adam had freely admitted that, these days, he was renowned for his poor listening skills. She had preferred to rely on the Satnav whereas Adam had pinned his hopes on remembering the way, even though twenty minutes into the journey he'd suddenly realised it was in fact a hotel of the same name in Greece that he had been thinking of.

'Greece! Can you believe it?' Adam chuckled, throwing her a side-eye. 'Greece!'

Kitty *could* believe it. Kitty *could* believe it because underneath that drop-dead gorgeous exterior, Adam was a prick. After they had driven in awkward silence, the moment Kitty had been dreading finally arrived. They had not even reached the hotel, and everything was already going to shit.

'I don't see why we have to discuss this now,' said Kitty.

'Because it's much easier if I don't look at you,' Adam was explaining, keeping his eyes trained on the road ahead. 'We need to clear the air before we arrive. It's about how we split up. You know, the wedding and all that?'

As if I would've forgotten? thought Kitty appalled. 'I think it's best if we don't rake up old...'

'Please, Kitty. I need this.'

She braced herself for his apology, hopeful for a short but harrowing narrative of self-loathing and shame. She'd waited long enough over the years, yet part of her was dreading it.

Oh God. This is really happening. Kitty suddenly realised that she needed it too. She needed clarity. She had never understood why he had jilted her a week before the wedding, and it had eaten away at her soul ever since.

After some moments, Adam cleared his throat and spoke in a quiet voice, sounding slightly robotic as though he'd rehearsed it many times before. 'The reason I had to let you go was because you would never have walked away otherwise. I had to be selfless and do what was best for you. So I gave you wings, to fly.'

It took a while for the words to percolate. Kitty slapped her notebook shut. She'd waited years to hear him explain himself properly. And now, even though she'd clearly asked him not to, he was coming out with this bollocks from the safe confines of the driving seat where she couldn't lean across to poke him sharply in both eyes. She was infuriated by him.

'Wings so that I could fly? WINGS? You sound like Bette Midler advertising sanitary towels.'

'What I mean is that I did it for you. You wanted out. I gave you an out and you took it. Without a backward glance I might add.'

Kitty could barely breathe she was so livid. 'How dare you! How dare you blame *me* for *you* dumping me a week before our wedding!' Years of pent-up anger exploded out of her system and vibrated around the car. 'DESPITE YOU BEING SUCH AN ARROGANT, SELF-AGGRANDIZING DICKHEAD, I WANTED TO BE YOUR WIFE!'

Kitty stopped ranting. She was utterly furious with him. Her lungs were billowing in her chest like bagpipes. She took in noisy gulps of air. Tears were spilling down her cheeks. She'd spent years forcing herself not to cry over him in an effort to move on. It had taken everything she'd had to get over the devastation and now here he was, about to undo years of hard work.

Wings! Fucking wings!!

Kitty stared back at him as she waited for the mother of all apologies and held her breath.

Adam took his eyes briefly from the road. He seemed to be weighing up her response. 'It was Westlife. The thing about wings. Not Bette Midler.'

They eventually arrived, tired, hoarse and quite sick to death of each other. They were still arguing at the hotel reception when Wilf, who they'd managed to lose within minutes of setting off, sauntered over to them.

'Where have you been? We got here an hour ago,' he said good-naturedly.

Kitty glared pointedly at Adam and bit her tongue. There was little point explaining to Wilf that his hero was in fact an illiterate moron with zero spatial awareness or sense of decency. Zero.

Adam stared coolly back. 'Anyway, if you can unload your stuff Kitty, I'll take the car with me over to The Plaza. They've booked me the presidential suite.'

'Of course *they* have.' Kitty wasn't about to be fooled. By 'they' Adam obviously meant 'himself'. Celebrity TV presenters often talked as though a third party were pulling all the strings. They were exhausting, the lot of them.

Typically, the crew would go on a few days ahead of the house hunters and would all stay in the same hotel but for reasons she was pretty sure she knew the answer to, Adam was five-starring it all the way while the crew stayed in smaller, cheaper hotels. Kitty would bet her life that he was the recipient of freebies in exchange for posting on social media. All terribly legal, but Kitty felt went against creating a camaraderie among the crew. Kitty suspected this shoot was going to be fraught with jealousy if they had to watch Adam enjoy all the trappings of celebrity while the others went without.

'What is that supposed to mean?'

'Nothing. Nothing,' Kitty backtracked. This was exactly one of those moments for which honesty was not the best policy, and yet she couldn't seem to stop herself. 'I just find it uncomfortable that's all. Never mind. Forget it.'

'What? What do you find uncomfortable?'

'Nothing. Forget it.'

It was like a red rag to a bull. He was so predictable. *Stop winding him up,* Kitty told herself.

'Forget what for fuck's sake?'

Please just zip it.

'All the freebie stuff you seem to blag in return for favours. It just leaves me... cold, I guess.'

Gah! There, she'd said it. Adam looked furiously at her, speechless for once. She let out an arduous sigh and plodded wearily back to the car before they could get into yet another heated exchange. A clip-clopping sound distracted her.

Kitty glanced towards reception to see Shiraz wearing a floaty chiffon kaftan hanging wide open to reveal Spain's tiniest bikini.

Three postage stamps would have been more effective. She would not have looked out of place in a 1979 Miss World competition. She was twirling her hair around her finger and biting her bottom lip. She peered at the two men over the top of her super-sized sunglasses. With her olive skin glistening with oil, she looked like she'd been there all week rather than just a couple of hours. Her sumptuous boobs were straining against the fabric like a dam about to burst free at any second. Kitty watched Wilf and Adam, their eyes out on stalks as they tried to politely train them to a spot high above her head.

Shiraz launched into telling Adam all about their journey to the hotel and their bitter disappointment at what poor facilities it had to offer.

'Kitty promised me she'd blag me a free spa pass,' Shiraz was saying with pleading eyes to Adam. 'But there's not even a pool here never mind a beauty salon. The place is a complete dump.'

'Oh, she did, did she?' said Adam latching dubiously onto this piece of information. He slowly turned his dark, accusing glare to Kitty. 'Kitty promised to BLAG you a FREEBIE? Well, isn't that just very HYPOCRITICAL of her?'

Kitty took in his gorgeous face, now livid, and tried to change the subject. 'One, this hotel is not *that* much of a dump, Shiraz, and two, why are you in a bikini anyway? We only have time to freshen up and then we need to head straight out after the production meeting. As per the schedule, if any of you had bothered to look at it.'

Making a point of ignoring her, Adam addressed Wilf and Shiraz. 'By the way, you can come over to my hotel and use the facilities any time you want. It's got a hot tub *and* a pool. I'd invite you Kitty, but I know how you despise anything BLAGGED FOR FREE!'

Kitty cringed as Adam shot her a disappointed look before marching over to the car to yank the door open with unnecessary force.

Once he'd left in an angry cloud of dust, most of which covered her from top to toe, tyres squealing once again, Kitty turned to ask Wilf and Shiraz for a hand carrying the heavy kit bags to her room. She had been dismayed to discover it was on the second floor and the hotel, in her bid to save money, was so cheap it didn't have a lift. Kitty's eyes darted around the reception area.

'Where did they go?' she asked the tiny receptionist who shrugged back in answer. Kitty was disheartened to see that physically, the receptionist would not be up to carrying anything more substantial than a small bar of soap even if, judging by the scowl on her face, she could get over the fact that Shiraz and Wilf had basically called her hotel a shithole right to her face.

Their scheduled arrival into Spain for the first happy day of filming was so far, not going according to plan. It took Kitty just over an hour to lug all of the bags and suitcases up to her room which was depressingly tiny and without a bath. It simply had a showerhead overhanging the toilet in a cupboard masquerading as an ensuite. She sat down on the bed and flopped back exhausted. Every bone in her body screamed at her. At that moment, she could have happily drifted into a deep and satisfying sleep, not caring in the slightest that she was still wearing her dirty travel clothes, her hair was half-tangled into what had started out as a casual bun but now looked like a crow's nest and her filthy, make-up free face looked like she'd just emerged from a collapsed office block. She couldn't move. She'd have to lie there for ten minutes until she regained enough strength to haul herself into the shower. She wiped the hair from her face and the sweat from her brow and closed her sore eyes, just as her phone rang.

'Kitty, where are you?' asked an annoyed sounding Shiraz. 'We're all here in reception waiting for the production meeting. AS PER THE SCHEDULE!'

Chapter 3

Kitty raced down the stairs lugging as many bags as she could carry. Her lungs could happily explode through her chest before she'd ever be accused of being late for their first official afternoon of filming. Otherwise, the crew would never take the schedule or her authority seriously.

'Kitty, my god, what happened?' Wilf gasped.

'Were you run over by a passing coal truck, perhaps?' asked Shiraz cattily.

Kitty's hands flew to her hair but as she frantically tried to tie some of it into a bun, the elastic band snapped, and it tumbled down her back. She wiped at her cheeks aware that Adam was watching her every move. He was smelling fresh from a scented bath, his hair damp, his clothes pristine and his face cleanly shaven. He had her so flustered, she felt a complete mess.

'Okay, down to business,' she said efficiently, pointing to a table in the hotel's deserted canteen area. They followed her over and sat down. 'The Network has commissioned us to produce four one-hour episodes for the next series of *Your Place or Mine?*. Couples are shown five properties and they each pick a favourite and then argue over which one to buy.'

Every single second felt like an eternity but by some miracle, she was managing to get through the whole production meeting without making direct eye contact with Adam. Everything about him was compelling, from the careful and speculative way he was keeping his eyes trained on her face throughout her entire presentation, to the arrogant, masculine way that he lounged comfortably opposite at the head of the table.

Kitty's emotions were all over the place. She should hate this man and yet... it had been so long since Kitty had felt the heady sensation of sexual attraction, that it was disconcerting to experience it while also explaining EU filming regulations. And even more distressing to discover that her ex-fiancé still had the power to set her pulse racing, even after all that he'd put her through. She risked a quick glance towards him and immediately regretted it. His eyes swirled dangerously with the promise of trouble.

Kitty swallowed, quickly turning her attention back to her notebook. 'The Network want to see glorious shots of the scenery, well-lit close-ups of the houses, the balconies with sea views, the pools and most importantly, aspirational but achievable living. We want to give our viewers hope.'

'But ultimately,' said Adam, cocking his head to the side, 'viewers want to see couples rowing on TV. Having tantrums, falling out, making up, sobbing on my shoulder.' For someone so utterly wide of the mark, Adam spoke with such confidence it was unnerving. 'We want them to take us on an emotional rollercoaster, we want to see grown adults bickering like children, showing us the worst of humanity, that kind of thing.'

Kitty rolled her eyes at his matter-of-fact attitude. To her ears Adam clearly had no idea about ethical programming. She looked forward to reminding him that uplifting, honest programming was their mantra, not gratuitous, vacant reality TV made only for the purpose of increasing viewing figures and pay cheques.

'Yes, spot on Adam. I agree completely,' Shiraz acknowledged with an air of finality, refusing to meet Kitty's critical stare. 'That's what I'd want to see.'

Wilf appeared to be lapping it up too. Kitty knew that if you constantly surrounded yourself with 'yes men' then this runaway degree of self-importance is exactly the sort of thing that might happen.

She cleared her throat noisily in warning, making a point to look each of them in the eye.

'No, not even close. We'll make *uplifting* and *honest* episodes, on time and in budget. I'll deal with any unexpected issues, liaise with the *inmobiliers* about the properties and generally keep you all to a tight schedule.'

Kitty felt pleased that she sounded more assertive than she looked and had used the one and only slightly impressive Spanish word she knew to make her sound on top of things. She also wondered when Jake would arrive to relieve her of duty. She wasn't sure how much more she could take of being in Adam's company. Try as she might, she was beginning to unravel.

'We'll film the lake and surrounding area for the montage this morning,' she instructed, getting up. Momentarily blinded by the brightness outside, Kitty pointed at the cars. The air was stifling as she clambered inside, the steering wheel too hot to touch. Tucking her wild hair behind her ear, the scorching heat caused a rivulet of sweat to trickle down her neck. At that moment, Kitty would have sold her first born for a cold shower.

She was relieved to hear Adam finally agreeing to travel with Shiraz who simply would not take no for an answer.

'No, Shiraz. It's my turn I think you'll find,' said Wilf sounding very put out as he clambered in with them. 'You sat next to him at the meeting.'

Kitty hoped that the bright, turquoise green of Lake Viñuela with the sun dancing around on its surface, the breath-taking beauty of the surrounding mountains and the captivating smell of fresh pine would help ease them into being friendly with one another. But she was wrong. The rivalry between Shiraz and Wilf seemed to have already taken something of a toll on Adam because he got out of the car and gave Kitty a weary look, as though she was somehow very much to blame.

'Come with me everyone,' she yelled, ignoring him. Celebrity presenters were notoriously paranoid and far too easy to upset. Especially this one. 'Wilf grab some mobile kit please. Shiraz, I think we'll go telephoto and wide-angled lens. Adam if you could grab the tripod, cables and leads that would be great, thanks.'

Within minutes, loaded up with bags, they were hiking through a forest towards a clearing that Kitty was familiar with. She ignored the moaning from the other three and, just as Shiraz declared that she was thinking of ringing herself an ambulance if Kitty made her walk one more step in her Gucci wedges, they reached the clearing and let out a collective gasp. The sight before them had been worth the hike. Shots like these came along once in a lifetime. The sun, the lake, the mountains, the light created a perfect storm of conditions.

Shiraz said in a choked voice, 'Get the tripod set up. The tripod, now! This is it, Kitty. I'll never get a better shot. This is the type of footage that wins awards.'

There was a mad scramble to set up the kit and after an hour they had everything they needed in the can. Kitty plonked herself down on the ground while Shiraz, Wilf and Adam went down to the lake edge to film some shots for his Instagram #livelaughlove #watersportstravelinsurancecover. Snippets of conversation about conceptual political juxtapose and Adam's plans to write an accompanying book trilogy floated towards her as she took a moment to plan the rest of the day's shots. She flicked through the list of properties plotting them out on her map, realising they could make up for lost time if they filmed the one that was nearby.

Kitty walked down to the water's edge.

'Hey guys.' She waved as she made her way down a little embankment towards them. All three turned to her in alarm. She just had time to hear Adam shout for her to stop when, too late, she found herself sliding down a steep ravine. Kitty flailed her arms about but couldn't prevent herself tripping on a thick tree root jutting from the ground, before being hurled straight into the lake. The shock caused Kitty to gulp in several mouthfuls of water before she felt herself being hoisted up. Gasping for breath, she took in Adam's concerned eyes an inch from her own.

He did not seem in a hurry to let her go.

He had a strong, firm grip on her. Their bodies tight up against one another. Kitty's ample chest was squashed against his. She felt her cleavage practically touching her chin. As if reading her thoughts, Adam instinctively tore his gaze from her eyes down to her chest which, from this angle, had the look of a baby's bum. He dragged his dark eyes back towards hers with some effort. It was a look that had disarmed her many times before. Before he'd jilted her at the altar. She felt unnerved at the effect the heat of his touch was having on her traitorous body.

'We need to talk.'

Kitty was momentarily lost for words as old feelings suddenly began to stir, causing confusion and panic but he was right, they did need to talk.

Shiraz darted over followed by Wilf scrambling behind. 'You're such a hero,' she gushed, prising him away. 'Now, let's get you out of those wet things, babes.' Shiraz was fussing, her hands splayed ready to strip him down.

Adam threw his head back and laughed.

From what Kitty could see, apart from two damp boob-shaped patches, Adam was still in pristine condition.

Perrie's warning pinged into Kitty's brain. She would have to make sure no hanky panky went on between Adam and Shiraz. She wouldn't trust either of them as far as she could throw them. It would all end in disaster anyway and from experience, Kitty knew that there was nothing worse than a camerawoman scorned. If Adam used her for a quick, meaningless bonk then Shiraz would crucify him with terrible lighting to make him seem old, bleary-eyed and double chinned.

Kitty had seen spats like this before. Ditto Wilf, although, she doubted he would have it in him. He'd need a few more years in the industry to become jaded like Shiraz. Kitty had a nose for hard people, and she sensed that about Shiraz immediately. She had a reputation for being a superb camera operator but after some due diligence, Kitty had discovered that, not unlike herself, she had a past littered with exes in almost every video production house she'd freelanced at.

'Back to the cars,' said Kitty, still reeling from the encounter. 'One more property before lunch. We should stick to the schedule.'

'Fine but I'm not doing carbs or gluten today. I'm Keto Paleo. And it's a raw food day for me so it'll have to be a salad box or an organic juice,' insisted Shiraz, looking to Adam for approval.

'And I need to eat soon, in my optimum nutrition window. Isn't that right, Adam?' Wilf was nodding like an excitable puppy.

Christ Almighty.

Kitty would rather stay wet and risk chafing than give either of them an opportunity to seduce Adam. She peeled clumps of algae from her shoulder. 'Shiraz, you come with me.'

'Adam can't eat this!' Shiraz gasped, horrified as the late lunch Kitty had pre-ordered was plonked down. 'Kitty, what were you thinking? Everyone knows he's on the 5:2 diet. Today's his soup and salad leaves, no-carb day. Isn't that right, Adam?'

'Yes, it is,' Wilf replied on Adam's behalf.

Jesus wept, thought Kitty. It seemed as though she could do nothing right. She gave Adam an exasperated look. What sort of prima donna had he become over the last few years?

At least Wilf and Shiraz now seemed to be on better speaking terms. Pity it was because they were uniting against her. Kitty outlined the new schedule and handed them each a paper copy along with the brief that she'd been given about the new house hunters. They all took a moment to stare at the names of the house hunters arriving imminently.

Shiraz's eyes darted over the sheet. 'They're Welsh,' she groaned. 'They'll drive a hard bargain and will demand top notch voos.'

'Voos?' Wilf asked.

'That's how the Welsh say views, isn't it, Kitty? VOOS. AMAAAZING VOOS is wah' they'll be aff-er.'

Everybody laughed at Shiraz's perfect attempt at the Welsh accent. Kitty was pleased to see Adam was showing signs of thawing.

'As a serious investigative journalist,' Adam said, waving his copy of the schedule at Kitty. 'I've faced many a hostile and difficult situation.' He paused for effect. 'I don't just front TV shows about people clearing out their sheds or fighting over how long to leave chicken breasts to marinate. I'm more than capable of dealing with the Welsh.'

Kitty gave him a sheepish look, making it obvious that she deeply regretted all the upset of earlier. He held eye contact with her before furrowing his brow in concentration as he glanced over the schedule. At least she seemed to be getting him back on side.

'You are kidding me,' Adam said, a few seconds later. He tapped at his notes with the back of his hand. 'How am I supposed to be taken seriously if I have to contend with this sort of thing?'

For once, Kitty felt for him. The Welsh accent was difficult enough to deal with but when they turned up with names like these, well it was anyone's guess how to pronounce them. Adam was understandably apprehensive.

'I think it's probably pronounced with a gargling sound,' Shiraz said.

'I reckon,' Wilf said, Googling it. 'I reckon you could call him Eef-ee-on-wee for short.'

'I'm not calling him that,' said Adam defiantly.

'It's very much part of a TV presenter's job description,' said Kitty. 'Talking to people and using their names.'

'I don't need you to remind me of how to do my job. I am the consummate professional, in *my* humble opinion at least. I just wish people would be reasonable when it comes to naming their children. I mean the wife's called Dee-wyn-wen-gog for fuck's sake. DEE-WYN-WEN-GOG!'

Kitty decided not to mention that in addition to the two days of gruelling tongue-twisters, he'd soon be on camera hurtling through the cobbled lanes of Malaga on a Segway wearing an unflattering helmet, elbow protectors and knee pads, screaming for people to get out of the way. Kitty glanced at him.

One step forward, two steps back.

'Are you doing this on purpose?' Adam asked Kitty, whose cheeks were aching from all the stiff-upper-lip smiling she was doing. 'Isn't this the sort of thing you iron out before the shoot?'

Kitty gulped, recalling Perrie's earlier warnings about Adam's penchant for persuading the Network to sack programme managers for far less.

'Excuse me,' said Adam abruptly, getting up from the table as his phone pinged in rapid succession. 'Back in a minute.'

Once she'd watched him disappear round the corner, Kitty turned to Shiraz and Wilf. It was time for Kitty to deflect attention away from her poor leadership skills.

'Now listen to me you two. This fighting over Adam's attention is getting way out of hand. You're clearly making him feel uncomfortable.'

They both glared at her wide-eyed.

'Us?' they said in unison.

Kitty nodded. Surely, it was plain to see?

39

'If anyone is making Adam uncomfortable Kitty, it is you!' accused Shiraz.

'Yes,' agreed Wilf. 'You've obviously still got a thing for him.'

Kitty looked at his sweet face. She'd clearly misjudged him the mean, two-faced fucker. 'There is nothing...' she said, trying to sound patient, '... *nothing* going on between me and Adam. Nothing at all. He means nothing to me.'

Shiraz and Wilf stared at her blankly.

Kitty reflected on the long and satisfyingly hot-blooded relationship they'd shared in the past. She was going to have to dig deep if she was ever to be convincing. 'I find him so... so deeply unattractive. Almost asexual in fact.' Kitty could hear the unconvincing tone in her voice.

'Yeah, right,' tutted Shiraz.

'The lady doth protest too much methinks,' agreed Wilf with an air of accusation.

Kitty knew she sounded ridiculous. Adam had clearly benefitted from thousands of years' worth of human evolution, but it seemed that once she'd opened this floodgate, it was not that easy to stem the tide. After all, what was so difficult about accepting that two ex-lovers, who were once very passionate, off the charts in the sexual athletics department Kitty recalled, and borderline obsessive about each other, could not conceivably work together as professional and platonic colleagues?

'Okay then. He might be one of the world's most handsome men, but underneath that magnificent exterior he's a humourless, self-righteous, nit-picking bore. Happy now?'

With her voice rising unattractively, she'd had quite enough of their childish bickering and narrow-mindedness. Perhaps now, she'd win them back on side.

'Now can we get past this petty jealousy and get on with our jobs please?'

'Ahem.' Adam was standing frowning furiously at her.

Cocking hell, thought Kitty feeling her blood pressure about to explode as she dared to meet Adam's ice-cold glare.

Chapter 4

Ten minutes later, Kitty was having to listen to Shiraz bleat on about the wonderful facilities on offer at Adam's luxurious hotel as she packed the car up. 'It really isn't fair, Kitty. How does he end up in the lap of luxury and we have to suffer in a cheap hostel that's no better than a crack den?'

'Okay, that's us ready to go,' said Kitty, ignoring the bait. Shiraz huffed sulkily, her sky-high wedges and a pair of skin-tight pleather jeggings making the simple act of getting into the car look like scaling a mountain without a rope. They'd only been driving for two minutes when Shiraz popped the question.

'What happened between you and Adam? You clearly have a messy history. What's the story there?'

Kitty glared at her.

'Shiraz,' she said, turning back to concentrate on the road ahead. 'Just because Adam and I have history does not mean that either of us want to talk about it. It's nobody's business but ours, okay? Adam and I have a professional, working relationship. Nothing more.'

Shiraz tutted. 'Well, seeing as you are supposed to be in charge, I should hope not.'

Kitty, not wanting to dignify this with a response, put all thoughts of Adam, the way he'd heroically pulled her from the water and the look he'd given her, firmly out of her mind. She needed to concentrate on the task at hand. The whole filming mission depended on it. She must not let any old feelings get in the way of that.

By the time they reached their destination Shiraz had made sure that Kitty understood something would *definitely* happen between her and Adam, but that she was *definitely* not in a position to say what exactly.

'I just think you should respect those boundaries and not let your own personal baggage with Adam interfere with whatever my new baggage with him might become, okay?' Shiraz said, picking at some imaginary fluff on her leg.

Once they arrived at the property, a remote hide-away, Kitty seemed to be on the receiving end of everyone's complaints.

'Nobody in their right mind would want to live in a dilapidated money-pit like this,' remarked Adam.

'You'd be surprised,' said Kitty. 'Some people love a 'much sought-after, tranquil, doer-upper' as we'll be calling it on air.'

'Adam's right. There's nothing around for miles. They could be here lying slaughtered in their beds, and no one would find them for years,' added Shiraz, coming up from the basement.

'Adam, mate, I don't know how you're going to put a positive spin on this place. It's giving me the creeps already,' chipped in Wilf.

'And there's no way I'm filming in the dungeon before you ask. It's haunted. I've just seen two ghosts down there.'

'Shiraz, it's a bijou basement ripe for conversion,' said Kitty brightly. 'For when the grandkids come to stay.'

'Why do the Spanish feel the need to leave piles of washing and old bikes in every room when the property is being filmed for international TV?' Adam said pointing to a pair of dirty pants lying on the floor. He looked around with a tragic expression. 'This is a disaster. A complete bloody shambles. Why does this have to be one of the properties?'

But even as Kitty was convincing them that the property was not as ominous as they all seemed to think, an eerie feeling crept over her. This was what happened when corners were cut, and budgets were squeezed. She would pick this up with Perrie on their next call. Looking at their miserable faces, she couldn't help but feel that her influence as leader was already on the wane, especially when at that moment, thunder clapped outside, and the heavens opened. They all turned to Kitty as though this was her fault.

'Great, now we're stuck here until it stops,' Shiraz said pouting. 'There's no way Adam will want to ruin his hair in this downpour, will you, babes?'

Kitty saw Adam hide his annoyance. She happened to know that if there was one thing other than references to his being lower in the TV ratings than her ex-boyfriend Maddison O'Reilly, Adam HATED being called 'babes'. A petty spark of joy ignited inside her.

'Okay team. Let's film the inside and use the reflectors and every working lightbulb in the place to bounce the light. We'll do sound-bites as soon as the rain eases off. Adam, can you read from the scripts for each room as we film, please?'

Kitty bossed them all into action to take their mind off the fact that she'd driven them to a cockroach-infested hellhole in the middle of nowhere and she could see the one muddy track out of there already beginning to flood.

'This weather and these damp walls will totally muffle the sound,' Wilf said gloomily over Shiraz's shoulder as she filmed. 'He's going to sound tinny.'

'Hmmm yes,' Shiraz was saying in a trill voice. 'The light isn't right either. It can add twenty years on...' She turned to wink at Adam as she set up the tripod. '... or *more* if I'm bearing a sizeable grudge. Like when I filmed for *Crap in the Attic*. The presenter was such an unbearable wanker.'

'Grudge?' Wilf asked.

'Yes,' Shiraz was clearly warming to the attention. 'If a presenter is difficult, I cut them off mid-sentence to make them sound a bit of a racist or a misogynist or a homophobe. And if I'm really annoyed, I can make them appear pro-Brexit.'

'I suppose I could do the same with some clever sound editing, couldn't I?'

Kitty, not altogether pleased that Wilf seemed to be soaking up Shiraz's advice like a sponge, felt the need to intervene. 'Fortunately, we are on a very tight schedule with literally zero room for professional grudges or malicious editing.'

Shiraz seemed to take this as a signal to shuffle over to Adam, linking his arm. 'Don't worry. We'd never edit you like that. Never.'

Adam grew pale, as though regarding the pair through a new lens. He looked moodily over at Kitty which gave her the immediate hump, but she forced a smile. 'Don't worry. I have everything under control. You're in safe hands. You'll look great.'

'Nobody could sell this place. Nobody. It's a complete joke. I thought this was meant to be a serious property programme?'

Kitty sighed inwardly. 'If anyone can pretend to love something, then it's you, Adam.'

Please refrain from talking. You're hardly ahead of the game. Don't throw it all away on a fruitless whim. Abort. Abort.

'Meaning?'

'Oh nothing.'

'If anyone is good at *pretending* then surely it's you,' Adam said stomping away.

Kitty was disappointed with herself. That was on her, and totally unnecessary. They'd always shared a tempestuous and passionate dynamic. One minute they'd be fighting over nothing at all and the next they'd be up against a tree ripping each other's clothes off.

'Why do you always upset him?' remarked Wilf.

'I'll see if he wants an Indian Head massage,' offered Shiraz.

And you two can both stop behaving like lovesick puppies, Kitty thought to herself, snapping at them both.

'Come on, it's stopped raining. We've no time to lose. Places everyone.' Kitty clapped her hands to get their attention.

'Come on, babes, let's get you back outside,' Shiraz said to Adam as she guided him through the door.

The kit was dismantled and reassembled in a frosty atmosphere. Kitty listened as Shiraz and Wilf made a fuss of Adam, adjusting his microphone, smoothing out his hair, pulling his shorts straight.

'Watch out for that big cesspit,' Shiraz warned.

'You mean the pool,' said Kitty. None of them were making this easy for her. 'Adam, we'll do a close up of you talking to camera before we go to adverts.'

Adam gave Kitty a supercilious look before turning to camera. 'Coming up after the break, what will our couple, with their stingy budget, make of this run-down country finca and its complete lack of appeal, its toxic green pool and its gloomy rooms?'

He took a beat to flick a smirk to Kitty. 'With such a poor selection of properties on offer, perhaps our couple will be wondering why they didn't go on *A Place in the Sun* instead?' Adam scowled at Kitty, 'There, will that do?'

He was clearly upset with her but if he wanted to jeopardise his career, let him. It was one thing for the viewers at home to slag off house hunters, while they themselves didn't have a pot to piss in, but quite another for the well-paid presenters to do it.

She closed her eyes and let out a long, gusty breath that sounded not unlike her soul deflating. The last thing she wanted to do was apologise to the man who had begun the long and harrowing succession of failed relationships that littered her recent past. She could no longer deny that she had terrible taste in men. Terrible. And now she was going to have to eat humble pie with the worst offender of the lot.

In as icy a tone as she could manage, Kitty boomed, 'Adam, a word in private please.' She marched off towards the house, relieved to hear him follow closely behind.

This was not how she envisaged the first afternoon of filming would turn out, but Perrie was right. She needed to keep it together. Once she'd marched down the dark corridor leading to the ridiculously narrow kitchen, she closed the door and faced Adam. She stood tall, wishing they weren't almost touching.

He screwed his eyes. 'We can't work together if you show me *zero* professional respect.'

Kitty lowered her lashes, her heart thumping triple time in her chest, her mouth dry as a bone. It was at times like these, when the universe appeared to be playing cruel jokes. Adam stood an inch from her, oozing masculinity and... what was that? Some kind of intoxicating pheromone? 'I will, I will. I promise. I'll show maximum respect. Hashtag maximum respect, in fact.'

Kitty tried hard not to stare at his muscular arms as he folded them slowly, cocking his head accusingly to the side.

'You see? You're doing it again. You clearly have a problem with
–'

'I don't,' Kitty blurted, keen to show how genuine she was. All
TV presenters loved the sound of their own voices, and ideally, she
should let him soliloquise uninterrupted, but nerves at his close
proximity were getting the better of her. The kitchen wasn't big
enough to swing a stray cat. Of which there were many lurking
around outside, she noticed.

'Kitty, let me finish. If you have a problem with us working
together –'

'I honestly don't. I assure you, I have everything under control.'
Except anything I say, think or do.

Adam clenched his jaw, flicking his hair from his face. 'If you
have a problem with us working together when we have so much
history and unfinished –'

'No, I don't.'

'For fuck's sake,' Adam roared. 'CAN'T I EVEN FINISH
A SENTENCE? You are so infuriating, Kitty!' He looked her
scathingly up and down. 'I'm not in the habit of working with such
badly dressed, hashtag bitter, merlot-soaked...' He could barely get
the words out. '... judgemental tyrants!'

Whaaaaaat????

All of a sudden, it was as though they'd never broken up. Kitty was back on familiar territory. For a grown man he could be
surprisingly child-like. Was he seriously trying to hashtag shame
her? She couldn't hashtag care less. She sincerely hoped that Adam

would not expect a response because she refused to be drawn into this type of ugly spat. Upsetting him every few minutes was becoming a less than desirable feature of her management style. Kitty wracked her brain for a mature and sensible retort.

'Well?' he said, sounding rather like a smug, newly qualified teacher. 'What have you got to say for yourself?'

'AND I'M NOT IN THE HABIT OF WORKING WITH PARANOID, COCK-FACED PRICKS,' she instinctively bellowed back.

Adam looked visibly shaken. Her heartfelt apology was somewhat losing its way.

'For all I know you're out for revenge. To ruin my career!' he shrieked, nostrils flaring.

Your career? How about you ruining my life? They took a beat to eye one another with suspicion. He was so petty-minded but if push came to shove, Kitty feared that deep down a tiny part of her would indeed sacrifice her career and all that she held dear, just to take him down a peg or two. She needed to hold it together for a few more minutes but when she saw him tilt his chin arrogantly away from her, something fundamental in Kitty snapped.

'Oh fuck off, Adam. Anybody would think it was *you* who had the moral high ground, not me.'

'Oh no, no!' He waved a finger in the air. 'No, no, no. YOU fuck off, Kitty. YOU fuck off! I DO have the moral high ground. I do!'

As she watched his beautiful face contort with disbelief, she was suddenly reminded that much was at stake. Perrie and Jake were

50

relying on her to save their business. Her beloved cockapoo Alma was relying on her for doggy wigs. She literally had mouths to feed. She couldn't abandon them. She locked eyes with him as he towered over her. Something about this whole exchange made no sense. How could he even possibly think he was in the right? Her heart had shattered into a million jagged pieces. Her life had never been the same after he'd walked away.

So, that's that, thought Kitty confused. *We both think we're in the right. But why? Why would he even think that?*

From nowhere, tears threatened to spill. She blinked them away.

Adam's voice immediately softened. 'Come on. Let's get this over with. We'll pick this up later. When we're alone.'

Adam opened the kitchen door to find Wilf and Shiraz, wide-eyed, riveted, looking on the verge of ordering in some popcorn. An uncomfortable hush settled, and precious seconds ticked by, while they all stood facing one another in the narrow corridor.

'Good. Good,' said Kitty. 'We're all here. Let's wrap this up.'

They trooped back outside.

'Action,' called Kitty, her mind elsewhere. *Why would Adam ever think he had the moral high ground?* He had jilted her, not the other way round.

Adam looked directly into camera. He looked exhausted and fed up.

'Coming up. What will our couple make of this worryingly damp Hellhole, on the market for a snip under a hundred and thirty grand?' Adam pouted at Kitty, 'There, will that do?'

She took in his sulky, attractive features. Two could play that game.

'Yes, that will do nicely. Thank you.'

They all jumped as a gust of wind rattled through them at force, knocking over the tripod and causing the front door to slam shut with a loud crack. Kitty ran over and tried the handle. She pushed her weight against it. It was locked. She patted her many pockets down in search of the house keys before peering through the window to see them lying on the table next to her phone and notebook, Adam's phone, the car keys and the pile of daily schedules.

'Great,' said Adam, shaking his head. 'So glad to see you have everything under control. Remind me, when does Jake get here to take over?'

Once she had called the estate agent on Wilf's phone for a spare set of keys, she instructed them to take shelter in the car. Luckily, Shiraz had had the foresight to keep her car keys in her jegging pocket, something Kitty feared she would never hear the last of, and suggested they go back to the hotel to greet the house hunters while she waited for the estate agent. She meekly waved them off. What a disaster. She was better than this.

'Let's put the table wherever a table shouldn't be,' advised Kitty. 'On those boulders near the water's edge.'

She was directing Wilf as to where best to have Adam talk meaningfully to the house hunters about their reasons to buy abroad and why now, at this late stage in their lives after they'd both endured several failed marriages between them and a string of failed online dalliances before finally settling for each other.

'It needs to be away from the prying eyes of passing tourists so that Adam can really drill down into why the couple are so obviously dissatisfied with Wales.'

Perrie, on the receiving end of Network instructions, had ordered tears and confessions and that was what they would get, no matter how unethical and demeaning Kitty found the practice. The Welsh house hunters looked ill at ease and quite understandably.

She helped Wilf lug the chairs, coffees and sound equipment across the sand. Shiraz was set up ready and tut-tutting about the light.

'We can't have Adam facing directly into the sun. Put him over there. It won't matter if the house hunters squint and show their wrinkles, but it will matter if Adam does. He doesn't believe in Botox you know. His smooth head is down to the collagen shakes he has for supper,' Shiraz said bossily.

Kitty waved her hand elaborately, relieved that she was almost out of ear shot. She had already bent over backwards and switched the order of the properties for him. It would cost another half day of filming time.

'Okay, sure. Whatever.' *None of it will matter anyway,* thought Kitty looking over at Adam who crossed his arms before turning sulkily away. *We'll not even get one episode filmed at this rate.*

'Excuse me,' called the house hunter. 'My wife says to tell you that she's afraid of water.'

'That's okay, Evan,' shouted Kitty. 'We're not going in.'

Sometimes house hunters could be unnecessarily difficult, but Kitty was prepared to overlook it in exchange for them agreeing to names that were easier for Adam to pronounce.

'She's having a panic attack just looking at it,' he yelled back.

Why had a fear of water not come up? Who had carried out the due diligence? Literally every property bar the earlier lice-infested, dilapidated villa had a view of the lake or the sea. It took them another half an hour to relocate the table to a side street. Still frosty with her, Adam was ignoring everything she had told him to do. Kitty could tell that he was taking the rejection of the five-storey townhouse on the edge of a busy main road with spectacular views of the sea from its spacious roof terrace, very personally. The atmosphere between the crew and the house hunters was awkward and unsettled.

'Are there any other negatives?' Adam asked the couple. 'Other than you don't like the style of it, the location, the fact it's not a south-facing property even though you'd not mentioned that before?'

'Just that,' Evan said in a confused way, 'it hasn't got a single thing we actually asked you for. Are you sure you're a real estate agent? I thought you did those food programmes. Didn't you set fire to one of the contestants?'

'What other phobias do you have?' asked Adam, tutting. They were sandwiched in between two tall buildings. The light was terrible. Their voices echoed off the concrete walls. They all looked stiff and uncomfortable but at least it seemed as though Adam would rise to the occasion and do what he was being paid to do. Kitty placed the cold coffees on the table and reminded them, for health and safety reasons, not to touch them.

'Just the water really,' Evan said, answering for his wife Dee. 'Oh, and peanuts.' The couple nodded happily to one another.

'To do with the house search,' Adam sighed. 'Any phobias to do with the house search?'

The couple thought for a moment and gasped.

'Oh, we nearly forgot. Roads. She has a fear of traffic so no town properties. She's not good with stairs either because of the arthritis, she's no good with heights so no roof terraces please and,' Evan said turning to his wife rather triumphantly, as though he was trying to pass an A-Level in the subject, 'you're no good with the heat either, are you love? Look at her, she's sweltering.'

Adam stared at the couple before directing a reproachful glare at Kitty. He was hiding it well, but she had never seen him this incensed.

'So, what you mean is, ideally, you'd both like a small, single storey barn conversion on a farm somewhere cooler, say for instance, in northern France?'

Evan perked up. 'Yes. That would be ideal.'

·♥·♥·♥·♥·♥·

Back at the hotel, Kitty sat down with the crew to get their thoughts on how they could salvage the day's footage. She set a tray of glasses and two bottles of wine down.

'They didn't even cry for fuck's sake,' Shiraz was saying. 'Even though Adam kept bringing up Evan's two dead wives and Dee's recent brush with bowel cancer. What do you have to do these days to get people to cry? Poke them in the eye with a shitty stick?'

'We'll just do an extra-long montage,' suggested Kitty. 'Perhaps they'll cry tomorrow when we take them to the haunted... I mean the remote finca.'

Kitty was desperate to get him on side. They had had one disaster after another between the weather, the inappropriate townhouse property and the couple's strong accent. Truthfully, Kitty knew what they had filmed was all garbage. Utter garbage. Unusable, pointless garbage. Day one of filming had been a complete shambles.

'You all did really well today under very difficult conditions,' she lied. Wilf was holding his head in his hands. Shiraz was picking at her nails. Adam was swiping away at his phone. It was essential that she gave them some encouragement and copious amounts of empathy. All great TV broadcasters did this sort of morale boosting. She must keep their spirits up ready for day two of filming.

'We'll nail it tomorrow. No worries. Who would like to join me for dinner? My treat?'

Adam, stony faced, picked up the bottle of wine, twisted the cap off, sloshed it into his glass and threw it down his throat.

He turned to Shiraz.

'Coming?'

Chapter 5

Kitty was up and ready before any of the others. She had had a late night emailing the footage to Perrie for editing. Then at 3am Perrie had rung back, screeching down the phone. She too had been of the opinion that it was all utter garbage. Stifling a yawn, Kitty was sure today would be a much better day.

The first thing she needed to do was get Adam back on side. They would all have to pull together to make this house hunt work. She rifled through the paperwork and dialled his number.

His phone rang and rang but Adam did not pick up. Kitty checked his Instagram to find out why not, hoping she wouldn't see photos of him and Shiraz in varying states of the morning after. She was relieved to see Adam was doing some yoga at sunrise, without Shiraz. Not just any yoga. He was enjoying a session of goat yoga with a select group of patrons and their goats. There were several photos of him smiling at baby goats, having his toes nibbled #laughteristhebestmedecine, one of him balancing a goat on the base of his feet as he held it high in the air #beatanxietytogether. Apparently, Adam was toying with the option to do naked yoga or

NOGA as it is commonly known, and he was asking his thousands of followers whether he should or not. Here was a man, already deserving of a UNESCO badge for outstanding genetic significance, volunteering to be the cause of a multitude of eggs shooting from ovaries around the world.

Kitty wasn't quite sure how she felt about it. As she perused pictures of Adam in Child's Pose with a pigmy goat trotting up his back, it seemed like the beginning of a substantial personal crisis, but at least he seemed to have cheered up. She would need to work hard to win back his trust. An image of Adam and the way he'd held her close and looked intensely into her eyes after he'd yanked her out of the water, popped into her mind. There'd been a spark. She couldn't deny it. And again, in the kitchen when they were telling each other to fuck right off, there'd been an undeniable frisson.

Kitty found Wilf sitting alone in the restaurant. They enjoyed an awkward breakfast while they skirted around the issue that Shiraz, whose phone was switched off, had clearly not returned from Adam's hotel. Kitty knew this because Wilf had been psychotically asking reception every hour the previous night to the point they had asked if it should now be a matter for the police. Kitty began to wonder where the polite, shy young man of yesterday had gone. Wilf was behaving like a deranged lover who was one pot away from boiling a bunny.

'To recap. The Welsh house hunters are in their early sixties and not too overweight which probably means they're moving abroad for a healthier lifestyle, plenty of walking, golf perhaps for him and close to amenities for her and of course, they will want the obligatory café culture so they can sit and people watch.' Kitty tried to coax Wilf away from obsessively checking the door. 'Because of the water, heights and road situation, they could probably take up cycling for a day or two a month until the novelty wears off. Let's show them some properties with all of that on offer.'

'Where's Shiraz?' he asked in a stern tone.

'Here I am,' Shiraz announced, coming through from reception looking very happy with herself.

Wilf looked visibly relieved to see Shiraz turn up alone and wearing a different outfit to the one she'd left in last night.

'Did I hear there's a situation?' Adam asked, wafting in looking equally as serene.

'No. No situation,' Kitty said quickly, thankful that Wilf no longer appeared remotely interested in pursuing lines of enquiry into anyone's whereabouts or wrongdoings the previous evening.

Not unless the reason you both look unnervingly happy is that you bonked last night.

Kitty's soul drooped at the thought. She needed to keep this scrappy team together at all costs.

'Evan and Dee,' Adam said smiling at the house hunters. 'Tell me why you want to live abroad. What is it about this sun-drenched paradise that drew you here from cold, wet, miserable Wales?'

Kitty bit her lip. It was nice to see Adam relaxing and having a bit of fun for a change. She wrote a mental sidebar to look up goat yoga and truly hoped that was the reason behind it.

'It's the voos, innit? We've come h'yur for the amazin' voos.'

Adam remained straight faced and carried on. Kitty detected a miniscule curve on his top lip. He was trying not to laugh. It would be all but invisible to anyone else, but she had spent many years peering closely at his mouth, kissing it, rejoicing in the feel of those lips as they caressed her body, revelling in the sweet sensation of them kissing her neck.

'Kitty!' Wilf was yelling. 'Kitty, do you want to do the communal pool first or the house?'

Kitty snapped to attention. She flicked her eyes away from Adam to Shiraz who was scowling at her.

'Pool! We'll do the pool!' Kitty shrieked, feeling the heat rise in her cheeks.

At the last property of the day, Kitty was relieved that all had run smoothly, and she'd managed to get away with her earlier embarrassment of being caught blatantly staring at Adam. Good job he couldn't read minds.

'So, this is music to my ears,' Adam was saying with a cheeky grin to Evan. 'You're saying you want something big but Dee, you'd like something cosy. Evan you'd like modern, clean lines but Dee you're after something with character and that authentic Spanish feel?'

Both Evan and Dee nodded their heads enthusiastically as Adam turned to camera with a mock look of exasperation on his face. 'And Evan you want to be somewhere fairly out of the way to enjoy the peace and quiet but Dee, you want to be within walking distance of all the amenities and café culture, is that right?'

'Yes, Adam tha's right. And the voos. Don' forget we must 'ave the voos.'

'Right. Gotcha. Short of buying you two separate places, I think I have just the property in mind, let's go, come on.' Then he winked at camera. 'Find out after the break if our couple can reach an amicable decision or will they come out swinging their fists, on *Your Place or Mine?*'

It was the moment Kitty had been dreading. She was taking the house hunters to do some Segwaying round Malaga castle before the last viewing. Unfortunately for Adam, they were bang up for it. She wasn't at all sure if he would agree, seeing as they'd have to wear helmets, and she felt sure he would not be happy if this interfered with his hair.

'I've neva-eva done this before Kitty,' said Dee in her singsong accent. 'It's so incredibly excitin' innit, love?'

'Oh yes, this is the stuff dreams are made of. We loves a bit of thrill seekin', don't we?' They were holding hands and giggling like school children as they helped each other with their pads and helmets.

Kitty caught Adam watching them from afar and her heart sank as he came marching over towards her.

'I'll do it, if you do it.'

Kitty wasn't sure what he meant.

'I'll do the Segway piece if you do the tour with us.' Kitty watched Adam fold his arms defiantly. 'We only need a fraction of it for the episode, but the tour is over half an hour long.'

She couldn't blame him really. She was always asking presenters to make fools of themselves for the show and they had no option but to do as they were told. Maybe she could win some brownie points here with Adam.

'Is this your idea of getting back at me? Fine. I'll do it,' she said, adding childishly, 'You're such a drama queen. How hard can it be?'

'You'll need a lot of padding if this is your first go,' said the instructor, securing the last pad to her body. Kitty could barely move for pads. She felt immediately ridiculous and once on top of the Segway, struggling to keep her balance, she very much regretted it. Within two seconds she'd swung out of control and had had to leap to safety. They watched as the Segway crashed into the tripod. Kitty received a sound telling off from the tour guide who insisted on putting something akin to a child lock on her Segway to control the speed.

'Harder than it looks?' Adam smirked, whizzing past as though he'd been born on one. Kitty watched him do a range of tricks and spins before realising he'd completely set her up. The house hunters weren't the only ones to be entertained at seeing Kitty flail about.

'If you can stop screaming for five minutes, please Kitty, while we get the shot that would be great,' yelled Wilf, running with the boom towards them. Kitty tried to turn round. She was going to hand the Segway back to the instructor. She would not be peer-pressured into it by Adam.

'Not that way for God's sake,' yelled the instructor. 'Or you'll...'

Kitty, on a collision course with the instructor, saw him instinctively reverse out of her way. This caused him to plough backwards through the house hunters, knocking them over like skittles with regrettable accuracy.

'I'll keep the camera rolling,' called out Shiraz, happily filming away. 'They love this sort of thing on TikTok.'

By the end of an excruciatingly long day of filming and a lengthy trip to A & E, episode one was almost in the can. The house hunters were in considerable spirits despite Evan on crutches, having sprained his ankle and Dee having to wear a neck brace and sling, having broken her arm. They surprised them all by putting an offer in on the ramshackle, haunted finca, which might not have been entirely perfect for anyone with an ounce of sense, given the lack of a bathroom, running water and nothing around for twenty miles, but Kitty was relieved.

Filming the montages had had to be put back an extra day so Kitty had decided to try again at a team building dinner before the arrival of their second lot of house hunters and was surprised to hear them all agree to it.

'I'll go if Adam's going,' said Wilf looking longingly at him. 'A sort of guy's night?'

'Or we could stay in?' Shiraz asked him seductively. 'Hot tub, again?

Kitty cringed at the thought of the two of them together. Adam's face, however, was unreadable. She chewed her bottom lip. Maybe it was best if they didn't go out. She really couldn't stand to see them drooling over each other and was just about to rescind the offer when Adam agreed.

'Oh well that's great.' Kitty imagined they'd grab a burger and fries at the hotel and maybe a few beers before turning in. No more than an hour or two tops. They had an early start the following day. She would make a point of reminding Shiraz.

'We need to go somewhere fancy, Kitty. Somewhere cargo pants are not allowed,' Shiraz said pointedly. 'Or boots. Or baggy T-shirts. Book somewhere that befits my miniscule silver dress and sky-high glitter slingbacks and afterwards we'll go somewhere that I can sexy dance for Adam. Meet back at reception for nine o'clock.'

Kitty watched Shiraz batting her eyelashes ferociously at Adam. She was clearly hoping for a strip club with pole dancing.

Not happening. Not on my watch.

'Leave it with me.'

·♥·♥·♥·♥·♥·

Just as she reached her room, her phone rang. It was Perrie.

'Say hello to mummy Alma, say hello to mummy wummy.'

Alma licked Perrie's face and then stuck her paw on the screen. Kitty wished she was back home, curled up on the sofa with Alma, a huge cheese scone and an evening of Netflix ahead.

'Show mummy your new ears. Flap them, yes flap them for mummy. What do you think?' asked Perrie.

Kitty admired Alma's ears, now sprayed pink and adorned with sparkles. Alma looked cuter than ever. 'She could win awards with those ears. Who's mummy's gorgeous-worgeous? Yes, you are. Yes, you are.'

'Speaking of awards,' said Perrie. 'I have news. Big news.' Kitty listened as Perrie outlined the conversation she'd had that morning. 'I sent off the dreadful footage with an apology that we'd redo the lot of it today but guess what? The Network execs love it! They think Adam is a hoot. They think his sulky and unprofessional demeanour is refreshing. In fact, they said that you must be a genius to make it seem like the whole crew were complete amateurs who don't know what they're doing. Apparently, it got lots of laughs from the Capital Network executives who were desperate for more.

They think it'll draw a huge cult following. Can you believe it? So basically, Kitty, they are telling us to keep doing what we're doing.'

Kitty felt immediately conflicted. 'They want us to keep making *bad* TV?'

'Yes. If that's what they want, then that's what we'll give them.'

'And what does that have to do with awards?'

'The Network want to win next year's Best TV Lifestyle Show.'

Kitty thought for a moment. 'I'll have to share this with Adam.'

'No Kitty, you can't. It'll alter the way he's carrying on. We have to do what the Network want, besides its Adam's choice to behave like a bellend, isn't it? I mean you're not driving him to be rude, are you?'

Kitty couldn't think of what to say other than to admit that yes, she probably *was* driving him to it.

'So, no, Kitty. Let him get on with it and say nothing. Now we have to go, don't we? Yes, we do. Alma and I have a thing to go to and we need to go walkies first, don't we? We're avoiding the meanie sausage dog next door. He laughed at your fabulous ears, didn't he?'

'The sausage dog laughed at her ears?'

'Well, no, but his awful owner did. He's so annoying. Anyway bye, bye mummy, luvoo!'

Kitty was on edge after the call. She felt uneasy at not sharing the information. *But then,* Kitty reasoned, *I am in charge.* Sometimes it was lonely at the top. That was what leadership often entailed.

Chapter 6

Kitty showered and took her time getting ready. She'd been aware that for the last year, particularly since she'd been dumped so unceremoniously by Maddison O'Reilly, that she'd let that side of things slip. She took a moment to inspect her naked body. She had to admit she could stand to lose a few pounds and her hair was extraordinarily dry, just like her nails. And if push came to shove, she'd admit that she'd gotten lazy with the razor. The last man to rummage around at the coalface was Maddison and he had insisted on a Hollywood. All off. Not one pube to be seen. He was the same himself and often made appointments for them to go together for hot waxes. He'd make her feel anxious about her overgrown flange and looking back, wished she'd never been so blinded by love as to willingly do whatever he asked.

She spotted some complimentary hair products and mini bottles of oils and lotions and got to work. She had an hour to transform herself into a clean, professional-looking woman who people might think cares about herself. Her mind wandered to Adam's Instagram posts. What had he said about his skin and nails never looking so good? Kitty decided she would order whatever it was he'd recommended because it sure was doing something great for him.

Once her hair was done, Kitty tackled her face. She'd brought minimal make-up but applied it anyway and even had a go at some eyebrows. Next, she wandered over to her suitcase and rummaged through the pile, pulling out a chiffon dress she knew belonged to Perrie and had been sneaked into her bag with good intentions. Trying it on Kitty could not believe the woman staring back at her from the mirror. This woman had sleek hair tumbling down across her shoulders, she had big eyes accentuated with only mascara and a flick of liner, her eyebrows had returned to frame her sun kissed glowing face. She twirled, liking what she saw. Her phone rang. It was Perrie video calling. Perrie tilted her head and took a moment to regard her friend.

'You don't normally get that dressed up. Anyway, the Network loved the rest of episode one. That bit at the end was hilarious, especially as Evan was so keen to get her onto a Segway and next thing you know she's wearing a neck brace.' Perrie could barely speak for laughing. Kitty remembered the moment only too clearly. Evan was caught looking at camera for a beat too long when Shiraz, distracted by Adam's gorgeous eyes, stopped rolling.

'I hope this next couple are as entertaining. By the way, can you see if Adam can get some happy tears out of them? And the Network lawyers would like Adam to say 'wriggle room' and not 'wiggle room'. For copyright purposes. Also, they've gotten wind that Maddison O'Reilly is up for the same award for that pet show of his. I wouldn't watch it myself, but Alma loves it, don't you darling? Don't you? But we still hate Maddison, don't we? She does this cute snarl when he comes on.'

Kitty was shocked at how hurt she felt at the mention of Maddison's name out of the blue like that. She had managed to avoid looking at his socials for two whole weeks while she'd been so distracted with work, but now all those feelings of longing for what once was, came flooding back. Despite herself, she still missed him.

'Yes,' Kitty nodded. 'We still hate him. Anyway, must go. I'm team bonding tonight. I really miss you both. I hope you're not having too much fun without me?'

Perrie with her long curls pulled into a ponytail snuggled into Alma with her matching afro doggie wig.

'I think you're beginning to look like each other. They do say that, don't they?'

'OMG. That's exactly what my judgy neighbour said. He doesn't believe in doggie accessories. And do you know what he actually said to me?' Perrie's eyes were wide with indignation as she covered Alma's ears. 'He doesn't believe in designer 'made to order' puppies. Can you believe that? He thinks it's unethical and that we should only take puppies from doggie rescue centres. What a pompous arse.'

Kitty was well aware of the true meaning of pompous arse. She'd had a significant number of relationships with pompous arses in her time and so, for that matter, had Perrie.

'So, your annoying neighbour is reasonably good-looking then, is he?' Kitty asked.

Perrie giggled. 'Hot as fuck, isn't he Alma? Enjoy your night, honey.'

Kitty clicked off the call and allowed her mind to wander to that devastating evening Maddison had walked through the door with Alma wrapped up in a blanket declaring he had news. Exciting news!

Kitty had leapt up to kiss him, she squealed with joy at the gorgeous bundle encased in his arms and when he nodded his head towards the fridge, she ran over to her small kitchen to retrieve the last bottle of prosecco from the fridge and two glasses. She poured the fizzy wine and took possession of the most adorable creature she'd ever seen.

'She's for you,' Maddison had said, swigging at the wine and pouring himself another then another.

'I love her. Thank you.' Kitty's heart swelled as she took in Maddison's skewed appearance despite the pristine tux and highly polished shoes. He worked hard at being Britain's number two most popular TV presenter and that night it showed. He looked tired. Kitty also realised that he seemed uncomfortable. For a fleeting moment she wondered if he was gearing up to propose. Couples often tested their relationship with getting a puppy first before taking the plunge, didn't they?

'Is this what I think it means?' she asked hopefully. Maddison turned his mega-watt gaze her way. It had disarmed many a woman and man in his time. The lavender eyes were striking enough but the enviable lashes that framed them gave him a unique handsomeness few could replicate. She'd known many male presenters go in for eyelash extensions over the last few years in an attempt to copy him, but none came even close. Maddison gave her a half smile and answered. Kitty had replayed the scene over and over in her head since that night chastising herself for asking. Wondering if she'd not asked would the moment of madness have passed and would they still be together.

'I think we should break up,' he'd said without any preamble. Maddison had such a wicked sense of humour. This was just like him, to come over late at night, looking all sexy, give her a puppy that she hadn't asked for or wanted, but that stole her heart with one look.

'Obviously, you can keep the puppy. Besides with me travelling so much it's not ideal. I've been given the main anchor job for 'Britain's Got Pets'. I don't know what the Network were thinking, dumping an animal on me like that,' he pointed to the bundle in her arms, 'but it's a one-off, designer breed apparently.'

Kitty's laughter died in her mouth. That was his exciting news? A new job? He seemed perfectly serious. He stood up and drained the glass.

'Don't look so upset Kitty-cat. We had a good run, didn't we? In a way, if it wasn't for you making me such a favourite with the public we wouldn't be in this position, would we?'

Maddison was blaming her for the break-up but before she had time to reply, he was letting himself out of the door advising her to get the puppy its jabs, a worming treatment and insurance cover before she took it out for any walks. Kitty scrambled to her feet and raced after him, the puppy stirring in her arms making it difficult to juggle the door. By the time she got it open, Maddison was gone. She looked down at the puppy, into the saddest eyes she'd ever seen and felt something warm in the palm of her hand. That was the second time she'd been shat on in as many minutes.

Rousing herself from the depressing memory, Kitty tried to focus on the night ahead. She needed to make a good impression and get the crew firmly onside. She glanced at the time. *Shite!* She was going to be late. She raced into reception to find three irate crew members who didn't give a toss about her new hair or her floaty dress, only that the taxi had tired of waiting and had left them high and dry.

'There won't be another one for over an hour. We tried ringing but you were engaged for over thirty minutes,' said Adam.

Kitty took a moment, fearing there would be a lot of ground to make up over the evening. Thankfully she'd had the foresight to drink the entire contents of the minibar while she was getting ready. It was just enough to make her work colleagues bearable, but not enough to make her resent them forever.

'I'm so sorry. I had to take an urgent call.'

'Someone very, very close to you better have died,' said Shiraz in a hard tone.

'We never had this at Sporadic,' said Wilf, turning to Adam.

'We can still make it,' promised Kitty, one hundred per cent sure that the restaurant would have given away their table.

'Good job you're paying because we are drinking Spain dry tonight,' threatened Shiraz. 'And you can kiss your early night goodbye.'

·♥ · ♥ · ♥ · ♥ · ♥·

Later that evening, a sobering Kitty had been dismayed to find that everyone round the table had said everything they needed to say to each other and were all drunk enough to repeat the same things again without really noticing. Distracted by the way in which the candlelight flickered across Adam's face to highlight his beautiful jawline, his chiselled cheekbones and his perfectly shaped lips, she reluctantly turned her attention to Wilf. He was regaling the entire restaurant for a third time with his hilarious story about home-brewed beetroot cider giving him the trots, while repeatedly reaching for a pint of beer that wasn't there. People were beginning to complain. Kitty suggested a change of scene.

They stumbled across a karaoke bar and Shiraz insisted forcefully that they all go in. Kitty had to endure not only Shiraz but Wilf too, as they fought over the microphone to croon love songs at Adam. Shiraz was singing an eighties power ballad on the tiny stage at the front while she trained her eyes on Adam to the point of making him uncomfortable.

'You make a cute couple,' said Kitty to Adam for want of anything better to say. He'd had a lot to drink but seemed oblivious as he collected stares from most of the people sat around the bar. Even Kitty could see that he stood out a mile. Adam was tall and athletic, he had striking features and hair that always managed to look freshly washed and a smile that lit up the room when he chose to use it.

'We're not a couple,' Adam shot back annoyed. 'Why would you think we're a couple?'

'Because you keep flirting with each other.' Kitty instantly regretted ever having made the comment. 'And she stayed over at your hotel.'

Adam rolled his eyes. 'She didn't stay over. I packed her off in a taxi at two in the morning when she refused to leave. It's like you're all obsessed with me. Besides, what's it to you? I'm completely unattractive and asexual if I remember correctly.'

And while he was making light of it, Kitty could tell that underneath she had upset him. Of course she had. He had an ego the size of a humpback whale. Of course he would be upset.

'I'm so sorry. I didn't mean it.'

Adam leaned over.

'Excuse me, what was that?'

He was going to make her work for it.

Kitty breathed in a sharp, woody smell. Adam had always smelled heavenly. 'I said I'm sorry. I lied to Shiraz to stop her thinking there was something going on between us. She was getting very jealous.'

Adam's face suddenly became serious. He was staring into Kitty's eyes. She was pleased to see that her revelation had landed well. She was becoming quite adept at apologising to him.

Just as he opened his mouth to say something, Shiraz, watching them intensely from across the room, ramped up the volume of her singing and blared across the bar that she would always love him, always think of him every step of the way but essentially, she would always, ALWAYS love him.

Even though she was absolutely plastered, she'd very obviously been blessed with the lungs of an opera singer and was belting out the tune as though not a soul was listening. At the piercing warble, Kitty very much wished she was one of those souls. Shiraz was now grabbing air and with closed eyes was lifting the microphone up high to sing the final notes into it.

'I will always love YOOO-HOOOO,' she pointed to him, her eyes snapping open, wild with longing.

'Nope. We're definitely *not* a couple. Nothing has or will ever happen between us. I'm very professional like that. Despite what you may have heard about me. If anything, I'm a bit afraid of her.'

They both took a moment to let that piece of information percolate.

'I'll do Mariah next for you Adam,' Wilf was yelling, hovering off to the side, barely able to lift his head from the table but looking determined to do one better than Shiraz. He bellowed over to the

DJ. 'Mariah! When a Hero Comes along. It's a song about Adam. Get the words up. Quick before I pass out.'

Kitty burst out laughing.

'Would you like to spend tomorrow afternoon with me?' Adam was dishevelled, his hair had that sexy, messy vibe and he was staring at her with big, dark, come-to-bed eyes. She was appalled to find that in her semi-drunken state, she wanted nothing more than to grab hold of his floppy locks and pull him towards her, lips first.

'After you finish filming in the morning. Just you and me? So we can talk properly.'

Alarm bells rang.

Kitty took a moment to think this through. If she said yes, then all hell would break loose. Wilf and Shiraz would be furious at being left out. Plus, she might send the wrong message to Adam. And somewhere deep down, she was still narked that he was yet to apologise properly. For some reason, Adam thought he was in the right. Kitty could only envisage a huge falling out trying to get to the bottom of that.

No, it was best all round that she didn't encourage him to explore the specifics of why things had gone so terribly wrong in their relationship, nor the subsequent humiliation and devastation of exponential proportions.

He reached across to take her hand in his. 'Please? There's something I need to know.'

The jolt of electricity that shot through her entire body was like a taser gun. Her pulse went through the roof. She lowered her gaze.

It was essential she play this cool. He must never know that he still retained the power to set her soul on fire.

'Sure. Fine. Whatever. Yeah. Sure.'

Shitting hell, she thought. *I sound like a lovesick poodle.*

Chapter 7

The following morning, as she waited at the breakfast table for her crispy bacon sandwich and Wilf and Shiraz to arrive, Kitty took a moment to reflect on how the team-building dinner had gone the previous evening.

'Why?' Wilf approached looking drained. 'Why is this happening to me?' he was asking no one in particular. 'Why do I feel so ill?' He was having difficulty trying to remember who had ordered the tray of flaming jalapeno vodkas at the club (him) or why he had a terrible feeling they'd ended up in A&E (also him) or why he had woken up with hair smelling of banana daiquiri and a top covered in blood. Feeling rough from lack of sleep and bitterly regretting his poor choices around how much alcohol he had consumed, he ordered a glass of water from a passing waiter.

Wilf creased his eyes at Kitty, the light too much for him as he plonked himself down heavily on the chair opposite. 'I hate myself. I feel poisoned. My mouth, it feels like I fell asleep tongue-first on a bed of rotting garlic.'

Kitty wondered whether to remind him about the spicy kebab he'd wolfed down at two in the morning, and listened, horrified, as he admitted to waking up with a stray cat licking something off his face and although fully dressed, he was not wearing a top that looked even remotely familiar. It was enough to put Kitty off drinking forever. Keen to divert attention away from her own failings, Kitty advised him to sit still and stare at the table while she ordered a strong coffee for him.

'Make that two coffees,' Shiraz croaked, pulling out a chair with a piercing scrape that made them wince in pain. 'Why did you make me drink so much?'

Shiraz was barely recognisable in oversize sunglasses and a silk scarf draped across her head and much of her face. If it wasn't for the inappropriately tiny stripper dress and towering wedges, Kitty might not have realised it was her at all.

'How's your nose?' Kitty asked Shiraz softly, ignoring the accusation.

'Still broken.'

They all took a beat to stare at each other before Wilf looked guiltily away.

Shiraz removed her sunglasses to reveal a thickly padded nose bandage, dark circles emerging under her eyes and lips set to a thin angry line as she scowled at Wilf.

'How many times do I have to apologise?' A sorry-looking Wilf hung his head. 'Why were you dancing right behind me while I was can-canning for Adam anyway?'

Kitty experienced a vivid flashback, Wilf had gone full showbiz.

As an uneasy calm fell over the table, Kitty eyed the two sulky faces on either side of her and passed them an itinerary for the shoot. It was time to dispense some nurturing nursery nurse style diplomacy. 'It was an accident. You'll both just have to let bygones be bygones.' Kitty made a mental note to look up the meaning of bygones as soon as she'd dealt with this spat. 'Which one of you is up to driving so we can film the montage this morning?'

'I can't,' answered Shiraz impatiently, before explaining that she had accidently swallowed her contact lenses during the night, but would rather not go into specifics. She picked up the menu, contemplating it thoughtfully. 'I'll just have a double mojito.'

'Get me the same,' agreed Wilf.

Kitty was appalled. 'I'd prefer it if neither of you indulged in a hair of the dog. Not until after we film the montage.'

'I'm afraid that ship may have sailed,' Wilf told them, waving Kitty's newly arrived crispy bacon sandwich around before devouring it. 'I left a pint of water out by the bed to drink first thing this morning. Only it turned out to be wine. A pint of white wine!'

Jesus Christ, thought Kitty forlornly as the last morsel disappeared into his mouth. It was barely eight in the morning.

'I wonder if Adam posted that video of me balancing tiramisu on my head,' said Wilf, clicking on his profile. Pictures of Adam flashed up onto the screen as he zoomed in.

Kitty took a beat to understand what was happening to him. He was being held down and tortured.

'Oh my god,' Wilf gasped. 'They've taken Adam.'

What did they do last night? Who did they upset? Kitty looked wildly about. *The Russians? The Chinese? Christ Almighty.*

Shiraz grabbed his phone.

'Wilf, you're such an idiot,' she tutted and pressed play on Wilf's phone. They all watched the video of Adam's face being pinched and pulled in all directions #facegym. Someone was stretching out his eyelids, pounding him with various implements of cruelty and his skin looked raw and shiny from the essential oils being beaten into it by a pair of muscular hands. They watched the short video nine times. It was addictive.

'Come on, let's get this over with. I'll drive obviously.' Kitty got to her feet. 'Shouldn't take us long to film what we need for the montage. Adam can do the voice-overs tomorrow.'

'Good. If we're not seeing Adam today then I'm going to bed for at least ten hours as soon as we get back,' announced Shiraz wearily knocking back the rest of her cocktail.

Wilf nodded, dragging himself up from the table. 'Great idea. Me too. Sorry Kitty. Looks like you'll be on your own today.'

As they made their way back from filming, Kitty had a sinking feeling that she had imagined Adam's offer of spending the afternoon together. She checked her phone. There was no word from him. He was obviously treating himself to a spa day or whatever that face thing was all about.

Fighting disappointment back in her room, she slipped into her swimwear and searched for some shorts and a top, all borrowed from Perrie. She might as well go to the beach for the afternoon. As she was dithering over whether to keep her hair piled up into a top knot, there was a knock at the door.

'Wow,' said Adam, filling the doorway.

Kitty pulled at her shorts self-consciously. The bikini was made entirely of dental floss and the shorts were no more than a denim thong.

I must remember to thank her.

They stood awkwardly staring at each other.

'Some night last night?' Adam said eventually, peering sheepishly past her into the room as though debating what to say next. 'Wasn't sure if you would remember.'

Kitty bit her bottom lip. This question a sudden minefield. Her mind a blank. She cleared her throat.

'Remember what exactly?' Kitty gulped waiting for his reply. He was so breathtakingly beautiful that even if she'd been roofied with horse tranquilisers and drip-fed Class A amphetamines, she'd still be able to recall if Adam Johnson had made a pass at her.

'That we made plans for today.'

'Oh. Plans,' Kitty breathed with relief. 'So, what do you have in mind for this afternoon?'

Adam turned his remarkably fetching profile to face her. Noble she would have said. His sparkling, mischievous eyes and proud features never ceasing to surprise. 'You'll love it. We're doing our social media.'

Kitty shook her head. No way on this Earth. She had high moral standards and plenty of them. Usually.

'Oh yes.' Adam was grinning.

She self-consciously finished packing her bag, pulling at her too short shorts to see if she could eek an extra inch out of them. She couldn't.

He was looking at her with that intensity she remembered only too well. 'Hashtag beauty is in the eye of the beholder.'

Kitty felt her cheeks flame. 'I'm not... this isn't for... I don't care what you think... or about your bloody hashtags.'

'Take the compliment.' Adam rolled his eyes playfully. 'Were you always this difficult?'

Back outside the reception of Adam's plush hotel, Kitty watched him shake hands with a keen, smartly dressed young man and pose for a selfie. Then he leaned on a gleaming quad bike in a variety of poses while the young man clicked away on his camera phone delighted.

Adam laughed. 'Hop on. You're about to become a social media whore.'

He revved the engine causing the quad bike to jerk to life and Kitty instinctively grabbed hold of him round the waist. She was immediately uncomfortable at the intimacy but had no choice as, within a few minutes, they were hurtling along a cliff-hugging coastal road that afforded a breath-taking view of the twinkling

Mediterranean far below. When they turned off the road, Kitty's excitement levels rose. The track was leading them down to a picturesque cove straight out of a brightly coloured Disney film.

As they pulled up to a beach shack nestled in the cove, Kitty was surprised to see it bustling with people. She jumped off the bike and followed Adam over to the shack. He exchanged a few pleasantries in English with people dressed in wet suits milling around and posed for some selfies. They lifted off a kayak from the rack and walked it over to the water's edge.

'Want to put your phone in the waterproof bag or keep it out for selfies?'

Kitty pretended to roll her eyes. 'You're obsessed. Have you thought about living in the moment? Just enjoying life as it happens? Not documenting it every second of the day?'

Oh my god, could I sound any more judgemental?

'Fine. No phones it is.'

Adam's eyes twinkled like the sparkles reflecting off the sea. Kitty quickly reminded herself that this was in no way a date.

She was technically his boss.

This was much more of a team building 'away day' if anything. She watched discreetly as he stripped off his T-shirt and felt her pelvis immediately twang.

Team building, she reminded herself.

·❦·❦·❦·❦·❦·

They clambered into a bright orange kayak and pushed off the shore with their oars. Kitty marvelled at the bright turquoise colour of the sea as they made their way over to some far-out fish farms. She watched as Adam's muscular back and shoulders pumped this way and that, as he handled the oar, powering the kayak to slice through the gentle waves like butter. Something caught her eye and before she could scream, a dolphin launched out of the water and plunged back into the sea right beside them. Then another and another.

They watched open-mouthed as for twenty minutes a whole pod of dolphins splashed around them. Kitty squealed with delight when one leapt right over their heads, missing them by inches. Adam swung round to face her.

'You okay?' he yelled. He was drenched. 'It's incredible, isn't it?'

Kitty nodded back speechless. Everyone had whipped out their phones to capture some of the magic and Kitty felt a pang of regret that she'd been so pious earlier. The last of the dolphins swam off and she had nothing to send to Perrie and Alma to show them how amazing the experience had been.

'You were right,' Adam said over his shoulder.

'Was I?'

'About the phones. Living in the moment. It's much more in-tense and satisfying. Usually, I'd be fiddling with my phone and would've missed half of what was going on trying to capture it.'

A thrill shot through her at the praise. Adam was flirting with her. He was inviting her to play a game of one upmanship.

'I'm glad you had such an... intense and satisfying... erm, experience,' Kitty said, managing to make it sound like she was giving customer service feedback.

Moment of one upmanship well and truly ruined.

When they arrived back at the water's edge, Kitty slid down from the kayak, feeling the sand soft between her toes, the water lapping against her thighs and the sun beating down on her skin. Instinctively, she leaned forward and plunged right in. She emerged to shake the cold water from her face and smoothed back her hair. In an unusual move, that Kitty put down to the aftereffects of Adam flirting with her, she found herself acting out one of those hair commercials where the woman rinses her hair in a lake and throws her head back, hair whipping in a perfect arc, eyes closed, lips parted, body glistening and all that jazz.

'Very impressive,' laughed Adam. 'Can you do it again for my Instagram? But possibly do it in slower motion, hashtag save our oceans?'

Adam really did have the most delightful laugh.

'This place is so beautiful. Where are we exactly?' Kitty asked, plonking herself down onto the soft sand after they'd returned the kayak.

'If you were on Twitter, you'd know that already.'

He lay down beside her. With his Roman nose, Mediterranean colouring and tight breastplate abs, he looked like a centurion. He whipped out his phone to show her his Twitter account. There was Adam posing on the quad bike back at his hotel which was clearly shown in the background and the bike's logo and company rep grinning away beside him #bikesforbigboys #mentalhealthmatters. Kitty was confused. He pointed to his top in the photo. Kitty wondered how she'd not noticed before. Adam was wearing a T-shirt with a slogan 'It's okay to feel like shit'.

'I'm one of the patrons for this charity and today just happens to be world mental health day.'

'Oh,' Kitty was taken aback.

Adam nodded his head. 'Yeah, it's all about hashtag taking a moment to reflect. Tomorrow is all about saving our oceans from plastic. I fundraise for these guys.' Adam pointed to the instructor. 'Besides, I'm tying in my posts with each episode we make.'

'Are you?' Kitty was genuinely surprised.

'Yes, of course. It's called responsible tourism?' Adam smirked. 'It's a win win. The towns, hotels and local businesses we visit get some great free publicity, and we'll get hundreds of thousands of followers watching the episode to see where we are. We'll release teasers a week before the run up to it airing on TV.'

'We?'

'Me and my talent manager.'

'Oh my god, that is so clever.' Kitty wondered why she was not on top of this already. She made a mental note to do some soul searching. While she had retreated into her comfort zone with a gin and tonic, she had let more than just her appearance slip over the past year obsessing about her break-up with Maddison. It was time to take a much-needed pivot out of her slump and back into being the creative innovator she used to be.

'Can I have a selfie?' Adam asked, sounding slightly cautious.

'With me? But why?'

Adam shrugged. 'For old times' sake?'

As they snuggled together, she forced her eyes not to roam over his superbly, defined abdominal muscles or down to his muscular thighs and prayed that he would not be able to hear her heart thumping wildly in her chest. She breathed in the salty tang of the sea from his skin and the heady scent of lemon and olives drifting on the air from the nearby groves.

Kitty gushed, 'Thank you. Today was incredible.'

Adam was still beaming as they pulled up at the hotel entrance to find, bizarrely, the same rep standing there waiting for them. Adam handed over the keys and discreetly slipped a wedge of notes into the young man's top pocket, his face alight with appreciation. Kitty would bet that although the bike had been a freebie, Adam had slipped him more than a week's rental.

Adam walked back over to Kitty. 'I've not enjoyed myself like that for ages. I forgot how funny and unself-conscious you are. You haven't taken one selfie all day or checked your phone.'

Kitty shrugged, acting cool.

'And we haven't argued once. That's got to be a step in the right direction,' he said playfully. 'Just like old times.'

Butterflies fluttered in her stomach. 'Can I buy you dinner?' she asked feeling a bit brave. 'I can show you how to eat at a restaurant without taking pictures of the food if you like.'

Adam hesitated.

GAAAH! She had misread the situation. Or *he* was misreading the situation. *Somebody* was misreading the situation and Kitty was mortified.

'Wait.' Adam reached out to gently take her wrist. His touch set her skin on fire. 'I was hoping... you'd like to stay here. For dinner. With me.'

Kitty gulped.

'Here? As in your hotel?'

Adam had managed to make it sound as though he was inviting her to strip naked and do the dance of the seven veils for him. Or maybe that was all her.

Team building, practical, cheaper in terms of expenses, Kitty ran through the justification in her mind.

'Sure. If anything, it'll be an opportunity to lay down the foundations of a solid work ethic going forward.' Kitty hoped the wobble in her voice could not be detected.

'Exactly what I had in mind,' Adam quipped in a way that suggested the exact opposite.

Chapter 8

Two hours later and Kitty would forever wonder what trickery of Adam's had led her to so easily be sitting in a white fluffy robe, quite naked underneath, eating the most appetizing meal she'd ever encountered while washing it down with a superb Sauvignon Blanc. She would wonder why when he had first suggested they try out the spa facilities at his hotel before dinner she had so readily agreed. She would wonder why she had been so willing to strip off, cover herself in Spain's softest towel and join him in a relaxing steam room. After padding back to his suite in hotel regulation robes and slippers, having enjoyed a free massage with essential oils and the best foot rub she'd ever experienced in her life, she'd agreed to have dinner in his suite. Just the two of them. With the lights dimmed and the music playing softly in the background. She'd not felt this relaxed or smelt this good in years.

'Oh my god, this is heaven.' She closed her eyes to savour each bite.

'Here taste this. It melts in your mouth,' Adam said, reaching over to put his fork to her lips. It felt like such an intimate action, loaded with suggestion.

Kitty hesitated for a moment, the smile once creasing the corners of his eyes had now disappeared. He was staring at her lips. Kitty slowly opened them and leaned in as Adam put the fork of food into her mouth. She chewed the food slowly, feeling extremely self-conscious at the obvious tension building between them.

'Sorry if I've overstepped.'

'No, no. You haven't,' Kitty answered quick as lightning, pulling her robe more tightly around her. The whole scenario was ridiculously romantic. 'But I think *I* have. All of this...' She swept her arm around the room. 'It's a little too... personal.'

It was reminding her of old times that she'd rather stayed forgotten. The best she could manage, in her emotionally incontinent state, was to accommodate him in a professional capacity.

'I'm okay with discussing what happened,' Adam said.

Kitty was vehemently not okay with it and slugged back her wine.

'Why don't we stick to talking about work rather than shameful mistakes I may, or may not, have made since you ruined my life and left me at the altar to be humiliated in front of my entire family.'

Why? Kitty wondered. *Why am I saying such things?*

'Shameful?' Adam said slightly taken aback.

'Yes. Exactly.'

Kitty suddenly had no idea what she was talking about.

'And you weren't quite standing at the –'

'I'm not up for a trip down memory lane during working hours, is that clear? Let's keep this professional and above board.'

Above board?

Kitty shifted in her seat and fiddled with the dressing gown belt. Why was she sitting here eating without clothes on? She wasn't from Finland last time she checked.

'Understood.' Adam was playing along. 'Although it's almost ten o'clock.'

She could hear the amusement in his voice. *Almost as though he knows that my mind is a terrifying mess!*

After a few moments of scraping her fork around the plate, she attempted to get the conversation back onto an even keel. 'The spa facilities here are very good. Are they tax deductible?'

Jesus wept.

Adam snorted but immediately tried to hide it. 'Perk of the job. It's my manager who does all the sponsorship deals and most of the Instagram posts. I just have to make out that I enjoy it all I suppose.'

'You don't?'

'No, I do. I do. It's just...' He shrugged it off. 'It's nice to see you so relaxed,' he said, changing the subject. 'I've been following your career.' Adam forked some food into his mouth. 'You've made some impressive shows.'

Kitty could feel her face glowing disloyally at the compliment. 'Not bad for a merlot-soaked tyrant, you mean?'

'And that's worse than a paranoid, cock-faced prick?'

'Who constantly questions my process,' she shot back.

His eyes fizzled with mischief. She'd missed that from her life. Adam was spontaneous and fun. No wonder she had not been enough for him.

'These recent mistakes you may have made because of me. Tell me about them. I want to help. Talk to me.'

Kitty was temporarily thrown. Naturally, she had not wanted to delve into her mistakes of the past with Adam but somehow, discussing her mistakes of the present felt even worse. Especially as she knew revealing her relationship with Maddison and the disgraceful way he'd treated her, would probably open a can of worms that should be left firmly sealed. Adam's rivalry with Maddison was very public knowledge. Her relationship with him was not. Kitty could feel the swell of resentment rise in the pit of her stomach. Ever since Adam had left her, she'd lurched from one bad relationship to another. She became immediately defensive.

'Help me? How can you help? You're the shallow hashtag *live, laugh, love* guy.' Kitty shook her head. 'As though life really is that simple.'

Adam's face immediately fell, causing her to take a beat. She was being very spiky. Sometimes she wondered where this sharp and unassuageable sense of justice came from. Wait, oh yes, it came from being publicly humiliated and the root source of that heartbreak was currently sitting opposite, dressed in nothing but a hotel robe, luring her out of her comfort zone while pretending that he had abandoned her for her own benefit, that's where. She bit her tongue as Adam allowed her words to hang in the air.

'You think my lifestyle is shallow and materialistic?'

'Yes, but I mean that in a nice way.'

'You think I only care about myself.'

Kitty had no words. She knew this to be a fact.

'Well?'

Abort. Abort. Alarm bells were going off in her head. As usual she ignored them.

'Not just about yourself. There're your millions of followers. You care deeply about them.' She noticed he was very fond of saying so on his Instagram.

A dark shadow crossed Adam's face as he studied her with his hypnotic, sharp-eyed gaze. It was very striking. Kitty had always been able to lose herself in his eyes. Sometimes for days.

'Well, Kitty, you're wrong. Hashtag *so* wrong.'

She fought the urge to giggle. Why could they never seem to agree on a single thing? Had it always been this way? Whatever, she was tiring of this continuous conflict between them and at this rate, she'd rather they discussed their failed relationship.

'Okay, I'm wrong.' Kitty picked up her menu to peruse the dessert options. 'You're not rootless and impulsive.'

'No,' he said after some thought. 'You're right.'

'Do make up your mind.'

'Are you saying that because of me you only go out with despicable, overly-attractive bigheads?' He cocked an eyebrow and flexed his bicep. He was playing with her.

'No, actually. I like the silent, bookish type.'

'What a coincidence because as you know, I'm writing a novel. It's a conceptual juxtapose. Bookish enough for you?'

In spite of her mixed feelings towards him, Kitty laughed.

'Please don't discriminate Kitty. It's beneath you. I'm allowed to be bookish as well as a muscular, well-toned sexual magnet. Ask my millions of followers.'

'Whatever,' Kitty rolled her eyes. She would not be drawn into his flirting games.

'Network executives are all under twenty-five these days. Forget CVs. It's all about your socials and how many followers you have. They are judgemental to an almost criminal degree, but they need to see that you 'get' them. That you can 'connect' with people.'

'Why can't they appreciate the amazing bloody standard of work I do and judge me on that?'

'Because they don't. I can help you build a better profile,' promised Adam. 'What do you say?'

'You mean you can help me become a proper Millennial?'

'I didn't say I was a miracle worker.'

Kitty smirked and took a moment to let this digest. While she was what might be diplomatically called boring and strait-laced, Adam was an expert attention seeker, a people person, an extrovert. As far as belief systems went, they were poles apart but that had always been their strength as a couple. They embraced their differences. It had made their relationship dynamic and exciting and full of growth.

'I'm sorry I called you a cock-faced prick. I misjudged you. I guess I'm... I mean, I *was... am* still angry at you for leaving me the way you did.' Realising she was straying into personal territory Kitty took a sip of her wine. 'Well, whatever, it's all water under the bridge now, isn't it?'

There was a slight tension in the air as Kitty raised her glass to clink with Adam's. She had no idea if it was water under the bridge or not. Having Adam this close, sharing an intimate dinner, it was all stirring up feelings that she'd long since buried.

'I'm not toasting that. And it's far from water under the bridge. It's more of a massive elephant in the room. Let's not pretend we can forget what happened, even if it does appear that we are trying to forgive each other.'

'Why would you need to forgive *me*?' Kitty drained her glass and went to pour herself another. The bottle was almost empty. 'Here... you take it. Maybe it's time for me to go.' She held it out to him, deciding she'd had enough to drink. It was loosening her tongue and she did not like it one bit.

Adam leaned over to the minibar and yanked open the door. 'Nope, things are just getting interesting.'

He pulled out a second bottle of wine and unscrewed the top, filled their empty glasses and raised his own to his lips, never once taking his eyes off Kitty.

'If you have to ask me why I'd need to forgive *you*, then from your point of view what I did was inexcusable.'

Kitty nodded, staring down at the table. Her heart was beating out of her chest. She'd buried all of this hurt and upset deep down inside for a good reason. She looked up slowly to find that Adam was holding out his hand to her across the table.

'We need to talk about it properly. There's something that you need to know,' he said, sounding rather subdued.

Maybe it was time to get everything out into the open. She took his hand. It felt warm and reassuring.

'This isn't going to be about the wings, is it?'

Adam smirked sadly and shook his head. When he opened his mouth to speak, they were interrupted by her phone ringing. It made them both jump and just like that the spell was broken.

The phone continued to wail like a new-born baby.

'Sorry. I should get this. It's Wilf.' Kitty answered the phone to hear Wilf shrieking down the line.

'Kitty! Where are you? There's been an incident.'

She put the phone on loudspeaker and listened as Wilf described how Shiraz, balancing a cocktail while taking a selfie on her phone, slipped in the bath and had landed on her already broken nose. 'She's screaming the entire place down. The hotel staff don't know what to do. We need you back here pronto.'

'Want me to come?' Adam said quietly.

Kitty was alarmed to feel herself thinking how lovely it would be to have someone there to rely on. Adam, no matter how much of a diva he had apparently become, had once been solid and dependable. She shook her head.

Adam looked disappointed.

'Stay here and finish your meal. I can handle it,' she told him.

'Of course you can.'

'I had a lovely evening. Thank you.' The sooner she got out of there the better. She was beginning to have feelings for him. She needed to nip that in the bud as soon as possible.

'This conversation isn't over,' Adam said, his face serious. Kitty nodded in understanding. She knew they needed to have 'the talk' but not right now while she was pissed and likely to make some bad choices. He was looking at her in a strangely familiar way and the best thing she could do right now was put some distance between them.

'Also, there's something I need to ask you. About the show and the feedback from the Network. They were being very cagey with my manager about the rushes. I thought you might have heard something.'

Kitty felt her stomach flip guiltily.

'Okay, I'll try to find out,' she agreed, shooting into the bathroom to put her clothes back on. Technically speaking, she wasn't lying, but now was not the time to tell him they were going to hang him out to dry.

When she came out, Adam got up from the table. His robe fell open to reveal a pair of tight-fitting boxers that left nothing to the imagination. She dragged her lustful eyes up to his, her heart skipping a beat.

'Thank you,' he said. 'I really enjoyed your company today. I wish you didn't have to go.'

Kitty hesitated.

'Me too.'

What are you doing? What the hell are you doing? Kitty asked herself ten minutes later as she jumped in a taxi.

Chapter 9

Kitty woke abruptly at six thirty in the morning. It was Perrie video calling.

'Morning mummy. Kisses for mummy.' Kitty watched as Alma scrambled to lick the phone. 'I think Alma's really missing you Kitty. We couldn't get her settled last night. No, we couldn't. No, we couldn't.'

Kitty watched Perrie slobber over Alma. 'Who's this 'we'?' asked Kitty astutely. Like herself, Perrie had the look of a woman who had been up most of the night. She hoped it hadn't been because of Alma.

'I'm sorry,' yawned Perrie. 'Late night. We had Ned the sausage dog and his terribly hot owner over for dinner. They wanted to make up for the wig incident by bringing wine over. He stayed until two in the morning. He's extremely... chatty, let's say.'

'Perrie! With the new neighbour?'

'Seriously Kitty. You would. If you could see him. You definitely would. He's smoking hot I'm telling you. And even Ned and Alma got on well. It was Ned who settled her. He fetched her Mr Stinky and they curled up in the doggie bed together. It was really cute.'

'I'm not sure I like the idea of Alma sleeping around, Perrie. It's not how I've brought her up.'

'I'm pretty certain her reputation is safe Kitty. If any of the other dogs try to slut shame her today at the park, I'll let you know. She's wearing her blonde ponytail and short skirt as a statement. Those other pooches will have to accept her for who she is and her choices. Alma's a feminist, aren't you? Yes, you are.'

'So has this terribly hot sausage dog man got a name?'

'Yes. He's called Ted. Ned and Ted, can you believe it?'

'Yes Perrie, unfortunately I can. You seem to be a magnet for hot men. Speaking of which, how would you feel about me letting Adam in on the whole Network plan and the feedback so far? I spent the evening with him last night and he –'

'Whoa there. Back up, you spent the night with Adam?' Kitty waited for Perrie to finish ranting. 'Kitty, I expressly told you no getting involved with the star of the show. It always ends in disaster! And you've been there before, so you should know that vain, arrogant TV presenters make lousy boyfriends. What were you thinking?'

'It wasn't like that,' said Kitty, while thinking that it could very easily have been exactly like that.

'Honey, I'd hate to see you get hurt all over again. You have awful taste in men. Why do they all have to be TV presenters? Why can't you aspire to a rich dotcom nerd or an American oil magnate or a Greek shipping billionaire like normal women?'

'Because I don't come across those men in my line of work. Anyway, nothing happened, and nothing *will* happen. It was all very innocent. We just need a bit of closure that's all. I think I need to actually forgive him. Maybe that way I can finally move on without this nagging feeling, this unresolved anger, this resentment against all mankind.'

'Honey, we're *all* angry at men. Deep down, we *all* secretly think that men are complete bellends out to shaft us,' Perrie said softly. 'The problem with hanging onto it is that it's terribly aging. You'll meet someone new and worthy of you. I know it. Get this job over with and we'll go out on the tiles trawling for a new man. And by the way, the Network seemed to love the fact that Adam couldn't understand a word of what the Welsh couple were saying. That bit where they asked him if they needed planning permission to knock down walls and he replied...' Perrie dissolved into giggles. '..."Aubergines and onions I think". What an idiot! Karma's a bitch as they say.'

Kitty clicked off the call. She felt very uneasy wondering once more whether to be truthful with Adam. The more she was getting to know him again, the more it was becoming a dilemma.

Meeting the crew for breakfast, Kitty could barely look at Adam. After she'd returned from the hospital, where unnervingly they had greeted her like a regular, she'd had one fantasy dream about him after another. All slightly erotic and disturbing in equal measure. For some reason, her subliminal mind had him licking her nipples, at sunrise on the beach, while they rolled naked in the surf. In the next dream, she was riding him on the seat of the quad bike legs akimbo. She'd even dreamt they were in the steam room with Spain's softest towel now acting as a pair of handcuffs, as she'd tied his hands up to the towel hook and straddled him vigorously. Finally, she'd been wanking Adam off mid-goat yoga, which to be fair was a slightly weird one but even so, Kitty could see that the fantasies were basically a porn version of Adam's Instagram, but at least she appeared to have the joints of an Olympic gymnast in them. She blushed when he approached the table as though he knew what she'd been thinking.

'Okay, no rest for the wicked,' Kitty announced, clearing her throat. 'Today we are off to the Sierra Nevada mountains, down near Granada. It's about a three-hour drive from here so we'll aim to leave as soon as possible after lunch. Here are your schedules. Here's what you need for the hotel check-in. Designated drivers are myself and Shiraz this time.'

'I'll come with you,' Adam said quickly to Kitty, before throwing Shiraz a determined glance.

'Fine,' said Shiraz through thin lips. 'Why would I care?'

'I need to go over a few issues with Kitty and I thought we might as well do it while we travel,' Adam said easily. Kitty detected an undercurrent of malaise between him and Shiraz who was now stamping away in her slingbacks, her great mane of black hair swishing angrily behind her back.

'Issues?' Kitty asked, not sure how she felt about it herself now that he had begun to infiltrate her dreams at night like a schoolgirl crush. One of the dreams had definitely featured her sucking him off on the backseat of the car she was going to be driving him in. From memory, she'd always been able to drive him wild with her signature tongue flick and agile wrist action. She shook the inappropriate, sexy thoughts away to find he was looking at her.

Kitty eyed him back suspiciously before realising that maybe he genuinely wanted to discuss the Network feedback rather than their failed relationship. She had, after all, made it clear that personal talk was off-limits during working hours.

What harm could possibly come from travelling together? she wondered, batting away an ominous feeling. Only, she supposed, that she had already jeopardised filming by offending him every five minutes since they'd arrived in Spain and now finally, they seemed to be getting on, it would be such a shame to ruin it.

'I've booked into the same hotel as you guys,' he said sounding a bit uncomfortable.

Oh God, thought Kitty, *this is getting worse.* In the shower that morning, she'd had the fantasy of him turning up unannounced to her room dressed as a bell hop, while for some reason she was standing naked, but for a wedding veil, on the balcony, with one foot on the balustrade, casually stretching like a ballerina. Again, legs akimbo while her full bush wafted in the warm night breeze.

Yes, in Las Vegas for some reason, with crowds of people milling about below them in Elvis costumes. It was simply baffling.

After a morning of filming segments for the links between house hunts, the 'coming up next after the break' voice-overs and a few rather awkward shots of Adam posing provocatively for Shiraz's benefit, they all went their separate ways to pack for the next leg of the trip. Back in her room, Kitty hurriedly packed her meagre belongings into her tatty case, gathering bits of kit to throw into the huge holdalls. She felt sure her nerves would betray her. Her phone sprang to life causing her to jump. It was the bank. That was never a good sign.

'Harmonia Films,' she gulped. 'Kitty McAllister speaking.'

Once she had clicked off the call, she buried her head in her hands. Kitty thought she was having an out of body experience. As though on automatic she dialled Perrie's number to explain what had just happened.

'I can't believe we put our own apartments up as collateral. If the bank forecloses, we're as good as homeless.' Perrie's voice was shaking. 'How could Jake do this to us? He's left us completely broke.'

'I'll ring him and find out what's happened. He must be in trouble of some kind.'

'No,' said Perrie. 'I'll ring him. You have too much on already. I'll ring you straight back when I know what's going on.'

Five minutes later, Perrie was on the phone again. 'He's checked into rehab for a gambling addiction. Gambling! How did we not see that coming? I could kill him. I'm so angry with him. I didn't even know he liked to bet. Did you?'

'No. No idea.' Kitty felt sick to her stomach. 'We'll figure it out, Perrie. Don't panic. Let's make sure Jake is okay first, and I'll sort out how we pay for it later. Ring him back. Tell him he's got our full support.'

'I'm too angry.'

Kitty took a deep breath. She understood completely.

'You were both there for me when I hit rock bottom, remember? Perrie, you brought me back from total self-destruction. If it wasn't for you and Jake, we'd have no film company. If we can survive that together, we can survive this.'

Relieved to hear Perrie finally agree, Kitty clicked off the call. She needed to get her head in the game. How had she been oblivious to Jake succumbing to this illness and gambling away her business, her livelihood, everything she'd worked so hard for?

'I'm fine with you travelling with me,' Kitty explained to Adam an hour later as they did up their seatbelts. 'We can talk about the episodes and work stuff but nothing personal.' Nerves were getting the better of her and she could hear her shrill voice sound as though it belonged to an old spinster headmistress.

It was essential for the sake of the show that she gave no hint whatsoever of being preoccupied with the imminent closure of her film company due to his brother's catastrophic fuck up, *nor* their break-up that she seemed unable to get over, *nor* his prior disappointing and confusing explanation involving wings, *nor* of her still finding him overwhelmingly attractive despite not having forgiven him. No hint.

Kitty could feel a light film of sweat form on her brow as she drove away from the hotel, Wilf and Shiraz having gone on ahead of them. Kitty listened in surprise to Adam's ideas for the house hunters and where, emotionally, he wanted to take them.

'I can see from the notes that they've got two sons, so I thought I'd ask about them early on and then come back to it during the table sit-down and really drag out any conflict around abandoning them to go off and live thousands of miles away in Spain,' Adam was saying. 'I think we can get some happy tears going in at least two of the properties. Then I could really go to town on them asking who wears the trousers and is it the one who actually inherited the money who should choose? That should get them arguing, then I think we'll nail what the Network is after, don't you?'

Kitty had not seen Adam this enthusiastic before and was enjoying his input. She felt a tiny twinge of guilt at not being able to tell him what the Network really thought of his performance. It might affect his presenting style and throw the remaining episodes out of balance. If she knew anything at all about programming it was that consistency was key. Viewers liked to tune in knowing what to expect week in, week out.

'I'd like viewers to take me seriously and respect my capabilities. Can we edit each episode to reflect that?'

After a few long and panic-filled moments, Kitty's phone sprang to life, saving her from answering him as it automatically went to Bluetooth. She swerved slightly as Jake's name appeared across the screen. She gave Adam an anxious look before trying to reject the call. There was no way she was ready to speak to him. The hurt and devastation that he'd caused to her and Perrie, never mind the business they'd spent every waking hour building up, was stored safely away until she could have a proper meltdown about it. Adam leaned forward and pressed accept.

'Jake? I've been expecting to see you, but Kitty says you've been busy.'

Kitty continued to stare straight ahead as an officious-sounding woman ignored him, asking if Kitty would like to accept the call. Kitty declined saying to tell Jake she was in the middle of driving on a narrow and dangerous mountain road with his brother and that she would ring back as soon as she could. She clicked off the call.

'Why is some woman ringing on my brother's behalf? Where is he?'

Kitty glanced briefly at Adam who had his brow furrowed. 'Is he in trouble?'

This drive was going to be tricky enough without the added complication of betraying one of her best friends. She took a moment to consider what to do.

'What's going on? Why did my brother suddenly get in touch after three years and beg me to do this show?'

Kitty gulped. It really wasn't her secret to share.

'Kitty, please tell me. I want to help.' And after a beat. 'Whatever he may have done... in the past... he's still my brother.'

This was the Adam she remembered. Knowing the conversation was not going to be an easy one, Kitty decided to focus on the immediate issues facing Jake, rather than delve into the family history between the two brothers, whose relationship had been fraught ever since the day Adam walked out on her, leaving Jake to pick up the pieces. Jake had been furious with his older brother at causing his best friend and business partner such heartache. He'd been wracked with guilt at being the one to introduce them in the first place and had never left her side since.

The car journey went as smoothly as it could under the circumstances. Adam had listened to every word about Jake's gambling addiction and deceitful actions in stony silence.

'And that's why you were forced to take this job working with me? You're bailing him out with your own money, as well as paying for his rehab?' Adam guessed correctly. 'You must really love him.'

'Well, it was difficult after, well, you know.' *You abandoning me at the altar!* 'We grew even closer I guess.'

Adam cleared his throat. 'How convenient.'

'What do you mean?'

'Nothing. Forget it,' said Adam sharply.

Christ, he sounds just like me!

'No, you don't. Don't play that game with me. Tell me what you mean.'

'You and he were... *are* an item.'

Kitty took her eyes off the road for a second. 'An item? As in me and Jake together? No way. Why would you even say that? He's your brother. I'd never think of him that way... no, never.'

Adam sat silently beside her.

After a long while, Adam spoke in a wounded voice. 'I need to speak to him.'

'Why don't I ring him later? It's about time you two buried the hatchet. And I have a few choice words of my own for him.'

Grateful for the quiet that followed, Kitty had not realised how treacherous the mountain roads would be. She hadn't factored in the stark change in temperature or road conditions. She had had Wilf on the phone several times complaining non-stop that Shiraz was complaining non-stop about the drive, and why had Kitty not warned them. An hour from the hotel they were headed to, the weather drew in and snow began to fall.

'It's hard to believe that a few hours ago we were driving in the glorious sunshine and now, it's getting dark and snowing,' Adam observed. 'Want to swap over the driving? You must be tired.'

Kitty nodded. Adam had visibly relaxed since their conversation and a warmth had come to him. 'It's time to stop for petrol anyway.

This journey is taking a lot longer than Google maps originally told me it would.'

'Let's stop at the next café or garage we see,' suggested Adam. 'I haven't seen any signs of life for at least half an hour. Are you sure this is the way?'

Kitty was suddenly not sure at all if this was the way. 'I've been following the satnav on my phone. Can you check that I'm still getting a signal please? Maybe these mountain roads interfere with it or something.' She reached over to the dashboard and handed her phone to Adam.

'There's no signal. Let's just keep on this road and hopefully something will come up.'

'I'm sure it will,' Kitty said, far from convinced but trying to sound much more confident than she felt. She flicked her eyes to the petrol gauge. They should have enough to get to the hotel. She hoped. As the minutes ticked by, Kitty felt herself growing anxious. Adam was unusually quiet too which had not helped. She turned up the radio to see if some music would help ease the tension. Even in the dusk light, the mountain views were ominously spectacular but the higher they climbed the more snow-capped they became.

'We've passed two cars in the last hour.' Adam was thrumming his fingers impatiently on his knee. '*And* they were going in the opposite direction. *And* we really need to stop for petrol.'

'I know,' said Kitty tightly. 'I know that.'

'*And* it's starting to get really dark. I don't like the thought of driving on these winding mountain roads in the pitch black with snow lying on the ground.'

Kitty held her tongue. She had had the exact same thoughts. She moved the car down a gear as they reached a steep bit of road, taking the hairpin bend very carefully. 'It'll be fine. Try not to worry. I'll get us there.'

Adam reached over to put his hand on her thigh. 'I know you will. I could always count on you.'

Kitty looked down briefly to where his hand lay burning through the light fabric of her trousers.

'Sorry,' he said, whipping it away. 'That was really inappropriate.'

But it was too late. The damage had been done and now as well as worrying about being lost in the mountains on treacherous roads with the weather coming in quickly, the light fading and running out of petrol, Kitty now had to worry about whether her thigh had felt toned when Adam had reached over to give it a squeeze.

Chapter 10

Kitty and Adam resumed their bashful silence as she drove, the tension cranking up a notch as the snow came down more heavily. She fiddled with the radio stations in search of a monotonous drone to fill the air, but only one station was picking up.

Why did Latino music have to be so sexual and passionate? wondered Kitty as the car became bathed in romantic crooning about beating hearts, trying to take things slowly and wanting to lick bodies up and down. Another hour crawled by as the cold darkness set in. The petrol gauge was dangerously low, and they had not passed a single car. With no signal on their phones and no way to turn the car round anyway, they had no idea if they were headed in the right direction or merely inching towards a sheer drop.

'There!' Adam shouted suddenly. 'Over there!'

Kitty peered through the windscreen at the lights in the distance. As they drew closer, a roadside café emerged through the snowfall.

'There's no petrol station but at least we can stop off and switch over the driving if you like,' said Adam.

Kitty nodded her head, relieved to be able to get off the road. Her nerves had been fraught at driving in the dark. 'Hopefully we'll be able to get directions and a hot drink.'

They pulled into the carpark at the front of the café and were reassured to see a few other cars and even a small 'Hostal, Bar & Restaurant' sign hanging above the antiquated wooden door. Even more comforting was that inside there were people sat at tables eating and chatting, a delicious aroma of garlic, herbs and sizzling chicken filled the air. It was enchanting. The wooden tables had standard issue red checked tablecloths with candles in wine bottles, wax dripping down the sides. The lights were bright, the atmosphere warm and cosy thanks to the roaring flames dancing in a huge stone fireplace bringing a much-needed warmth to their bones.

'Thank God,' she said to Adam. 'I really thought we were going to get stuck on the mountain and I'd be forced to eat you when you froze to death.'

'Charming. I'm glad you kept that to yourself on the drive up. Which bit would you eat first?'

Kitty ignored the open invitation to flirt back. They sat down at a table and soon found out a couple of American tourists, sat opposite, were in a similar predicament.

'You guys trying to get up to the ski resort?'

Kitty nodded.

'Oh honey, let me save you a ton of fuss. There ain't no way you'll get there tonight. We checked. The lady over there said it's too dangerous to drive in the dark, so we booked a couple of rooms here. We're gonna head back out in the morning.'

Kitty thanked the two women.

'I'll go and book two rooms,' Adam said. 'Can I get you a drink?'

Kitty nodded. 'I'll just have a crate of red wine please. I need to keep a clear head.'

Adam treated her to a honeyed, silky laugh. The tension seemed to drain out of him.

Kitty winked. 'Perhaps I am a merlot-soaked tyrant after all.'

Adam walked over to the lady behind the bar. She was regretfully shaking her head and saying 'sorry' in Spanish. She poured Adam two massive glasses of wine, and he brought them over.

'There's good news and bad news I'm afraid. The good news is she's still serving food. The bad news is that she has no rooms left and there's nowhere nearby that we can stay. They're open all night, so we can stay sitting here as long as we keep ordering food and drinks and don't fall asleep.'

'I suppose it's better than freezing to death in the car.'

'Let's order some food and spend the night talking about our feelings.' Adam had that twinkle in his eye, the one that could steal her breath away. In that moment, it was as though time had stopped. 'Starting with why you won't let me explain why I think our relationship had to end.'

'I've changed my mind. This isn't better than freezing to death in the car.' Kitty got up, waving her phone in the air for a signal. The lady behind the bar shook her head and pointed her to a pay phone on the counter. Kitty scrolled through her contacts and rang Shiraz.

'Where are you?' Shiraz shouted down the phone. 'We had a nightmare getting here. The hotel was not where the satnav said it would be. The roads were effing terrifying. The snow is belting down. My nose is five times its normal size. I did not pack for this kind of weather. I'm thinking of suing someone. I'm completely traumatised, and I feel like it's all your fault, Kitty. You're supposed to be in charge.'

'Well, I'm glad you and Wilf have arrived safe and sound. We'll sort you out with some warm clothes tomorrow. Make sure you get some food and a good night's sleep. We'll see you in the morning.'

'Why? Where are you and Adam? In some luxury hotel, I suppose? I knew it. I knew there was something going on between you two.'

Kitty explained that she and Adam were stuck at the roadside restaurant and that they'd have to sit ordering food at their table all night as there were no rooms available, and it was too dangerous to drive in the dark with so much snow building up on the road.

'You have to sit up all night? Well, that's a relief at least,' Shiraz huffed. 'If it's the one we passed earlier with the string of lights outside, you're not too far away. About twenty-five minutes I'd say, so I'll see you both in the morning.'

Kitty hung up relieved that at least Shiraz and Wilf had made it safely to the hotel. She picked up the handset and dialled the last number to ring her mobile.

'Hello, can I speak to Jake Johnson please? It's Kitty McAllister. Yes, I'll hold.'

A few minutes later, Kitty's heart went out to Jake. She listened to his tearful apologies and promises to repay the money. Kitty wasn't a hundred percent convinced and when he begged her to keep it quiet for the sake of the company's reputation and future, she warily broached the topic of having confessed to Adam. He had not taken the news well, but instead had warned her not to fall in love with him again.

'That's your concern right now? Not the fact that the bank could take our homes? Close the business?'

Jake wasn't making any sense, and she was keen to get off the phone. When she said she hoped that the door was open for the brothers to address their own issues, he hadn't sounded keen but neither had he been opposed to it.

There was now only one blot on the horizon that threatened the new peace. Kitty knew the matter of her and Adam had to be broached sooner rather than later, and it would require some delicacy, but she had run out of steam and was determined there was no way, under any circumstances, that she would be drawn into discussing it tonight. Even under this bizarre scenario of being stranded and forced to sit up straight and listen to Adam, a professional talker, for ten hours until they could head off again. Kitty marched back to the table determined that this must not be allowed to happen.

Adam had other ideas. He was busy perusing the menu. His hair had fallen into his eyes. He brushed it casually away unaware that every single woman in the near vicinity was watching him. He was one of those men that naturally drew the eye. One of those impeccably groomed men from top to toe, even after a gruelling, mountainous trek. He threw her a warm smile which caused her heart to promptly melt.

'I need to tell you something about Jake,' he said resignedly.

'I'd much rather you didn't. He's not exactly my favourite person right now.'

'Okay, fair enough. That's understandable. We Johnson men seem to have a habit of letting you down. Let me walk you through my thoughts for your social media instead.'

Kitty drained her glass. Maybe it was time to show Adam she'd moved on and that whatever had passed between them all those years ago, was no longer an issue. No one needed to know she had been experiencing hot flushes, tingles and sexually graphic flashbacks every few minutes while he had been talking. She wasn't sure how much more of the emotional turmoil she could take. One minute she was overwhelmed with lust for him and the next she'd be seething with bitterness and anger at the way he'd ended things. For the sake of professional harmony, at least until the end of filming, it would be better for her to give him the impression that theirs had simply been one of those relationships that had been enormously improved by the buffer of several years of not being engaged to one another.

'Okay. Sure. Why not?' she said, relieved that at least for the next ten hours they would be on safe territory conversation-wise.

Kitty was unsure as to how exactly the topic of one's appalling social media profile morphed into Adam confessing to crippling doubts about whether he was being true to himself. Perhaps it had occurred somewhere between the first and second bottle of red wine and Adam revealing that he no longer had the constitution for the drink that he once had, not now that he was occasionally vegan. He was pinning her to the seat with an inebriated stare.

'Brace yourself Kitty,' Adam said, slurring slightly. 'Real strength is in our weakness. I'm going to expose myself.'

'Please don't.'

'I'm going to be vulnerable in your presence and I'd like you to acknowledge my lived truth. I was so obsessed with making a living over the years that I forgot to make a life. That's my *lived* truth. *My* lived truth, Kitty. Can you believe it?'

Kitty *could* believe it. For a professional talker he was making what could have been a somewhat useful conversation into something altogether much harder work, requiring translations and explanations of popular culture references that she couldn't hope to keep up with.

'*My* lived truth is that I'd like you to speak English please and not in hybrid American clichés.'

'Look at me,' he said, reaching across to take her hand in his, 'I'm going to explain my truth of what happened... so please, just listen. Listen with your eyes.'

'My eyes?'

She'd need another drink if this was the path he was going down. A large one.

Kitty, four glasses of wine in, was staring at Adam's beautiful mouth, realising bitterly that she'd made a grave error of judgment, a humungous mistake, in travelling with him.

Why? Because as she watched him swaying around beside her, she was overcome with the realisation that she fancied him. She really, really fancied him. She was powerless to deny it any longer. Powerless. And by the way he was carrying on, Adam was also realising that he too may have made a humungous mistake in *not* marrying her, which made her fancy him even more.

'Take our lavish, over-the-top, celebrity-style wedding. You seemed so anxious at the time.'

'I mean what bride wouldn't be?' she asked him. 'You invited two hundred people. I knew seven of them. I wanted a small intimate wedding on a beach, you booked Westminster Cathedral and a horse and carriage.'

'You see the problem is I fell in love with you,' Adam said, shaking his head in disbelief. 'Then in love with myself... then out of love. Out of love.'

Adam thumped the palm of his hand against his forehead as the realisation sank in.

'Except I didn't, did I Kitty?'

'Didn't what? I'm a bit lost off.'

He placed his hand over hers, his eyes wide and incredulous at the simple realisation. 'I never fell out of love with you.'

Kitty perked up.

'And really, maybe I just need to accept that perfect love may not actually exist. Our perfect love didn't exist. I blamed my brother. I blamed you. Everyone but myself.'

Disappointment flooded through her as Adam lost her in a string of contradictions.

'Except that it *did* exist. It *did* exist.' He was stage-whispering to her.

Kitty, exhausted and in danger of becoming numb to it all, was then forced to witness an incoming tide of self-recrimination and braced herself with another top up. Adam seemed furious with himself. She watched helpless as he muttered into his drink.

'I'm a fool, Kitty. A moronic fool.'

Nobody could argue with that.

'What I did to you was despicable. DESPICABLE!' Adam slapped the table, sending a stray olive into the air.

Kitty felt relieved that by glass five and a Limoncello chaser, his Hulk-like rage had subsided and was surprised to find that she had every sympathy for him. How had neither of them ever really acknowledged the fact that they had simply been young and acting on impulse?

'Why didn't we simply *talk* to one another about it, Kitty? Why? I'm a talker. A professional talker for God's sake!'

Luckily, by glass six, with the red mist of fury completely dissolved, a giddy clarity had emerged as they drank themselves sober and between them a flurry of apologies ensued.

'I think I'm to blame,' Adam said, looking rather surprised at himself. 'We're like two wrongs that make a right.'

'Yes,' Kitty agreed. Adam appeared to have a PhD of some sort in Psychology.

'It was all my fault, Kitty.'

'Yes. Yes, it was.'

'No, don't blame yourself. I was the fool. It was all me.'

'Yes, I'm agreeing with you.'

'People make mistakes, don't they?'

'It's what makes us human, Adam.'

'So, it's both our faults?'

'If it means you'll stop talking, yes. We were both to blame. But you more than me.'

Adam had a soft, soberish look in his eye.

'I'm so very sorry you know.'

His words flowed through her like a soothing balm, dissolving toxic emotions as they went.

He leaned over to gently thumb away the tears rolling down her cheek.

'You needed to hear that years ago. I'm sorry you had to wait.'

Some hours later, sleeping in the car and risking freezing to death seemed like a very good idea. Kitty could barely keep her eyes open. She felt her cheeks being patted.

'Stay awake Kitty.' Her eyes pinged open.

'YES!' she yelled. 'I'm not sleepy. I'm not sleeping. I'm not going to fall asleep. I'm completely... not asleep...'

'KITTY! WAKE UP,' Adam shouted again. 'We've already been warned once. We both just fell asleep.'

'Did we?' Kitty glanced over to the lady behind the bar who was staring disapprovingly at them. 'We'll order more coffee. And more wine. No. More coffee. Coffee is what we need.' Kitty dragged herself up and walked unsteadily over to the bar.

She staggered back to Adam. 'I'm not sure I'm going to be able to stay awake.' She picked up her glass and tipped it down her throat.

'Me neither,' he said blinking, picking his wineglass up and copying her. 'Just to warn you, this coffee tastes off.' Kitty watched Adam's forehead thump loudly onto the table. 'It's no use, Kitty. I can't do this. Surely it must be morning soon.'

'Here, you'd better take these.' Some keys clanked down in front of them like a Christmas miracle.

'It's only a single attic room but seeing as it's not even midnight yet, we figured you'd need it more than we do,' said the American couple, smiling. 'We'll bunk in together for the night. Besides, we really can't take listening to you anymore.'

There was a pause as Adam, overcome with emotion, tried to offer the couple a billion pounds Stirling to repay them for their generosity. His eyes were glassy with tears and his lip wobbled as he blinked them back. He struggled to his feet and raised a hand to his forehead in salute.

'God bless America,' he bellowed, arms outstretched. 'Let's make America great again. Oh, say can you see... by the light... by the... star-spangled...'

The couple gave Kitty an understanding look as they scuttled away.

After tripping up the narrow staircase, giggling like a pair of little girls, taking it in turns to shush each other and taking an age to get the key in the door because Kitty's fingers had turned to water and the key kept slipping through them onto the carpet, and every time Adam bent down, he fell over into the perfect shape of a chair.

'Stop sitting on me every time I get down to look for the... what am I looking for again?'

She tried to get up but found she simply did not have the strength what with her spine now like a strand of overcooked spaghetti.

'Where are we?' Kitty whispered, sinking heavily into him. Adam looked up at her, his cheek against the carpet. 'Emotionally, I mean.'

'Aha, found it.' Adam unfolded himself and took Kitty with him to an almost upright position. He waved the key around. 'Now which room are we in? So many doors. How many doors do you see?'

Kitty squinted at the wall. 'One.'

Kitty fell through the door and straight onto the bed. The room was approximately the size of a bathmat. She took in the shabby, narrow single bed, the small table with an old lamp on it and the tiny slit for a window in the sloped eaves.

'It's beautiful,' gasped Adam.

Kitty nodded as she patted the empty space on the bed beside her, tiredness seeping into her bones as sleep took hold of her.

She woke after what felt like a thousand years later, feeling instantly rejuvenated. 'Oh my god. How long have I been out?' She blinked at her phone, still in her hand where she had left it, to see she'd been asleep for less than three minutes.

Adam was awake beside her, grappling with his shoes. He flung them in the air where they landed with a thump and a crack to something that sounded breakable. Whatever it was, it turned out the light.

'Who did that? Where are my shoes?' Adam asked, grasping wildly at the air by his feet. 'They've been stolen, Kitty!'

He was extraordinarily drunk.

Kitty pulled his arm and felt him sag into the space beside her, his head sinking into the pillow with a contented sigh. She focussed on the rise and fall of her chest, every sense in her body aware that lying beside her was Adam Johnson. After all this time. Her body still fit perfectly against his.

'You should never have left me,' Kitty said, experiencing a profound moment of clarity. Adam froze. After an eternity he answered her.

'I think a part of me has died every day since. I feel thin without you. Like I'm just watching a version of myself living this fantastic life, but I can't feel the joy, there's no depth, no substance. Then I'm with you Kitty, and suddenly it all makes sense. Everything means something.'

The last thing Kitty remembered was the trickle of tears rolling down her cheeks as she closed her eyes to let sleep take her.

Chapter 11

There was a loud knock at the door and some rumblings in Spanish. Kitty woke with a great gasp to find her heart thumping and her leg completely numb. She tried and failed to open her eyes. She poked Adam in the chest from her position snuggled up beside him. She was lovely and warm under the duvet cover and could see no reason to move. She poked Adam a little harder as the knocking became more insistent.

'Adam,' she croaked. 'The door.'

Adam stirred, their faces were less than an inch apart. Alcoholic fumes billowed from his lips. Kitty tried again. She was feeling very weak and even the energy it took to jab him in the chest was draining.

'Adam.'

Kitty reached her hand up to cup his cheek, just as the knocking stopped. He nuzzled her nose, grazing her lips with his. Kitty in a dreamlike state was flooded with endorphins. Her lips involuntarily parted and before she quite knew what was happening, she and

Adam were kissing. Light, feathery, other worldly kisses. Kitty kept her eyes clamped shut, her mind spinning.

This isn't happening, she told herself. Her heart was beating wildly. I'm still fantasising. She felt his tongue slide gently against her lips before his mouth trailed down to murmur words into her neck. It sent shivers across her skin and caused a heat to rise from her lady parts.

Kitty felt the light touch of Adam's fingers caressing, touching and stroking her soft skin as they writhed slowly against one another. At some point during the night, they'd both lost their outer clothing and were wearing only underwear. She felt him go hard, grinding deliciously against her. She relished in the slow build-up of sensation until it was like an electrical current running straight through her. She'd always loved a good dry hump. Adam groaned gently. Their kiss deepened as he shifted to roll between her legs, his body undulating, simulating sex. Her soft moans seemed to tip him over the edge. Adam reached round to release her bra and caress her breasts as they tumbled out, filling his hands. His thumbs grazed her nipples in such a lazy, sensual way that her entire body felt on fire. Her cupid's tunnel tightened as he rubbed his fingers gently against it, causing a tingling sensation to pulse out through her whole body in the most sensuous way. She shuddered to a climax.

Her body sagged contentedly into his, a soft, ethereal sound escaping from her lips. It was warm and familiar. He gave her his full weight as their arms and legs entwined.

Realisation settled on them as if in slow motion.

Kitty's eyes sprang open.

As she stared at him, Adam began to blink rapidly before his eyes came to focus on hers.

There was not enough room in the tiny bed for either of them to make any sudden moves, besides every nerve ending of Kitty's had relaxed, her entire being had gone soft. They stared at one another trying to focus with somewhat muted expressions. For once, Kitty was at a loss for what to say. Adam appeared to be the same.

'Maybe this is just a dream,' Kitty whispered, closing her heavy eyes. 'Yes, a dream.'

Relief flooded his face. He wrapped his arms around her, and she drifted off to the sound of his steady breathing.

The next time Kitty woke, it was with a banging head. Adam still had his arms clamped round her. She could hear a phone ringing and shuffled over Adam's lean body to peer over the edge of the bed. It was on the floor. Kitty's fingers felt numb as she struggled to pick it up. The exertion was making her head snap with jabbing pains. Prising her eyes open, she was dismayed to see it was a video call.

'Who are you? Where is Adam?' a flame-haired woman barked angrily.

She winced as she took in the enraged face, the liberally applied mascara weighing down two large, come-to-bed, green eyes and thick amber hair glistening as the woman bobbed about shrieking.

Adam had not mentioned that his manager was a woman. She gingerly turned the phone to face a sleeping Adam. He let out a gentle snore as he held on tighter to Kitty causing her to fall into his armpit. The lady on the phone did not seem impressed. She screamed down the phone at him, causing Kitty to hold it at arm's length.

'WHAT THE HELL IS GOING ON?'

Adam's eyes sprang open. 'WHO? WHEN?'

He took a moment to give Kitty a bewildered look. He peered down to the phone being held somewhere by his chin.

'Take it,' said Kitty. 'It's too heavy for me.'

'I don't want it!' croaked Adam.

'It has a loud lady on it.'

Adam and Kitty heard the lady scream dramatically before she hung up.

Adam rolled onto his side to spoon Kitty who was already purring gently at the feel of him snuggling into her neck. Her traitorous body stirring, sensing pleasure. She sleepily pressed up against him, weakening with desire. She decided she might stay here in his arms forever.

'Your manager is very attractive.'

'Who? Nigel?'

'Ah,' said Kitty as realisation dawned. 'She's your…'

'I'M STILL FUCKING HERE YOU MORONS!' shouted Rebecca just as the loud jangling of keys at the door caught their attention. A second later a cleaner appeared in the doorway pointing to her wrist as though she was wearing a watch. There was too much happening at once.

'Shitting hell,' gasped Kitty, leaning over Adam. It was almost lunchtime. They were way behind schedule.

'ADAM, YOU LYING, CHEATING, SHIT BAG!!!'

Adam, pale faced, looked down at the angry woman on his phone and promptly switched it off.

Twenty minutes later, they sat in the restaurant staring at the two plates of eggs, sausage, tomatoes and toasted bread that had been put down in front of them.

'It'll do us good I suppose,' said Kitty. She looked sadly up at Adam. His face had the tinge of a green hue to it. He nodded dumbly. They ordered more coffee and paid the bill. Kitty found it hard to believe that merely a few hours earlier they had both been swept away on a riptide of white-hot lust. Walking outside they paused to face each other.

'I want you to know that Rebecca and I...'

Kitty put a shushing finger to his lips. More fool her for falling for his charms. She should have known, but she was too hungover to get into a slanging match with him over it, and so via the medium of telepathy, told him that for a variety of professional reasons, what had just occurred that morning, the very obvious, bone-shakingly erotic effect they had on each other, the seismic orgasm brought on by the expert dry humping and the accidental adultery... must never be spoken of, ever again.

Adam nodded in agreement. Kitty raised a tiny smile, remembering how they had always been in tune this way.

It took Kitty over an hour to drive the twenty minutes it was supposed to take to the hotel. First, they'd had to stop for Adam to hurl up sausage onto the roadside. Then they'd had to stop for Kitty, too weak to climb out, to be sick out of the window. She'd taken them both by surprise as she ejected a jet of yellow fluid from her throat with the force of a power hose. Then they'd had to stop in a layby while they both closed their eyes for two minutes before swapping over the driving because Kitty suddenly had no recollection of where they were headed or why. Adam then drove so slowly that a family out hiking with two young children walked past, waving as they overtook them. They limped the vehicle into the carpark as Wilf came running towards them.

'Flat tyres?' he was asking. 'Engine trouble?'

Adam wound the window down, looking at Kitty then back to Wilf. 'Yes.'

'Which one? Tyres or engine?'

Adam rubbed his temples, as though the pressure of thinking was about to make his brain burst through its casing.

'Flat... erm... flat,' began Adam, just as Kitty realised that lying about the tyres would be tricky as they'd be *visibly* intact.

133

'Engine! Yes, flat engine,' she croaked.

Adam gave her a distressed look.

Kitty felt rather at sea herself. How would they explain the previous evening and late morning shenanigans? It was highly unprofessional at best, and Kitty wished she was almost anywhere else when the looming figure of Shiraz, thick eyebrows knitted together over the nose bandage, ploughed towards them.

'Engine trouble, my hairy backside,' she spat at Wilf. 'Look at the state of them.'

Kitty steeled herself. She may as well have a huge neon sign above her head with 'ADAM RECENTLY FINGERED ME, AND I LOVED IT!' written for all to see. She got out of the car, reaching for the roof to support her as the ground momentarily subsided. She blinked a few times until Shiraz and Wilf came into clear focus. Her stomach rumbled violently. Kitty's hand flew to her mouth as a jet of bile sprayed the window screen causing the wipers to start automatically.

'FOOD POISONING,' bellowed Adam, his head suddenly jerking up. 'Food poisoning! That's right. Food poisoning. We've both got food poisoning.'

He got unsteadily out of the car and dashed towards the hotel, disappearing into the Gents. Kitty, in great need of porcelain herself, flew after him.

After running the cold tap and splashing her face repeatedly, the soothing balm of freezing mountain water calmed her heaving stomach. Kitty shivered at her pale, shrivelled face in the mirror.

She'd put herself at around seventy years older. Leaning her head against the cool enamel of the sink, she hunched over until the sickly feeling had fully subsided. After what could have been seconds or hours, her mind still foggy, Kitty made her way to reception to check in. Adam was lying face down on an elaborately embroidered chaise longue with one leg sprawled on the floor and an arm around an expensive-looking vase, watched by several receptionists wearing worried expressions.

'I'd like to check us both in please,' she whispered, mortified. 'Sorry. We've both got... erm, food poisoning.'

The receptionist tutted and handed over two key cards, pushing a bowlful of mints towards her.

'What...' mumbled Adam, as Kitty placed a hand on his shoulder. 'What? Why... why do we do this to ourselves?'

Kitty took his arm and hauled him up to a standing position. He was looming over her swaying. Somehow, she managed to get him over to the lift and up to the third floor. Getting into his room had been a struggle but once in there the mood suddenly shifted.

Christ Almighty, thought Kitty.

'Right then. I'll leave you to it,' she said, trying to get past him. They awkwardly tried to sidestep each other. She felt sure he must sense the heat radiating from her whole body. She was on fire.

He swiped up a complimentary bottle of water and handed it to her, taking another for himself.

Kitty was acutely aware that here they were again, alone, in a hotel room and, even through the thick haze of a hangover, yes, he looked dishevelled, yes, he looked weary and yes, he could barely stand up straight, but oh my god, he looked extremely fuckable, shower permitting. Kitty gulped. Adam tore his eyes from hers to the huge, sumptuous, impossibly inviting bed covered in cushions that were begging to be thrown to the floor. It was nothing short of sensual torture. Kitty wondered if she was still dreaming and against her better judgement bit her lower lip gently. It did look extremely comfortable.

'The woman on your phone. The angry one,' Kitty said wearily. 'She's pretty annoyed for someone who isn't your girlfriend.'

'It's complicated.'

Kitty followed his stare to a large painting on the wall above the bed. It was of a church, its doors thrown open to an explosion of confetti falling over a couple of newlyweds, laughing as they emerged hand in hand. A feeling of deep sadness seized her as she imagined what might have been if, instead of rejecting her three years ago, Adam had gone ahead with the wedding. She wouldn't have spiralled, wouldn't have been robbed of her sense of self-worth and wouldn't have begun to doubt her professional capabilities.

'Are you okay?' Adam was watching her with a look of concern.

Kitty's hand flew to her chest as she bent over struggling for air. She was about to have a panic attack. Like most jilted brides, any reminder of happy couples tying the knot seemed to bring it on. All of a sudden, she was fed up of it. She took in a deep gulp of air. This was not happening. Not anymore. It was time to get over it.

'I can't keep making the same mistakes,' Kitty said hoarsely, reluctantly putting up a trembling hand to stop him folding her into an embrace.

She had been haunted by his rejection of her for too long.

'We can't. I'm sorry,' she said bleakly. She just had time to see Adam's look of disappointment as she left the room, surprised at how it tugged at her heart strings.

He. Is. A. Taken. Man.

You are the programme manager.

Get. A. Grip.

Chapter 12

The next morning Kitty awoke determined to put the bizarre events of the last few days well and truly behind her. She had been so wracked with guilt over what had happened between her and Adam during the overnight stay at the roadside hotel, that she couldn't face the planning meeting that Shiraz had booked for them, mainly because it was to be held in a steaming hot tub. He might be unforgivably handsome and positively explosive on the sexual front, but that was no excuse to succumb so easily. Even after stoically deciding to end things in a mature and amicable fashion, she had been visited by lurid dreams of Adam's engorged manhood satisfying her over and over, as she quivered beneath his touch. One of the dreams had been spectacularly vivid with him bending her over the ornamental chaise longue, pounding her from behind while the receptionist tutted and shook her head disapprovingly. In another, she sat at the edge of a hot tub, clipboard in hand, legs spread wide. Adam was butt naked, his head enthusiastically between her legs, licking and sucking her like she was made of chocolate trifle, as she experienced wave after wave of tingling ecstasy. This dream had been so powerful that she'd orgasmed in her sleep and had woken, panting with beads of sweat dripping down her back. Her dumplings throbbing to the beat of her heart.

It was all getting way out of hand. She needed to put as much distance between her and Adam as she could.

Shiraz had posted photos of the meeting the previous evening on Instagram. Wilf, Adam and Shiraz soaking in a jacuzzi with a glass of bubbles in their hands. The top of Shiraz's bikini seemed to have pinged off amidst all the planning and discussion. This was on her. It was poor team management and all her own fault. She'd have to have words with the crew about their unprofessional behaviour.

There would be no more fantasising about Adam. No more distracting him away from filming. No more battling with her moral compass as to whether to mention his angry, flame-haired, 'it's complicated' girlfriend to Shiraz to put a stop to her persistent chasing of him. Things were getting silly. They were grown-ups after all.

The only issue she had difficulty with was whether to mention the Network's intentions to hang Adam out to dry in order to win this year's TV Lifestyle Show Award for '*Your Place or Mine?*'. In the meantime, Kitty would focus on the next episode and try to make it more heart-warming and feel-good than the last, and hopefully edit Adam in a better light. Filming for episode two was beginning that day and she was waiting in reception to greet the new couple.

'Morning.'

Kitty watched a sleepy Adam ruffle his hair and stretch out his arms to inappropriately reveal his taut stomach to all waiting at reception. Kitty had to admit he was insanely attractive with his perfectly symmetrical features and glossy, dark hair. He oozed appeal on every level. Kitty dragged her eyes back to his face.

'What's the plan for today, boss?'

'Well,' Kitty battled to clear her mind. Adam was usually last to arrive, so she felt temporarily thrown. 'We have our new house hunters arriving any second now and –'

'By the way, reception asked me to tell you that some woman has been ringing the hotel for you,' said Wilf, slinging an arm round Adam. 'She's rang twenty-nine times. It might be important.'

Shiraz followed close behind wearing a purple spandex ski suit and white fluffy boots. 'Adam, who's this stalker woman that keeps calling? I bet you have crazy women chasing after you all of the time, am I right?' Shiraz cackled, sliding up close to him.

'We'll protect you from stalker woman,' said Wilf keenly. We'll never leave your side. Not for a single minute.'

Kitty detected a sound of weariness in Adam's tone as he thanked them for agreeing to basically out stalk the stalker. Kitty handed out sheets of paper to them.

'Well, I think that's everything covered. Call sheets, locations, properties and crazy psychotic stalkers.'

'OH MY GOD THERE HE IS! HE'S THERE. IT'S HIM!'

Kitty and Adam swivelled round to see the new house hunters charging at them like hungry wildebeest. They stopped abruptly a foot away from him, panting with excitement.

'I CAN'T BELIEVE THIS IS HAPPENING. ADAM JOHNSON IN THE FLESH. AND HE'S GOING TO FIND THE HOUSE OF OUR DREAMS!' said one of the house hunters wearing an outlandish, multi-coloured, bobble hat with neon green earflaps made of, Kitty wanted to say, old leg warmers from the eighties. People often felt ski slopes were the perfect venue for expressing their zany inner truth, style-wise.

'How was the naked snow bathing this morning?'

Kitty looked from the house hunters to Adam in alarm.

'We follow you on Instagram,' said the house hunter. 'You are so right with your advice to listen with your eyes. It's a real gamechanger.'

Kitty found the adoration a little unnecessary but was pleased that Adam was taking the fuss in his stride.

'We've never had identical twin brothers on the show before,' Adam said good-naturedly, politely holding out his hand to shake both of theirs. The house hunters erupted into giggles.

'We get that all of the time, don't we?' said one to the other.

'We're actually husband and wife.'

They all took a beat to let this land.

'Follow me,' said Kitty, 'Let's get you both checked in.'

·♥·♥·♥·♥·♥·

'But they look exactly alike,' complained Adam once the couple had disappeared off to their room. 'It's like owners eventually looking like their dogs. Is that what happens to couples when they've been together too long? They've got the same short haircuts, the same matching outfits and the same bloody walking shoes. If it wasn't for those bizarre hats, I'd not be able to tell them apart.'

'Maybe they just like 'two for the price of one' offers at the hiking outlet?' said Kitty. 'And not *all* owners end up looking like their pets.'

Adam stopped and eyed her slowly before his lips curled into a knowing smirk. 'You never got yourself a pet? No way.'

Kitty nodded.

'You always swore blind that you'd never get one. Too much responsibility. Which animal doesn't require any sort of care? Did you get a pet rock?'

'She's a gorgeous cockapoo if you must know and I love her very much.'

'I don't believe it.'

As if fate were listening, Kitty's phone rang. It was Perrie on video call.

'Morning yummy mummy. Guess who had her first kissy wissy yesterday with Ned. Yes, you did, didn't you? It was so sweet. Ned brought her a pig's ear wrapped in a pink bow, and Alma went all glassy eyed and they spent the entire evening curled up in the

142

basket, snogging and licking each other. Mind you, so did me and Ted, only not in the basket wink, wink. Ah, hello Adam, didn't see you there. How are things? House hunters arrive, okay?'

Kitty listened as Adam and Perrie exchanged brief but awkward pleasantries.

'So, this is the doggy woggy I've been hearing all about,' teased Adam.

Perrie held up a wriggly Alma for Adam to admire. 'Isn't she gorgeous?'

Adam nodded and gave Kitty a side glance. 'Adorable. She looks just like her yummy mummy. Same dress sense. Same approach to kissing.'

Kitty bitterly regretted the fluke occurrence that Perrie had chosen the high ponytail, the dark blue onesie and red coat combo for Alma today. Kitty glanced down at her dark blue skinny jeans and red padded ski coat. Her hair was tied up in a high ponytail. Adam may have a point.

'By the way Adam, great job on the rushes so far. Keep up the good work. The Network are loving it. I hear you'll be milking mountain goats while wearing traditional lederhosen for the 'look what fun things you can do here' segment.'

'Actually, Perrie,' said Adam, his face becoming serious. 'I've been discussing with Kitty that perhaps we could go for a less trivial angle, you know? Really drill down into the psychology of why we think buying a house abroad will fix our problems. Maybe even delve into the politics behind Brexit and the knock-on effects for

143

ex-pats. We could even do a piece on the financial red tape and do a sort of 'Rip Off Britain' style exposé? What do you think?'

Kitty held her breath. She knew exactly what Perrie would think.

'Cool, Adam. All great suggestions. Leave them with me but for now, more of the same yeah? Okay, gotta go. Bye.'

Adam looked hopefully at Kitty. 'That went well don't you think?'

Kitty nodded her head. *That did not go well in the slightest*, she thought, smiling guiltily at Adam. A noise distracted them in the foyer.

'Which one of you is the man?' Shiraz was asking the house hunters.

Filming the search during four days of blizzards had been excruciating. Not only was Adam having trouble telling the couple apart, but they were clearly not interested in any of the properties.

'So, for our fifth and final property, how can I improve on this three-bedroomed chalet with its magnificent mountain views, a minute's walk from all of the facilities you said you needed, and coming in well under budget?' Adam asked patiently.

The whole crew could see he was struggling to keep his pecker up.

'I'm not really sure Adam,' said the male house hunter sadly, blowing on his fingers to keep them warm, his wife having long since lost the power of speech, her teeth chattering too loudly for the mic boom.

Wilf had had nothing but complaints to make throughout filming. Shiraz was also complaining bitterly about the cold seeping through her fluffy snow boots that looked more like a flimsy, fashion boot than sturdy all-weather footwear. It was not going at all well. 'I think we'll have to rule them all out.'

'For fucks' sake,' Kitty heard Adam murmur under his breath. 'And can you tell me why?'

'It's the snow!' he said, suddenly realising that he could no longer bear sub-zero temperatures.

'CUT!' Kitty yelled. 'That's enough for one day.' She eyed the couple who were looking miserable beyond words and reassured them that she would figure something out.

Later that day over lunch, Adam poked his fork at Kitty. 'They're going to make a fool of me, aren't they? This episode is going to put me right back to square one with everyone thinking I'm a joke.'

Kitty had never seen Adam this despondent. She tried her best to reassure him. Adam reached out across the table to squeeze her hand in gratitude.

'We've got your back, mate,' chipped in Wilf.

'And I'll make sure it's those twins who look like fools, not you, babes,' said Shiraz.

Kitty wasn't going to correct her again. Shiraz had been referring to the house hunters as twins all week. Nothing anyone could say was going to dissuade her.

'No one is going to be made to look like fools. Trust me,' Kitty said, getting an ominous feeling that these might be famous last words. 'Shiraz, did you manage to pick up the hired lederhosen costumes from reception? We'll be milking a herd of goats this afternoon when it stops snowing.'

After they'd finished a rather miserable dinner without Adam, who'd said he was unable to join them due to lederhosen-related frostbite and preferred to order room service, Kitty instructed everyone to pack up their stuff ready to leave early the next day. Back in her room, she rang Perrie.

'It's fucking genius Kitty! The whole thing could've been scripted. You couldn't make it up, could you? Couple dreams of living in the Sierra Nevada only to find that they hate the snow. They can't even bloody ski! And don't get me started on the three of them in lederhosen. I bet I can guess who made Adam wear the tightest ones. They left nothing to the imagination. Even my eyes were out on stalks. He looked bloody furious.'

Kitty listened to Perrie honking with laughter down the phone. 'He has no idea which one is which. That bit where Adam says, 'Is your wife a good cook?' and she says, 'I *am* the wife'. He looked about to explode with frustration. '

'So, we're going to have to show them a house in the sunshine. We'll have to move back to the coast I'm afraid. It'll cost an extra day and I'll have to put the extra expenses on my credit card. But instead of filming the millionaire's mansion on the slopes as planned, we could do one overlooking the Med and that'll mean we can claw back a bit of time.'

'Good idea. I'll clear it with the Network. I have a bit of room on my credit card too but not much. If we can scrape by until the last episode, we should just about manage. We need this to be a roaring success. Just make sure it stays funny. We can triple our fees after this.'

Kitty clicked off the call. A steady trickle of anxiety crept through her bones.

'Designated drivers are me with Wilf and Adam with Shiraz. Here are your schedules and hotel details,' said Kitty the following morning, as they prepared to leave in search of sunnier climes. 'The house-hunters have left already by train. They hate driving apparently.'

'But those houses they wanted to see were all ones only accessible by car or snowmobile.'

'I know, Adam. I know,' soothed Kitty. 'It's just one of those things. People can be quite bonkers. We'll get back on track today. Shiraz, as soon as we arrive, you and Wilf will head out to film for the montage. I'll check out a few millionaire mansion options and

Adam, you can stay at the hotel pool if you like, rehearsing the scripts.'

Kitty thought Adam deserved a treat after the few days of hell the house hunters had put him through. She still hadn't quite forgiven herself for behaving so unprofessionally and was determined to put any awkwardness behind them. Adam hesitated before getting behind the wheel and Kitty noticed he seemed sheepish.

'Well actually,' he said, looking at Kitty then Wilf and lastly Shiraz, who was already in the passenger seat next to him. 'I'll be checking in to another hotel. It's quite nearby yours so there shouldn't be any issues.'

'Five star I expect,' piped up Shiraz. 'Quite right, babes. You are a star after all. Does it have a nail salon for me, yeah? Pin me the deets.'

Wilf sounded disappointed. 'But I thought we were going to hang out, do a Turkish baths together and a mani-pedi?'

'Sorry mate, but well... Rebecca's coming to stay.' Adam threw Kitty a pained look. 'She wants to talk things through after... well, you know.'

'I KNEW IT. AFTER WHAT?' Shiraz bellowed, pinging her accusing glare from Kitty to Adam and back again as though she was watching a table tennis championship. 'AND JUST WHO THE FUCK IS THIS REBECCA?'

Kitty jumped in the other car, dragging Wilf behind her, and sped off, tyres squealing. She thought it best to let Adam sort that mess out with Shiraz himself, and tried to ignore the sinking feeling of disappointment growing inside. Her head was telling her that she'd had her moment of closure, he'd apologised, given her one last deep and satisfying orgasm to remember him by, and now it was time for her to move on. Whatever Adam got up to was none of her business.

So why did her heart not feel the same way?

Chapter 13

Kitty endured the road trip back down the mountain with Wilf who was obsessively speculating over what might be going on in the other car with Shiraz and Adam. Every so often Wilf would get the giggles and Kitty would have to remind him that, ethically speaking, as part of the crew he was every bit as responsible for team bonding and welfare as she was.

'Shiraz *so* has the hots for Adam, but he *so* has the hots for you,' laughed Wilf. 'Even though you literally threw up on his face. It has been driving her crazy since we got here. He's just not that into her. Why doesn't she get it?'

Kitty bit her tongue. She would not be drawn to idle gossip. Besides, it would be terribly unprofessional. Both as a manager and as a traumatised ex-fiancée, she must not be one of those desperate types, clingy for information. She would remain aloof.

'It wasn't over his face, exactly. Most of it went on the wind-screen. It was the food poisoning, remember?' Kitty still cringed thinking about it.

'And now there's this Rebecca on the scene. He told me she's a dancer in a musical. A dancer! Imagine how Shiraz will take that?'

Kitty would rather not.

'When I get my chance to be a presenter, that's exactly what I'll do. Play them all. A girl for every episode then I'd be off. Not even a goodbye. Not even a follow on Instagram,' Wilf was fantasising. 'He's so awesome.'

'There's nothing going on between me and Adam,' interrupted Kitty, who could take no more of his nonsensical chauvinism. 'And even if there was, I'd never succumb to his charms that easily.' She was more than prepared to be damned to Hell for the lie, but Wilf was stirring up old insecurities.

'The point is that he can have any woman he likes. He makes them think they're the sole object of his desire, they fall at his feet and then he moves on to the next one. That's what matters.'

Kitty's heart pinched. For her own good, she would need to keep her distance from Adam Johnson and his magnetic charm. Thankfully she was a formidable woman and could train herself to be impervious to his lure. *Once bitten, twice as shy.*

'This looks much better than that last shithole,' Shiraz said the moment they walked through the door of the next hotel, that would be home for the filming of episodes two and three. Shiraz thumped straight towards the lift and put her hands on her hips. 'Right, Wilf check me in, I'm off to lie down... Wilf?'

'He's being sick outside,' said Kitty, trying not to look the receptionist in the eye. 'Car sickness. Mountain roads.' At this rate they were going to get themselves a reputation, and not a good one either. 'I suppose I'll go and unload the cars then. *Alone.*'

'I'm too...' Shiraz threw Adam a dirty look. '... too disappointed to lend a hand.'

Kitty bristled at Shiraz's icy tone. She knew an emerging professional grudge when she saw one.

Unusually, Adam helped unload the car and even seemed to Kitty, slightly embarrassed at leaving to go and check in to his five-star hotel on the other side of town. They worked in silence, both of them careful not to make eye contact. Kitty was feeling extremely self-conscious. Despite herself, she was experiencing a strange sensation in the pit of her stomach, leaving her quite chewed up and tearful at the thought of him leaving to go and administer sexual favours to his lady friend.

'Are you okay?' Adam asked quietly.

Am I okay with you going off with another woman, even though I very clearly told you nothing would ever happen between you and I? Of course I'm not.

'I just wanted to explain about...'

'You don't have to. It's fine,' Kitty interrupted.

It is absolutely not fine. Obviously.

'Well it feels as though it isn't fine.'

'It is fine.'

How can he think this is possibly fine?

'You don't sound fine.'

Christ. He is like a police Alsation sniffing for drugs. Now, read my mind and tell me you understand my concerns.

After a moment, Adam gave up. 'Fine. Have it your way.'

Watching him drive off and disappointed in his lack of telepathic ability, Kitty dragged the kit over to the lift and after three trips she had finally managed to get it all in her room.

Keep it together, Kitty. You are here to work, not to take a trip down fantasy lane with your ex.

Not wanting to linger on her unwelcome reaction to Adam, she got busy ringing around the estate agents and tourist offices, planing places of interest with which to intersperse the house viewings.

A few hours later, Kitty was sweltering as floor to ceiling windows reflected blinding light straight into her eyes. She followed the estate agent into the main room.

'What did you say the show is called? A Place in the Sun? Is very good show. I love it. Is best show on teewee.'

'NO! No, ours is called *'Your Place or Mine?'* It's a completely different show. Completely different concept. The couple have to fight over the property at the end to see who wins. It's more of a drama with a social commentary feel.'

Antonia looked disappointed. 'Sure. Whatever. But programme is still just people looking at houses they don't want to buy, no?'

Good Lord.

'As you can see, the house has been designed to maximise the space. Bringing the outside inside because you British, you want to feel like you sitting in garden when you sitting on sofa.'

'Outside inside. Yes. Yes,' finished Kitty impatiently. She'd seen three millionaire mansions and all of them looked the same. *Boring. Boring. Boring.* She needed something with the wow factor if she was ever going to salvage this shambles of an episode. They only had one house left to show the weird twin couple which meant the showstopper would have to be all singing all dancing in order to liven it up.

'Antonia, haven't you got anything really striking or decadent? Like in a bonkers way? Something that will shock the viewers.'

Kitty was desperate.

'We do have something coming up, but it's... I don't know how you say... but it isn't yet on the market. I can text the owner now and ask if he'll allow the cameras in?'

'Yes please,' said Kitty. 'Can we see it today?'

'He lives abroad. I have the keys in the office. But I warn you. It's a bit... erm... well I wouldn't exactly call it...'

'Don't care. How much?'

'Ten million.'

'Perfect. Let's go.'

As soon as Kitty stepped foot in the millionaire's mansion, she knew it was the one. It was so over the top opulent that seeing was believing. Perrie would love it. The only problem she could foresee would be Adam keeping a straight face. Kitty revelled in the tour, snapping away on her camera.

'Antonia, show me that vulgar leopard print bedroom again. No! Let's do the gold cinema room then that dodgy Fifty Shades-type gym,' squealed Kitty, getting carried away with so many outlandish features to choose from.

The pretty Polish estate agent shook her head, laughing. 'It's hideous, no? At first we all think this is typical German with their brains full of sex and need for walk-in fridge for all the sausage.'

Kitty nodded along, remembering the mirrored ceilings in just about every bedroom and bathroom. She followed Antonia to the vast kitchen and watched as she opened the largest fridge she'd ever seen. It was crammed with booze of all types.

'But then we think it's the Russians because everything is so gaudy and golden with rich, deep colours everywhere. Desperate to show wealth.'

Antonia reached in, helped herself to a bottle of designer water and slammed the fridge door shut with some effort before she clip-clopped into one of the open plan lounge areas.

'Even this hideous green and many shades of purple sofa it costs twenty thousand euros. This extravagant paper lamp, two thousand euros! Is old French newspaper!'

Kitty watched as Antonia pointed disapprovingly to a variety of lavishly over-priced sticks of furniture. 'Who needs coffee table shaped like giant peach? Who?'

Antonia beckoned to Kitty. 'Come. I show you pool area. Is only nice thing about whole place.'

Once through the remote-control patio doors, the heat hit Kitty like a blast of air from an oven, causing her to appreciate, at least, the personalised state-of-the-art air conditioning the owner had installed.

'But then we find out it is British owner! British! They normally very boring with houses. Always the same. Lots of glass for light. Obsessed with light.'

Kitty couldn't argue there. She'd seen it all in her time. She grinned as Antonia put on a fake British accent.

'We must have space for dogs because we love them more than our own children, and vegetable patch for being off-grid and self-sufficient because even though we stinking rich, we want to live like poor people.'

Kitty was half-listening while she took in the breath-taking views from the pool. Its terracotta-paved area, dotted with plush sunbeds and parasols, looked like one of Adam's five-star luxury hotel Instagram photos.

'And we must have the views. Spectacular views from kitchen sink. Why kitchen sink? And kitchen, it must be open plan because they afraid of guests talking about them behind their back if shut away cooking all the time, even though they have enough money to eat out. Look, pool is fabulous, no?'

'It's exactly what I need.'

The whole place reeked of someone desperate to show they were successful. The elaborate décor and sensual trappings had the feel of a Playboy mansion. The artwork was suggestive, the ornaments borderline erotic and the owner had carelessly left out his whole collection of pornographic magazines in the bathroom, indicating he was partial to a jolly good orgy.

Yes, thought Kitty, *this is perfect.*

'Can you meet us here at around two-thirty tomorrow? We are filming a property about a fifteen-minute drive from here beforehand. I'll need the owner to electronic sign these papers. Can you scan them over?' Kitty handed a wad of papers to the estate agent. 'Who is it? Anyone famous?'

'No. No one we ever heard of but perhaps in UK he is a someone. Mad his son oh really? You have heard of him?'

Mad - his – son - oh - really. The words echoed round her brain.

'Is pronounced Maddeeson Oh Reilly, I think,' said Antonia looking at her notes. 'Is woman's name but he is a man. He is teewee presenter.'

Oh. My. God.

Kitty thought her heart actually stopped for a few seconds at the horror of her exes Adam and Maddison, two huge personalities, confronting each other.

Chapter 14

Kitty stared wide-eyed at the estate agent as she locked up the doors. 'Will the owner be here tomorrow?'

'No. He ask me to show house for him.'

She drove back to the hotel in a daze. Maddison O'Reilly. *What were the chances?* For reasons she was not entirely sure of, she decided it would be best to keep that snippet of information to herself for now, and not share with Perrie or the crew. She pulled up to the hotel at the same time Wilf and Shiraz were returning from filming the montage.

'Did you get everything?'

'Yes, but the town square is typical Spanish and quite dull,' Shiraz said, sounding bored. 'Nothing but a few old fellas with missing teeth sitting around playing cards in tracksuits and lots of stray dogs. I'm thinking we should do a night shoot. Inject some razzle dazzle, maybe?'

'I saw a sign for a jazz club stuck to the toilet door earlier. I think Adam would probably like it.'

'No, Wilf,' said Shiraz. 'We don't need him for this montage.'

Pleased that Shiraz seemed to be over her obsession with Adam, Kitty imagined a bit of distance would do them all good.

'That's settled then. We'll do a night shoot tonight. Meet me in reception at eight.'

·♥·♥·♥·♥·♥·

That evening, Kitty met Wilf and Shiraz in the hotel foyer to load up the mobile kit. She hadn't heard from Adam all day and had felt awkward contacting him. She imagined he'd be busy if an angry girlfriend was flying in to sort out their relationship.

Kitty looked Shiraz up and down. There had clearly been some crossed wires as to the nature of a night shoot. Unlike Kitty, Shiraz was dressed to go clubbing. Silver hot pants, silver shoe-string vest top, sky-high wedges, legs of a giraffe, eyes of a panda, nose of a proboscis monkey protruding from the bandage.

She looked at Wilf.

Cocking cock, thought Kitty. Wilf was also groomed and ready for a night on the tiles. Kitty suspected the two of them would dump all of the kit on her, go off dancing at the soonest opportunity and she'd get a call at three in the morning to go and rescue one of them. Then they'd be too hungover and exhausted to do their jobs properly the following day. She would have to nip these plans in the bud.

'Mr and Mrs Holden have opted to stay in tonight and search for properties on the internet because we have to be up first thing tomorrow. So, we could all do with an early night.'

'Who?' asked Wilf.

'The Twins,' answered Shiraz in a bored tone.

'Are they still here? Oh well, I hope they like the final property,' said Wilf as he piled into the car. 'It's in a nice area. Close to amenities. It's got lots of outside space. It's under budget so they can put their own stamp on it. They're getting a lot of bang for their buck.'

Kitty and Shiraz both giggled at the same time. 'Spoken like a true presenter-in-the-making,' said Kitty, loading the last bit of kit into the car.

'I've booked us a table at Destination by Dino. It's supposed to be the only decent restaurant in town. And then after there's a club we can go to. And after that there's a sort of speak-easy where they do fabulous cocktails served in edible glasses. And then after that there's an underground illegal bar cave selling Absinthe. Surprising for such a dumpy town.'

Say what you like about Shiraz, thought Kitty, *but she's extremely thorough.*

'No,' she told them. 'We're working, we're not on holiday. We'll eat. We'll film. We'll have an early night. We have a big day of filming tomorrow.'

'Aren't we picking up Adam for dinner though?' Wilf asked as they parked up in town.

'No, he's not coming.' Kitty hesitated as the atmosphere turned immediately frosty. 'He's messaged to say he's taking Rebecca out for a meal.'

·♥·♥·♥·♥·♥·

Kitty could never possibly have imagined how terribly wrong the following day could have turned out. The first indicator was Adam texting to apologise he would be late and would meet them at the property, and under no circumstances were they to go and collect him from his hotel.

The second was that the house hunters had turned up looking like they were going on safari. They had comically matching outfits and hats, socks pulled up to their ample knees, khaki shorts hoiked right up past their bulging waistlines, bright pink shirts already showing sweat patches and Jesus sandals. Kitty could only imagine the Tweets they'd receive.

The third indicator, the worst in hindsight, was that Shiraz was not the only one nursing a grudge.

'And we had hoped that Adam would dine with us last night. He had fillet of sole for dinner with a low-calorie dressing, didn't he?' remarked Mrs Holden. 'We'd have loved that, wouldn't we?'

'Yes, love. But we could see from his Instagram that he was enjoying a couple's massage followed by a moonlight forest bathing experience, wasn't he?' said Mrs Holden to her husband, who shook his head sadly.

'Forest bathing?' Kitty regretted asking the moment the question escaped her lips.

'Very romantic. Then of course he went dancing, didn't he?' Mrs Holden sighed dreamily. 'If only we'd known.'

'We have a beautiful property lined up for you today,' squeaked Kitty, desperate to stop them babbling. She could sense Shiraz stiffen nearby. Molecules of fury being released into the air.

'Couples massage? Moonlight forest bathing?' Shiraz choked out.

'Everybody, cars now please! House hunters with me!' Kitty boomed, ushering the house hunters into the car.

Kitty pulled up outside the property and was relieved to see it had oodles of kerb appeal. She heard Mrs Holden let out an enormous squeal as she got out of the car and ran towards it. Kitty was soon disappointed to see that the cause of the excitement was Adam, looking like a movie star with his legs wide apart and his shiny locks flowing in the breeze. He slowly took off his sunglasses and flashed his mega-watt smile at Mrs Holden.

'You look ravishing Mrs H,' he soothed. 'Nice sombrero. We could all get under that. Now, excited to get in?'

Mr and Mrs Holden, positively preening under the attention, followed Adam into the property like a couple of baby ducklings. Kitty felt relieved as she unloaded the car. She might be able to avoid Adam for at least an hour while they set up.

'Would they consider a project?' Adam asked. Kitty studied him. He looked like a movie star who had hardly slept. Although, she'd sneaked a peek at his Instagram to see he'd been picking up plastics from the beach at dawn #alonetime #savetheseas #easypayfinance, who knew what he'd really been doing that morning? Kitty would rather not know than ask.

'Kitty?' snapped Shiraz, who looked as tired as Adam. 'Adam is asking you if they'd consider a project and you're looking at him as though he's about to press charges.'

Kitty gave herself a sharp mental slap in the chops to stay on track. 'Sorry,' she yawned, 'Miles away. Late night *working*.'

Adam continued, 'Kitty, about last night. The reason I couldn't have dinner was –'

'It's fine,' Kitty interrupted. The last thing she wanted to appear was jealous. *But how could he be so blasé about it?* thought Kitty.

'I would have come to the shoot but –'

'You were couples massaging and forest bathing, we know.'

'Please don't interrupt. The reason I couldn't –'

'I told you it's fine. What you do is your business.'

Why am I like this? Why?

'For fuck's sake, Kitty. You are so infuriating. Whatever you think I was doing, I wasn't.' Adam strode off leaving them all to gawp after him.

'He seems tense,' said Shiraz about to follow him.

Quickly taking charge of Adam's welfare, Wilf barked at them. 'No Shiraz. I'll do him a shoulder massage while we do his sound-bites over by the pool.'

Kitty's spirits sank. This fighting for his attention was beyond acceptable. She yelled over, 'Adam? Make sure you mention talking turkey and getting more bang for your buck. The Network want to associate you with an authentic property specialist. They also wondered why you weren't asking the couples about wriggle room more often.'

Adam's face dropped.

'And I suppose I need to bang on about each property being a contender, do I? I have done this presenting lark before, Kitty. I know what I'm doing. I'm not a poor man's Maddison O'Reilly whatever you might think,' he hollered over his shoulder in what Kitty would say was quite an immature tone.

At the mention of Maddison, Kitty dropped the clipboard she was carrying. She scrambled to pick up the escaping papers. Adam raised his eyebrows pointedly and turned back to Wilf.

He was clearly annoyed.

Oh well, another step backwards it is, she thought to herself. TV presenters were so volatile. Their egos often so fragile. No wonder they were ever so slightly bonkers. She took a moment to stare at him. He looked on the surface like a man who had it all together, but Kitty wasn't so sure, especially after the way he'd confided in her at the snow hotel. Especially after they had shared that... special moment. She blinked away the thought.

She must stop annoying him. She must *stop* feeling bitter about a past life that had not gone to plan, *accept* the reality of what did happen and *move* on, allowing only the present to occupy her thoughts and heart. Hashtag live in the moment. Yes. That's what she would do. Starting immediately.

'IF YOU CAN TEAR YOUR HORNY EYES AWAY FROM ADAM FOR TWO SECONDS, I NEED YOUR HELP OVER HERE KITTY,' bellowed Shiraz. Wilf and Adam looked up sharply. Kitty froze like a deer in the headlights.

'Shiraz, honey, keep the noise down please,' called Wilf. 'Adam, we'll have to do that take again.'

Kitty spun round to face Shiraz. 'I was checking the angles and the... erm, sunlight, exposure, light exposure.'

'That's not what it looked like to me.'

She needed to face this mutiny head on. She'd worked with the likes of Shiraz before. These contractors liked to come in and take over just because they'd worked for the BBC or Netflix.

'What is your problem?' Kitty asked, hands on hips.

Shiraz pursed her lips, glancing briefly over to Adam.

'Keep it professional please, Shiraz. You have a job to do.'

'I will, if you will,' Shiraz huffed before stomping off in her sky-high wedges and her skin-tight dress halfway up her backside.

What sort of outfit was that to wear to work?

Kitty glanced down at her regulation baggy khaki shorts with lots of handy pockets, her plain T-shirt to blend into the background and walking boots, in case she dropped kit on her toes.

And how did I just become public enemy number one again?

Kitty shook her head. It was like playing emotional tennis against all three of them. She would mention how high maintenance this crew was to Perrie next time she called her.

Determined to get everything back on track, she first needed to stop Wilf commandeering Adam. He was pumping him for information on being a TV presenter. If there's one thing a TV presenter hates, it is normal people thinking they too can become TV presenters.

Kitty set about collecting up the leads and cables to hide them from shot. Still mortified at Adam sulking with her, she deftly hooked the microphone pack on the back of Adam's shorts while he continued to chat with Wilf. Adam took the lapel mic and scripts from her without so much as eye contact. Kitty straightened his collar and removed a leaf from his hair. Adam silently pointed to his backpack with his thumb. Kitty lifted his shirt and adjusted it before tucking him neatly back in. Next, he pointed to a line on the script and frowned. Kitty reached into her pocket for a pen and scribbled it out, before scuttling away without a word spoken.

The two men disappeared into the house with the excited house hunters.

'So, tell me.' Kitty heard a sharp voice behind her. 'What exactly is going on between you and my boyfriend?'

Kitty felt her entire stomach drop and snapped round to see an angry, pencil-shaped, copper-haired woman charging towards her and gulped. She'd recognise that furious face anywhere.

'I've been watching you from the car for ten minutes. You have to know someone very well to be able to ignore them like that.'

Chapter 15

Knocked sideways, Kitty struggled to find the right words and after a beat too long opted for a panicked smile. 'Hello. You must be Rebecca. We've all been looking forward to meeting you. We hear you're in a musical.'

Rebecca studied Kitty for a moment. 'There's obviously something going on between you. And where's this Shiraz I've heard all about? She can fuck off an' all.'

Kitty watched Rebecca fold her arms and tap her long toes impatiently on the terracotta floor tiles. She glanced down to see that even though she was wearing jewelled flip flops, Rebecca must be over six feet tall. Kitty became momentarily fixated with the length of Rebecca's toes. They looked like an old man's fingers. She was saved from answering by the honking sound of Shiraz laughing by the pool.

Rebecca's head jerked round like an apex predator and, considering the size of her hooves and gangly tanned limbs, she performed a rather graceful pirouette and darted towards the sound.

Surprisingly, it took only ten minutes of shouting for the air to be cleared between the two women, before it seemed to Kitty, like they were suddenly and unexpectedly becoming BFFs. Shiraz gave Kitty a superior glare before they began marching in her direction.

'READY TO ROLL!' she boomed, thinking quickly. Adam emerged with the house hunters, casting an apprehensive eye around to take in what was happening. 'QUIET ON SET. HOUSE HUNTERS LET'S HAVE YOU OUTSIDE. QUICK-LY. Adam, take us from 'What will our house hunters make of my final property' please. AND ACTION!'

Kitty could feel the sweat dripping down her back as Rebecca stamped off towards the garden area, where she continued to distract proceedings as much as possible by taking numerous selfies leaning against a palm tree in a variety of poses that required the lifting up of her short skirt to reveal a toned thigh that went on for miles.

Kitty glanced over at Adam with the house hunters. He flicked her the briefest of looks and Kitty thought she saw something that resembled an apology in them.

All the time they had been opening up to one another, and he'd had a girlfriend the whole time and not once thought to mention it! Not even to Shiraz to stem her relentless pursuit.

What seemed like an eternity later, Kitty was relieved to hear Adam, sticking to the script, summing up on camera, 'Well, what a house hunt it has been. Our couple are playing their cards very close to their chests. First, they wanted to be in the mountains with views of the slopes. Next, they wanted a chalet away from the action. Neither of them liked our third property, and they ruled out the seven-storey townhouse project in the village centre with its own crypt. There's just no pleasing some people. Fingers crossed this final garden property in the sunshine, with sea views, is a contender.'

'CUT!'

Kitty shouted instructions for everyone to pack up the kit and make their way to the millionaire's mansion. As Adam approached, she decided to dodge him. She was all riled up over Rebecca's arrival and felt sure Adam would be able to see her true feelings written all over her face.

You've played me for a fool, mister.

Kitty put it to the back of her mind and hurried over to the house hunters. 'I've ordered a taxi to take you back to the hotel so that you can decide whether to buy property five or not.'

'We don't want to buy it.'

'Well, at least have a think about it. Maybe one of you likes it and the other doesn't, and you can argue about it tomorrow on camera?' Kitty said, trying to keep her tone light.

'But we both hate it, don't we?' Mrs Holden said, nodding to Mr Holden for confirmation.

Kitty tried to be patient. 'The programme is called '*Your Place or Mine?*' she reminded them. 'Can you at least pick a favourite property each and pretend you might want to buy one of them. For camera?'

169

Mr and Mrs Holden clearly didn't like this idea. A thought suddenly came to Kitty. 'Do it for Adam, please?'

The couple cheered instantly. 'Okay. We'll do it. We'll do it for Adam.'

Kitty looked gratefully at their round, smiling, innocent faces. Their crush on Adam was quite cute really when you thought about it, she mused.

'But only if he'll have dinner with us tonight.'

Kitty's heart sank. *The manipulative little bastards. He'll never agree to that, especially not now his angry, long-toed, skyscraper of a girlfriend has flown all this way to spend time with him.*

'Of course I'll have dinner with you,' said Adam swooping in to charm the pants off them. 'And by the time I've finished with the pair of you, you'll be begging to buy a house from me. Shall we say seven? I'll meet you at your hotel reception. How's that?'

There was a very imposing tone to his voice. He had the underlying vibe of a man not to be toyed with. They'd all taken a beat to appreciate it when the taxi swung into the drive and beeped.

Adam and Kitty were relieved to wave the couple off and stood facing each other.

'Manipulative little bastards,' Adam murmured, causing her to smirk. Despite the mounting feelings of disappointment with her exceptional ex-lover for bringing his personal baggage to work with him, at least he was speaking to her.

'Where's Rebecca? I feel like she might stab me with something sharp.'

'She probably would but she's in the car, napping.'

Kitty gave him a quizzical look. 'It's not even lunch time.'

'She has eight naps a day. It's because she doesn't eat. She needs to stay thin. For the musical.'

'Oh. Right. Of course. Is it about pencils?'

Adam chuckled. 'Listen, about Rebecca. I'm terribly sorry. I tried to talk her out of coming but, well, she's... and earlier. I shouldn't have lost my temper. It's been a rather confusing time.'

Kitty nodded understandingly.

'We're not an item. No matter what she says. I didn't even invite her here. She just turned up.'

'Well, if she's a recent ex then she's bound to feel suspicious. She must be desperate to win you back.'

Adam lowered his voice, giving her a thoughtful look. 'You never were. Not once. I had women throwing themselves at me all throughout our relationship, and not once did you ever accuse me of cheating.'

Kitty swallowed, unsure of what to say. 'Because we were happy together, weren't we? There was no reason to cheat.'

Kitty experienced a pang of loss. Theirs had been one of those fun relationships, filled with laughter even when there was nothing to laugh about.

'I miss those days.' Adam sighed as though catching her thoughts.

Quite unexpectedly, tears sprang to her eyes.

'We need to talk, Kitty,' he said softly.

She hurriedly looked away from him and dashed to the car.

Oh my God, pull yourself together. Do not keep making the same mistakes over and over again.

Fifteen minutes later, they arrived at the millionaire mansion. Antonia was waiting at the end of the palm-tree lined driveway to greet the arrivals. Kitty got out of the car and went over to introduce the rest of the crew. Wilf's eyes lit up as he took in Antonia's striking East European looks and raised the back of her hand to his lips. *He was becoming more and more like his idol every day*, lamented Kitty.

Antonia reciprocated the flirting, giggling coyly. 'Would you like a private tour first before you set up the camera things?'

Wilf nodded enthusiastically, raising his eyebrows in delight as Antonia reached slowly past him to demonstrate the doorbell. They all listened to the elaborate sound of a woman sighing at the height of orgasm. Wilf and Antonia swiftly disappeared through the grand, over-sized door and into the mansion.

'What sort of prick lives in a house with a doorbell like that?' Adam said in disbelief.

'A very rich prick,' said Shiraz. 'Who lives here?'

Kitty's cheeks burned. 'Oh, some Russian oligarch I expect.'

'Well, I hope he's single,' said Shiraz, barging past them into a plush hallway, featuring a fountain of a naked couple entwined around one another with the water squirting tastefully from the man's erect penis.

Charming. Simply charming.

Maddison must have bought this place after they'd broken up. That, or he didn't bother to mention it to her.

Thank Christ he is not here, she thought for the hundredth time that morning.

'Whoever he is, he's a sexy bugger all right,' boomed Rebecca marching up the stone steps, fresh from her third nap of the day. 'I'd do him.'

'Hashtag me too,' quipped Shiraz as the two women erupted into peals of giggles.

'That's not what that...' Kitty watched Shiraz throw a casual arm over Rebecca's shoulder as an erotic artwork of two women kissing caught their attention. She had bigger concerns than these two ruining a global movement to empower women after thousands of years of patriarchal injustice. Episode two was in desperate need of rescue and this place was the key to providing a memorable viewer experience. It was wasteful extravagance of the highest order. She needed to remain focussed.

She felt Adam at her side making her body tingle. He smelled of bergamot and fresh lemons. Images of him soaping himself extravagantly in the shower pinged into her brain. She needed to put him right out of her mind.

'Where's the double walk-in fridge?' Rebecca demanded of Antonia as she breezed back into the hallway with an ecstatic Wilf at her side. 'They always have a stash of booze in places like this. Shiraz, champers?'

'I don't mind if I do, babes.'

Adam gave Kitty a look of alarm. She leaned in towards him, whispering as Rebecca, Shiraz and Wilf followed Antonia into the vast kitchen and hospitality area. 'How come Rebecca isn't angry with Shiraz?'

Adam nodded thoughtfully.

'It's so unfair...' Kitty's words died on her lips as Adam lightly grazed her hand with his.

'Rebecca thinks you're still in love with me. Are you?'

Kitty stumbled backwards. 'What? Absolutely not. No way,' she hissed, her face on fire.

Adam was looking at her intensely.

He knows I'm lying, she thought helplessly. *He knows I'm lying.*

Chapter 16

Kitty, dazed from Adam's shock revelation, contemplated the debauched scene that lay before her. They'd only been at the place twenty minutes and already Antonia, Shiraz, Wilf and Rebecca were playing topless volleyball in the pool. They were splashing about as though they owned the place. She was losing her grip on this team. Unless this counted as a collaborative approach to decision-making. Yes, a strategic collaborative exercise. That's what this was.

'No more than an hour for lunchbreak then it's back to work,' she called to them, desperate to seem in control. 'And not everyone wants to see you all waving your magic tits around.'

'I have to avoid tan lines. For my job?' Rebecca shot back.

As a dancing pencil?

'It must be so difficult filming in this heat. Especially when you have to work alongside judgemental stick-in-the-muds. Shnooky wooky, come and play!' cried out Rebecca to Adam.

As if Shiraz calling him 'babes' wasn't bad enough, the Adam she knew absolutely detested pet names like these. She threw a furtive glance his way. Adam was stretched out on a lounger a few along from her, eyes closed, pretending not to hear them. There was an awful lot of silicone bouncing around. The girls had all had a generous feel of each other's boobs to compare implants and scar tissue. Like a kid at Disneyland, Wilf was struggling to know where to look first.

When she could bear it no longer, Kitty got out and busied herself at the far end of the pool with one of the cameras, while they shrieked and splashed, consuming bottles of grog that cost more than her monthly mortgage. Adam strolled over.

'Kitty, why don't we do some shots for your Instagram? You haven't posted anything up in over a year. The Network will assume you've died.'

'Not a good idea.' She nodded over to Rebecca.

Adam cast a glance over his shoulder. 'She doesn't seem too bothered.'

Kitty thought he sounded genuine.

'You're definitely not a couple? It's not... complicated?'

'No. Not anymore, no. That's what I was trying to explain to her last night, but she had already booked a load of ridiculous things for us to do. It's all for her social media. She's an influencer.'

'Oh. Right.' She followed Adam into the house. 'Let's do it then. In the interests of the show and increasing viewer traffic.'

Who was she kidding? Adam was wearing nothing but a pair of swimming shorts that clung to his body like a second skin. She looked down at her tiny bikini. 'I'll just cover up.'

'Don't on my account,' Adam said, his tone light. 'Besides. You look fantastic. Natural and confident.'

Kitty was buzzing from head to toe with the compliment. She wondered whether to mention Shiraz's fake boobs and Rebecca's unnaturally long toes but decided she might sound petty.

'We'll take some shots and decide later whether they are suitable for Instagram or whether they go straight into my private collection.' Adam's eyes were so effervescent with mischief that Kitty shuddered in anticipation.

They left the others boozing in the pool to go through into the formal lounge area. Kitty's mind was buzzing from Adam's revelation. Whatever she might have thought was *not* going on between her and Adam, was nothing compared to the tense atmosphere and the lingering looks they were now giving each other.

Adam looked her slowly up and down. Kitty found she was thrusting out her chest and sucking in her belly. She found she was biting her lower lip and tilting her head to one side in a coquettish manner. Adam directed her to strike a number of poses on the many ornate chaise longues. He moved her arms slightly this way and her legs slightly that way. One time he gently parted her legs so that he could get the right angle. Kitty was embarrassed to find she shivered all over from his touch.

'Private collection,' he confirmed, his eyes creasing with mirth.

She took some photos of him in various yoga poses on tiger skin rugs and on the balcony off the main stately room. They had both agreed that their casual state of undress was a nice conceptual juxtapose to the formality of the place. He had asked her to get in real close, in order to capture his meditative glow. Her boobs had accidently brushed against his cheek as she removed a strand of hair from his magnificent forehead. He'd had to steady himself by gently grabbing one of her buttocks. The closeness made Kitty grateful that she'd sprayed scented sun oil over herself after the pool.

Next, they decided a less formal room was needed and went down to the spa area. He took some of her voguing in the jacuzzi. He asked her to squeeze her boobs together suggestively and look up into camera with a sexy look in her eyes.

'Private collection?' she asked huskily as steam billowed around them.

He took some of her face glistening with water droplets. He'd had to wipe some of them away from her mouth with the tip of his thumb. Kitty had felt strangely disconnected from reality as he sensually traced the outline of her lower lip.

Squeals drifted through the air to remind them that they were not alone, and time was ticking.

In order for Adam to come across as your run of the mill beefcake next door, they decided that the kitchen is the real heart of any home and Kitty took one of him posing naked with only a food blender hiding his meat and two veg from sight.

'Definitely private collection,' he said.

Then deciding that perhaps they might get better light upstairs, he took some of her kneeling suggestively in front of one of the free-standing gilded mirrors on the landing. She took some of him lounging on a huge round bed. It was covered in bright red silk, not quite the same but similar to his swimming shorts. They both agreed that the clash of colours would not look great on camera. Kitty watched as Adam stepped easily out of his shorts to slide beneath the silky sheet. Kitty found it necessary to lie beside him to get a shot of him through the ceiling mirror.

He took one of her kneeling on the bed with both of her thumbs hooked into her bikini bottoms, pulling them ever so slightly down to her recently tidied pubic area.

'I miss a full bush,' Adam said playfully, staring at her crotch. 'You don't see them anymore these days.' Adam looked like a hungry wolf about to pounce.

She took one of Adam lying in thought, with the red silk sheet grazing his rock-hard buttocks. Kitty took a moment to admire them. She edged towards him to get a close up of his lean torso. She had never seen a more resplendent body. The white-hot sexual heat emanating from him was palpable. Without thinking, she licked her lips. When she met Adam's gaze his eyes had grown dark, and his pupils dilated. His breathing had become ragged, and the silk sheet was exposing an enormous erection beneath.

'Show me the tattoo.'

'Show me yours.'

Kitty watched Adam slide the sheet down to reveal a tattoo, nestled in his impressively manscaped groin. She had a flashback to the moment they both went for their post-engagement tattoos, hers the ornate lock to Adam's elaborate key, convinced they'd be in love forever.

They stared at each other for what seemed like eternity before he reached out for her, and she fell into his arms. Within seconds her bikini top had evaporated, and they were rolling around together in the silk sheets. He was kissing her neck and pressing himself into her in a deliciously erotic way. He rubbed his hard on against her in exactly the right spot to cause a pulsating heat to spread through her body. His lips moved slowly from her neck down to drop kisses on her nipples. Kitty's mind was swimming as she arched into him. She knew that this was very wrong and unprofessional on so many levels, not least because her most recent ex-lover Maddison had probably done the exact same thing to someone in this very bed, but a burning heat was radiating out from her, and passion was clearing her mind of all things.

'I want you,' growled Adam. 'So much.'

Before Kitty could comment on the less-than-ideal timing or morality of the situation, Adam peeled her bikini bottoms easily from her quivering body. She gasped as she felt him slide between her legs, his tongue trailing circles round her thighs before she felt it tickle the tip of her Lady Gaga, creating a storm of pleasure to rage inside her. It sent waves of spasms through her as he did it again and again, applying a little more pressure each time. Within seconds Kitty was shuddering to a climax and gasping for air, her mind a complete and utter glorious blank. Adam covered her mouth with his own. She could taste herself on him. It was one of the most erotic experiences of her life. She was lost in the moment. Lost in his eyes, lost in the sensation, lost in the lightning bolt of sexual heat. She pulled an inch away and was relieved to see desire clouding his face. He kissed her again with such depth of passion that Kitty felt literally swooped away.

In that moment, all she could think about was giving him the same intensely gratifying pleasure he'd given her. She slid slowly down his body, kissing and stroking him, greatly turned on by the sexual excitement she was causing. He let out a desirous moan as she grazed the top of his silent flute with her tongue, but just as she was about to reciprocate fully, they heard a commotion outside in the pool.

They stopped to listen. A new voice had joined the others and the squealing had stopped. It was a man's voice, deep, smooth and silky.

'I recognise that pompous accent,' said Adam, sitting bolt upright. 'Fuck. I'd know it anywhere.'

Shit. Shit. Shit, thought Kitty.

That deep, smooth, silky vocal sound was the unmistakable voice of Maddison O'Reilly.

Chapter 17

Kitty flew to the balcony and peered over the edge. Antonia jumped out of the pool and raced towards Maddison full of apologies. She was quickly followed by Shiraz and Rebecca who both seemed extraordinarily keen to introduce themselves without a whiff of an apology. Maddison was gawping at the topless women before him.

'I LOVE MY LIFE!' he roared, throwing his head back. 'Now, someone get me a drink. I have some catching up to do. YOU!' he barked at Wilf. 'Who are you? Get me some champagne and then come and explain yourself. How did a little prick like you end up with these three stunners in my pool?'

Wilf jumped out of the pool and ran towards the kitchen. Kitty sensed Adam behind her.

'I hate that showy bastard. How did we not know this was his fucking house?' Adam was livid. 'And this is his fucking bed! Jesus Christ!'

'Erm, well...'

Adam gave her an incredulous look.

'You knew? He's a total fucking arsehole,' spat Adam without letting Kitty explain. 'I worked with him years ago. He's arrogant, self-centred and a complete prat.'

Kitty wasn't going to disagree, but neither was she about to get into the 'hows' and 'whys' of her past relationship with Maddison and how they'd managed to keep it such an industry secret, him preferring to take hired supermodels to the big flashy award shows rather than her. If it wasn't for the fact that he'd routinely made her head spin in bed, she might not have put up with it, but at the time she'd been desperate to block out the devastation that Adam had left behind.

'Come on, quick. Let's go down. We can say we were running the lines.'

'Fine' said Adam sounding pissed off. The tender moment they had just shared already a distant dream. 'We'll have to film the millionaire's mansion segment elsewhere.'

Kitty's heart sank. *Here we go, yet another obstacle to overcome. A huge, egotistical, mountainous obstacle.*

Kitty and Adam raced down the stairs. They were zigzagging through the many ridiculous sofas in the open plan lounge when they spotted Wilf watching them from the kitchen. Wilf raised an eyebrow at them and carried on filling the champagne flutes.

'Drink?' he asked them, managing to make it sound like he was asking if they'd enjoyed some great sex recently.

'No thanks,' shouted Kitty, rapidly stepping away from Adam as though he was on fire. They stopped at the patio doors to hear

Rebecca boasting that her soon-to-be-fiancé was also a big shot TV presenter, and had Maddison seen any of his work.

Kitty mouthed, 'Fiancé?' at Adam, expecting him to contradict what Rebecca was saying but disappointingly, he was standing staring at the group, his face unreadable.

Kitty's heart sank. Adam may be angry with Rebecca's blatant lie, but he was probably angrier at her for not telling him that this was Maddison's villa. Their public rivalry and dislike for one another had gone on for years.

How had she managed to get into this situation? She stowed Adam's sort-of-adultery away in her brain for later, unconvinced that the relationship with Rebecca was completely done and dusted, seeing as she had flown over under the impression that they were very much still a couple, and a proposal was in the offing. Adam was clearly not being honest with either of them.

Kitty knew full well she had played more than a willing part in the antics upstairs, but she was single. She was a SINGLE LADY. Therefore, free to do what she liked. It didn't matter that Adam had actually put a ring on it, because he'd also taken it back off again. Kitty promised herself she would go over the semantics later once she'd gotten this awful afternoon over with. Two past lovers under one roof and barely a pleasant thing to say about either!

'Let's get this over with then. Smile for the camera,' she said tightly.

She had a few bones to pick, starting with Antonia, who had promised her faithfully that Maddison would not, repeat would not, be home today. Not only that, Antonia had sworn to her that he would not even be in the same country. Kitty felt as though Antonia was somehow to blame.

Antonia, however, felt that it was Kitty who was very much to blame. So did Shiraz and as it transpired, so did Rebecca.

Kitty walked outside into the blazing hot sunshine to see the girls protesting to Maddison. Not one of them had thought to put a top on. Maddison had his back to her. She grabbed up her kaftan from the lounger.

'So, what you're all saying is that Kitty brought you all here, and encouraged you to make yourselves at home, splash about in my pool, get naked and help yourselves to all of my very expensive champagne? Do you know, in most countries that's called breaking and entering?'

Even to Kitty's ears, this did not sound very good. She was surprised to feel Adam squeezing her hand.

'Leave this to me. I've got this,' he said quietly, his face no longer thunderous. 'I'll say it was me. He's the sort that would cause a whole load of trouble.'

An overwhelming surge of respect for him enveloped her. Kitty yanked him back.

'Thanks. But it's okay, Adam. I've got this.'

'Of course you bloody have.' Adam shook his head in resignation. 'But I mean it Kitty. If he gets out of line, I'll...'

'Hey, Maddison. What's Britain's favourite TV presenter doing flirting with my crew?' she yelled over, forcing a bright smile.

'Kitty! Tell him this is all your fault!' bellowed Shiraz. 'That's her. She's in charge.'

Maddison swept round, piercing her with those stunning lavender eyes of his. For a second her heart jolted.

Muscle memory, Kitty told herself. *It's only muscle memory.*

She strolled casually over to Maddison. Her floaty kaftan top wafting open to reveal the string bikini. Maddison's eyes roamed hungrily over her body.

She cocked her head, 'Please stop teasing the girls and let them get back to bouncing around.'

Maddison laughed. 'Kitty-cat! God, I've missed you,' he said, grabbing her by the waist, dipping her backwards and sticking his tongue down her throat.

Kitty struggled out of his embrace. He smelled of stale beer and he was sweating with the heat but more so, Kitty suspected, at the excitement of a pool full of half-naked women.

'Let's get out of this heat first,' she said, luring him away from the girls who were seething. 'And you can tell me what you're doing here.' She flicked a glance at Adam who stood open-mouthed, looking like he'd just been told he owed a fortune in back tax.

If Kitty was going to get away with this, she was going to have to ooze some of that confidence that Adam was talking about. She linked an arm through Maddison's and rubbed it affectionately as they walked back into the house as though they were old friends with much catching up to do. Maddison stopped next to Adam. Kitty felt him bristle.

186

'Don't I know you from somewhere?'

Adam's jaw tightened. Maddison hated competition. Kitty had seen him routinely crush the confidence of rival presenters as though it was merely a fundamental part of his job.

Adam folded his arms and straightened to his full height, causing Maddison to mirror the action, rather like primates in the wild.

'Are you still looking for work, or have you gone behind camera?' Maddison said in a childish tone. 'You always seemed kinda stiff and uncomfortable in front of it.'

'Adam, I think you've met Maddison before. He and I used to erm, work together.'

'Of course. Who would forget a guy with such a delightful woman's name?'

'It's the French-Canadian spelling,' Maddison said tightly. 'It's unisex if you must know.'

Kitty dragged him away, mouthing an apology to Adam over her shoulder.

'So, this is a surprise.' Kitty tried to sound matter of fact. 'We weren't expecting you to come in person.'

Maddison stopped to give her a sly look. 'I saw on the paperwork that you were directing, Kitty-cat. This isn't a coincidence, is it? You knew I'd come.'

'No, absolutely not.'

'You knew this place belonged to me, right?'

'Well, yes but –'

Maddison sneered. 'I'll get changed and then you can tell me why you've lured me here and why you're working with that arrogant wanker.'

Unbelievable, thought Kitty aghast. *Un-fucking-believable.*

By the time Kitty raced back outside to explain things to the crew, Adam and Rebecca were long gone.

'Where's Adam?'

Wilf, Antonia and Shiraz looked up from drying off.

'He went off in the car with Rebecca. She didn't even want to go,' Shiraz said.

'I assume that means no more filming today?' Wilf asked Kitty before smiling adoringly at Maddison as he emerged from the villa in a fresh shirt. 'Mr O'Reilly, I'm such a huge fan of your work. The rapport you have with the nation's pets is... well it's... magical. They seem to obey your every command.'

'Just like their stupid owners,' Maddison sniggered. 'Stay for a drink, we'll talk turkey, that's what you guys say, isn't it?'

Wilf's and Shiraz's eyes lit up.

Please no.

'We can film in the morning with me on camera. That'll boost the ratings, won't it? I mean you'll get none with that asshole presenting. Always taking himself so seriously and he's so vain. Who has hair that shiny for Christ's sake?'

They all watched as Maddison barked with laughter. 'Stay for dinner. We can discuss the segment. There are so many features to this house that will blow the viewers' minds. I have a slide from

188

the bedroom straight down into the hot tub. What do you say?'
Maddison looked at Kitty pleadingly with those mesmeric eyes of
his and before she knew what she was doing, Kitty almost agreed.

She shook her head firmly. 'We still have so much to –'

'Great idea,' said Shiraz, cutting her off. 'We'd love to stay for
dinner.'

Wilf, a few sheets to the wind, nodded enthusiastically in agreement.

'We have a schedule to stick to,' said Kitty eyeing the others. *Had
they forgotten who was in charge around here?*

'I've watched every programme you've ever made.' Wilf's eyes
shone up at Maddison. She knew this would be music to his ears,
but only as long as Wilf didn't tell him of any aspirations to steal
his job. 'We even studied you at college.'

Maddison's lip curled. 'Really?'

'Yes. You're a module on powerful body language. Is it true that
when you speak, you can hypnotise people by accident?'

Kitty needed to stop Wilf from gushing, but Shiraz stepped in.
'Wilf, stop pestering Maddison. He's just our sound engineer,' she
said by way of apology. 'I do the camera.'

Kitty experienced déjà vu as she watched her in action.

'I'm Shiraz. I'm silky and smooth and sometimes a little fruity.'
She let out a tinkling laugh and switched her eyelashes to a slow
setting. Kitty was amazed Shiraz could get away with such an obvious line, but it seemed to have a one hundred percent success rate
because Maddison reciprocated the flirting with a wink.

189

'I bet you are. Now, Wilf, tell me all about this fabulous module you studied at college. Shiraz, honey, grab another bottle of fizz. Let's move this meeting to the jacuzzi and then I can claim it on expenses. It's down as a meeting space. Meeting space!' Maddison chuckled over his penchant for tax evasion. 'HMRC get nothing out of me, I can tell you. Not one penny.'

Kitty stared aghast as he stripped down to a bright, canary yellow thong, flinging his clothes to land wherever. Apart from a tiny paunch, he'd stayed in great shape.

'Should I go then, Mr O'Reilly?' said Antonia nervously.

Maddison looked her up and down. 'Certainly not, you can tell me exactly how much money I can make off this place. And whether I should keep renting it out? I can get up to ten grand a week, can't I, sweet cheeks?'

Wilf beamed at Antonia who looked shyly back. That was settled then. The evening would be spent sucking up to Maddison and his inflated sense of self-importance, which evidently was still located somewhere in the nineteen seventies. Kitty's mind flicked to those magazines and the graphic pictures of bodies indulging in an orgy of epic proportions and the bed upstairs covered in red silk. Once again, Kitty felt that she might be slightly losing her grip on things.

This house oozed sex. She briefly wondered if she'd been possessed by the house earlier in some way. She had a searing flashback to Adam sliding his tongue sensually over her.

'Kitty?'

She snapped out of her fantasy to see the group looking at her.

'Is that a yes?' Maddison was asking.

'Yes,' she said instinctively. She must stop zoning out like that, inwardly praying that she hadn't just agreed to allow him on camera with Adam.

'Great. Antonia, baby. Get us all some nose candy for after dinner, will you love?'

Jesus Christ, Kitty thought. *This job was impossible at times.* 'No. I'm putting my foot down. Maddison, we're in the middle of a shoot. Please don't lead my team astray.'

'It's a bit late for that, don't you think? They're already guilty of breaking and entering. Not to mention stealing a grand's worth of Pommery. And all under your orders I believe.'

Kitty sighed. She knew where he was going with this. He'd always had questionable morals.

'You wouldn't want to offend the host by turning down a simple invitation to dinner, would you?'

'No but...'

'Good. It's settled. Your charming company in exchange for the use of my home and me dropping all the charges.'

Kitty wasn't sure if he was joking, or whether she would have a legal leg to stand on if he wasn't.

'Fine.'

She resolved to flick through her extensive collection of leadership podcasts later, in the hope of finding one to deal specifically with staff issues like this. Staff who willingly stand back while their boss is openly blackmailed into an uncomfortable situation.

Chapter 18

Kitty stared at Maddison, sandwiched between Shiraz and Antonia, from across the vast dining table. He was many things. Exceedingly generous, flirtatious, confident, charming and dangerously unpredictable. She would need to keep her wits about her to keep him onside until filming had finished the following day. Maddison was keen to ensure everyone around the table seemed like the most important person in the world. He was skilful at that. Kitty knew that better than anyone. She listened to them vying for his attention.

'Tell me more about how you got into presenting,' Wilf was asking him. Maddison looked momentarily distracted and Kitty suspected it was because he was stroking Antonia's thigh underneath the table. Neither she nor Shiraz had thought to put any clothes on and were having dinner in their bikinis. Kitty looked down at her plate. Maddison had ordered in some very messy Chinese food. She'd had to witness both women sucking up noodles while trying to make it look sexy.

'I want to know more about how you spend your free time. Is there someone special we should know about?' Shiraz was asking him, batting her lashes and for some reason twirling her hair down between her breasts. Kitty had noticed Shiraz touched them a lot while talking. Maddison dragged his eyes from her chest to where thick make-up and a nose bandage were trying to disguise two black eyes and a swollen nose, before turning to look directly at Kitty.

'No. There's not been anyone special for quite some time.'

'How long has it been?' asked Shiraz stroking his arm sympathetically, cocking her head to one side. She was effectively putting herself forward for the next someone special.

Not taking his eyes from Kitty, he crooned, 'Twelve months, two weeks and four days, isn't that right, Kitty-cat?'

Shiraz and Wilf followed his eyeline to Kitty.

'You are shitting me!' yelled Shiraz. 'For fuck's sake! What is wrong with all of you men?' Shiraz threw her chopsticks down huffily, causing Maddison to burst out laughing.

'So sweet of you to care.' He fixed her the O'Reilly look, and Shiraz seemed to melt. Charmed by him. He could get away with anything. She saw his arm move ever so slightly beneath the table. Kitty remembered only too well the damage those fingers could do.

'Time for dessert? Antonia honey, did you get the goods?'

'I think I'll leave you all to it,' said Kitty faking a yawn, grateful she'd not touched a drop of alcohol. 'I've got to be up early to go and get the house hunters for breakfast and persuade them to get upset and have a huge row on national TV for the amusement of the general public.'

Maddison roared with laughter. The last thing she wanted to do was watch this four engage in a drink and drug-fuelled party. She had spent the last year checking his Instagram and obsessing about him coming back to her full of apologies, in an attempt to get over yet another rejection. For a while Kitty had even worried that she was perhaps in some way *drawn* to rejection. Perhaps she went out of her way to choose lovers who would be *guaranteed* to dump her. And now here he was, yet she wanted nothing from him. Not even an apology. She felt nothing for him.

Progress has been made.

She pushed back her two-thousand-euro velvet covered chair and stood up.

Maddison's face fell. 'No Kitty-cat. I want you to stay.'

'You know me. Work comes first.'

She knew this would resonate with him. He'd said it to her often enough. Luckily, Shiraz was demonstrating how she could top up his champagne by making it look like it was coming from between her boobs while Antonia retrieved a small bag of white powder from her handbag on the floor, wiggling her pert bottom high in the air a few inches from his face. Maddison's eyes swivelled from boobs to bum cheeks back to boobs and Kitty spotted that this was very clearly her window of opportunity to escape.

·♥·♥·♥·♥·♥·

The next morning, Kitty sat across from the house hunters in the hotel dining room as they described how perfect dinner had been the previous evening with Adam.

'He paid for everything you know,' said Mrs Holden.

'And he showed us how to manage our finances with that clever money app he sponsors. We're downloading it today, aren't we love? And we've ordered the face cream he uses, haven't we?'

Kitty smiled. Adam had kept his promise to them. She hadn't been at all sure he would. Relieved, she asked the pair what they'd like for breakfast.

They giggled. 'We'll have organic poached eggs on mashed sustainably farmed avocado on locally sourced rye sourdough,' said Mrs Holden winking at her husband.

'There simply isn't any other way to start the day!' he said proudly. 'Adam has changed our lives, hasn't he?'

Kitty stared in disbelief. TV presenters and their influence. *Mind boggling. Simply mind boggling.* She texted Adam to thank him for his generosity towards the house hunters and arranged to meet him at the millionaire's mansion. They would film both the end sequence for the house hunters there, by the infinity pool and also do the 'look what you could never afford in a million years' mansion tour. Shiraz and Wilf had not returned back to the hotel last night, weren't answering their phones and Kitty could only hope that they would be at Maddison's place ready for this morning's shoot.

She waited nervously for Adam to reply. For Kitty, neither scenario was ideal, but if she wanted to stick to the schedule then sacrifices would have to be made and egos swallowed. There was no time to find another mansion. The crew had a lot of ground to make up. They needed to wrap up episode two and make a start on episode three the next day.

Her phone pinged. Three little words. Kitty stared at them, her heart sinking.

'Find another house.'

He sounded pissed off. Very pissed off. Kitty dialled his number and waited for him to pick up. It was time for her to step up. She was done pandering to TV presenters. She had a job to do, faceless Network executives were counting on her to do it, banks were counting on her to repay monies owed, friends were counting on her to dig them out of huge financial holes and her adorable Alma was counting on her for a lifetime supply of doggy wigs.

Eventually he picked up his phone and all Kitty had to do was remind him of who they were both trying to help. His brother Jake, however much damage he'd caused to Kitty's business and whatever he may have done to upset Adam in the past causing them to not speak for three years, would need them both to rise above it.

She was dreading the day ahead, but not as much as seeing both her ex-lovers on camera together. It was clear that they detested one another which, last time she checked, did not make for great on-screen chemistry. She hoped that she could get away with showing as much of the mansion as a montage with Adam narrating over the top.

Once at the mansion, she made the house hunters a coffee and sat them out of the way before she heard the crunch of Adam's car arriving. He was uncharacteristically punctual, she had to give him that. Adam strode through the house and greeted the house hunters warmly. Today they were dressed in matching lemon tops, paisley shorts and white knee socks pulled right up to their knees.

'You've swapped the sombreros for oversized tennis visors today. And they match your shorts. How clever,' Adam observed cheekily as he approached them. Mrs Holden tugged the tip of her visor and collapsed in a fit of unnecessary giggles.

'We bought one for you if you'd like to wear it. It matches ours,' said Mr Holden kindly, holding it out for Adam.

'How delightful,' said Adam coolly, taking it from him. He looked somewhat horrified behind the eyes. She had remembered him saying on Instagram that it took roughly fifty minutes each morning to achieve his look, hairwise. 'Unfortunately, because of issues with the ... but definitely I'd love to wear this yes, if only...'

He spun round to face her.

'Sorry Adam,' Kitty said, diving in to rescue him. 'It'll ruin the continuity. And set a terrible precedent. We can't have house hunters thinking they must bestow gifts. I'll have to ask you to leave the visor off for this shot.'

Adam tipped his head at Kitty. He was clearly annoyed that she had not relocated to another mansion but obviously valued the rescue. She didn't dare assume that he was also a bit jealous about her having been in a relationship with Maddison. He was probably pissed off that Rebecca was telling everyone who'd listen that they were practically engaged.

'Adam, could I grab you for a second please?'

'Is it to tell me we are relocating?'

Kitty shook her head. 'No, but I need to...'

Adam, pretending not to hear her, walked off towards his car.

'Fine. Be like that.' Kitty thumped into the mansion in search of the crew. No one had so much as come to greet them when they'd arrived at the villa. She found them scattered all over the house. She found Wilf and Antonia sprawled on the floor of the cinema room. The giant TV screen was frozen on a close up of three unnaturally flexible women enjoying each other. One of them looking as though she was on loan from the Cirque de Soleil.

Kitty prodded Wilf with her toe. 'Get up please and commence the working day,' she said as loudly and forcefully as she could.

Wilf snorted himself awake and into a sitting position, his hair stuck at right angles to his face, his haunted eyes swivelling about. 'Where am I?' he whispered.

'Get dressed. We shoot in ten minutes out by the pool.'

Kitty was in no mood to take any prisoners today. He was ashen and looked as though he was going to need a lot of coffee to pull himself round.

'Where's Shiraz?'

'Who?'

Jesus Christ.

'Forget it. Pool in ten.'

Kitty bumped into Adam on her way from the cinema room to find Shiraz. 'I wouldn't go down there if I were you. Things got messy last night.'

Adam stiffened, looking right through her as though she wasn't even there. 'Well, I wouldn't know, would I? I was doing my duty and *working* last night. For the sake of the show. Because I am a professional like that.'

Kitty was immediately miffed at the insinuation. Adam had no right to be on his high horse, not today. 'Well, I wouldn't know either Adam, because I was also doing my duty last night and editing the montages for the show. Because I am *also* professional like that.'

Adam glared at her as though weighing up the truth in what she was saying. 'I saw Shiraz's Instagram. It sure looked to me like you guys had quite the party after we left.'

'I imagine they did look like that. Fortunately for me, I don't believe everything I see on Instagram.'

Adam took a beat to let this land. Kitty was quoting him back to himself and she wondered whether it had worked. 'So, you didn't spend the night?'

Kitty shook her head. Part of her was excited to see that this bothered Adam but part of her felt very differently. 'Where's Rebecca?' she said, a hint of jealousy creeping into her voice.

'Napping in the car,' said Adam, staring straight at her. 'Like I told you, we're not...'

'She's gone!' bellowed Wilf, running towards them.

'Who's gone?'

'Antonia. She's gone,' Wilf cried dramatically, tearing up. 'One minute we're making quick sweet love up against the popcorn machine and the next she's checking her phone saying she's late for a showing. Not even a goodbye. Not even a phone number. Who does that? I'll never get over this. Never.'

Kitty and Adam watched him wiping the tears from his cheeks.

And would it be too much to hope you are also upset because her disappearance will jeopardise the mansion segment, throwing us right off schedule?

'Wilf, mate,' said Adam reaching out to squeeze his shoulder. 'Is there a small chance you're still extremely high?'

'Yes,' whimpered Wilf. 'Maybe. I fucking *love* you two. And you two loving *fuck* each other.'

Kitty and Adam stared aghast at one another.

'No, sorry,' Wilf said, suddenly cheering as he laughed to himself. 'And you two fucking *love* each other. That's right. Come here you two. Bring it in.' Wilf launched at them, grabbing them up into a hug.

Kitty leapt back, mortified.

'Okay, that's quite enough. Now put some pants on and I'll make you a coffee,' she said, not daring to look at Adam. 'Wilf, any idea where Shiraz got to?'

Kitty was dismayed to see that Wilf was still struggling to place the name.

'Want me to come with you?' offered Adam.

Kitty nodded. She dreaded to think what she would find upstairs. They reached the top of the stairs just as Shiraz was click-clacking her way towards them. There was a slight pause as they all stopped to stare at one another. Under the glassily ambivalent glare of Shiraz, Kitty decided some small talk might be in order.

'Nice night?'

Kitty received a stern-lipped response.

'So-so.'

Small talk over, Kitty snapped into manager mode. It shouldn't bother her a jot what Shiraz and Maddison got up to. Not a jot. She'd be a fool to feel anything but ill-will towards Maddison after the way he behaved. *Good riddance.*

'We are filming in ten minutes out by the pool. Grab a coffee and meet us there.'

'Where's Maddison?' Adam asked her. Kitty could hear the strain in his voice. He was no more looking forward to this than she was.

'How would I know?' Shiraz answered enigmatically, giving Adam a pointed look. 'Jealous?'

'Not at all. I was rather hoping to discuss whether the lack of one single redeeming feature in this whole place was deliberate or not. You couldn't give this place away for free never mind sell it.'

Good grief, thought Kitty. It seemed as though she was the only one among them with a scrap of professional dignity at times. 'Okay, let's film the house hunter's final scene with Adam. Let's get some tears going if possible. We'll worry about the millionaire's mansion segment later.'

It had taken Adam several goes at digging around into the house hunter's private lives to dredge up a modicum of emotion. He'd mention Mr Holden's recent heart attack, Mrs Holden's estranged sister, their twenty-year ongoing feud with their next-door neighbours before finally, he hit the jackpot. 'You've two grown-up sons and seven grandchildren, haven't you? What do they think of the move to Spain?'

Mr and Mrs Holden went very quiet. Mrs Holden lifted her watery eyes to Adam. 'Yes, we have two sons. But they're not currently speaking to us, are they?'

Mr Holden shook his head sadly. 'We had a huge row.'

'Over you both looking like twins?' Adam said, gently prying. 'Are they ashamed of you?'

The crew held their breath. Adam was worth every penny. The atmosphere on set was intense. Kitty took in their podgy, guilt-ridden faces.

'Yes, they are. That's why we are leaving the country.'

'That seems a bit extreme,' probed Adam softly.

'We were caught dogging, Adam.' Mr Holden blurted. 'Have you heard of it? No, I don't suppose you have. No one was as surprised as us to discover it doesn't involve dogs.'

Mrs Holden hung her head. 'A friend suggested we try it so, you know, we turned up with Poppy, and someone filmed her because she was the only dog there and suddenly everyone was laughing and we had no idea why and then it went viral, didn't it love?'

'CUT!'

'Jesus wept, you couldn't make it up, could you?' Kitty howled with laughter as she and Adam waved the couple off in a taxi.

'Thank God we have The Gays next for episode three,' said Shiraz. 'They might be the pickiest of house hunters, but they always put their hands in their pockets.'

'Shiraz, please don't call our next house hunters by their sexuality but yes, with any luck they'll be ready to buy,' Kitty said hopefully. 'And to bicker about it beforehand.'

'Maybe we can all go to a gay club when they get here? They love to dance, don't they? Who's up for that?' said Shiraz.

Kitty shook her head wearily, adding stereotyping to her list of workshops to attend.

'I love a gay club,' said Rebecca, climbing out of her car to stretch and yawn. 'Great idea, lovely. Now, who do I have to blow to get a decent coffee round here?'

'That would be me,' came the unmistakable smooth voice of Maddison O'Reilly.

Chapter 19

.

Kitty noticed Adam turn the colour of a ripe plum as Rebecca threw her head back and laughed like a drain. Apparently, Adam found her offering to give his TV nemesis a blowjob in exchange for a hot drink, not quite as hilarious. Kitty thought she sounded rather like a strangled pigeon but decided not to say anything. She jumped in, to salvage what she could.

'Here's the situation. Antonia has disappeared off to another property, so Maddison you'll have to step in and show Adam around the house. We'll do a montage of all the main rooms,' Kitty rattled on before either man could protest. 'So, Maddison if you could do the meet and greet in the hallway, take us through to the lounge with the clap on clap off giant lava lamp shaped like a, well whatever it is that's on the coffee table, then we'll head to the master bedroom to take in the Ancient Greek-style marble ensuite and end at the pool with the magnificent panoramic views.'

'How long will Antonia be?' Adam asked forcefully. 'Surely it makes more sense to wait for her to come back. She's the expert in selling houses, after all. Even ones this vulgar.'

Kitty gulped, sensing the testosterone billowing from him. Adam was not a man to be toyed with.

Like water off a duck's back, Maddison had a laconic retort at the ready. 'What's the matter? Afraid your presenting skills won't match up to mine?'

Kitty waited patiently for him to stop laughing at his own, the world's pithiest retort. 'She's not picking up my calls.'

'That's because she's doing some errands for me.'

Oh my fucking God. He's set us up.

'Let's keep to the new schedule. Sorry Adam,' Kitty said, hearing him tut loudly. 'Places please!'

Once both men had smoothed back their hair in the floor to ceiling hallway mirror, and assumed matching power stances, standing with their legs a ridiculous width apart, Kitty called for Shiraz to begin filming.

'Neither of you are opera singers. Stand normally please. And action.'

She was dismayed at the hostile atmosphere as both men read their lines. The number of times Kitty had had to remind Maddison not to wink at camera reached ridiculous levels.

'Please, Maddison,' she pleaded. 'Only Adam is allowed to look into camera. You must only look at him. Otherwise, the viewers will become confused and upset and they will write angry letters and emails about it. They demand consistency.'

Maddison winked. 'I'm sure they will make an exception for Britain's number one TV presenter.'

'Number two,' corrected Adam flatly.

'Okay, Maddison, go from telling us why you want to part with such an over-the-top, pleasure-seeking...'

'Cry for help?' Adam injected.

Kitty gave him a stern look. '... villa.'

She couldn't wait to get this over with. Both men reminded Kitty of a pair of alpha male baboons.

They'll be beating their chests and baring their teeth in a minute.

Firstly, Maddison had disagreed with Kitty and demanded that they film the segment in rooms of his choosing. Which they did, only for Maddison to then change his mind once the unflattering light failed to highlight his best features and decide that the best rooms would be those that he (that Kitty) had originally suggested.

Adam was clearly struggling to keep the boredom from his voice, nor could he hide the disdain for the vulgarity of his surroundings, from his face. Maddison countered this with an elaborate show of prowess, demonstrating whenever possible his skills. They wandered through the kitchen.

'Not to toot my own horn but I'm actually a trained, Michelin-starred chef.'

Kitty was growing impatient. 'I don't have to remind you that anything you say that is factually incorrect must be reshot and we really don't have the time, Maddison. Or the money for lawyers.'

They passed through the living room where he pointed to a rug on the wall.

'I killed this lion myself. With my bare hands.'

She heard Adam muttering expletives under his breath. She couldn't blame him. They went out to the pool.

'As a linguist, I'm good at speaking in tongues,' Maddison winked at camera.

This was news to Kitty. Surely, she'd have noticed that he was multilingual during their time together.

'Yes, I speak the international language of love. Have you noticed that an orgasm sounds the same the world over? Even in Mongolian.'

'CUT! FOR FUCK'S SAKE, MADDISON.'

'Sorry Kitty-cat. We'll do it again. Roll camera!' Maddison shouted brightly, waggling his eyebrows at Shiraz. Then to Kitty's horror, they all watched as he stripped off, in less than two seconds, to become a blur of leopard print thong diving into the pool. And as if that wasn't bad enough, he goaded Adam on camera into becoming his performing monkey.

'Come on, it's refreshing. Let's race. Or are you too scared I'll show you up?' He looked into camera with a raised eyebrow. 'I'm a qualified lifeguard. Like on Baywatch. And I can hold my breath for five minutes. Do you know how handy that can be, ladies?'

Maddison then proceeded to thunder down the pool doing butterfly stroke like an Olympic athlete, slicing through the water to perform a somersault at the end before gliding like a shark back to the edge. Kitty gave Adam a worried look, inwardly pleading with him not to rise to the bait.

Keen to see both men strip off, Rebecca, Wilf and Shiraz goaded Adam to join in. Her heart sank as she watched a tight-lipped Adam smile rigidly for camera.

'No, Adam, don't. We really don't have time in the schedule for –'

'LOOK AT ME,' Maddison boomed. 'I'M LIKE A TORPEDO. ADAM, YOU WOULD NEVER CATCH ME ANYWAY.'

Wilf and Shiraz were capturing the whole scene with awestruck faces.

'Let's do the rest of the tour without him,' instructed Kitty. 'Everyone, follow me.'

'I'll give TEN THOUSAND pounds to the charity of your choice if you race me.'

Everyone turned to stare at Adam.

'For fuck's sake.' Adam turned to Wilf and Shiraz. 'Did you get that on film?'

Shiraz nodded and kept rolling.

'Right, let's make him pay,' Adam mumbled before ripping off his microphone and diving in. The next few minutes had been excruciating to watch, as both men thrashed up and down the pool, proving nothing but causing a tidal wave of water to soak the crew and equipment instead.

'CUT!' yelled Kitty, finding the spectacle utterly ridiculous. 'Very good children, now, please can we get on with it? I have a very tight schedule to keep to. Maddison, you owe Adam ten thousand pounds. Happy now?'

To her relief both men were keen to emerge from the pool. Kitty watched them gasping for air as they tried to cover up how tiring their competitive, testosterone-fuelled splash-about had been.

'I'd say it was a draw.' Maddison winked at camera, flexing his pecks.

'No. I won fair and square, but not bad for someone of your age, Maddison, I suppose.' Adam retaliated crisply as he towel-dried his hair and magnificent body. 'They say fifty is the new forty.'

Maddison, turning puce, was quick to deny it. 'I'm thirty-six.' He flicked Kitty a look of warning. She had attended his lavish forty-seventh birthday party just before he broke up with her. She had pretty much spent their entire ten-month relationship organising it.

'Shiraz, please stop rolling. Let's go to the master bedroom and wrap this up quickly.'

Maddison led the crew to his gaudy, mirrored, lothario's lair. Adam looked about with a frosty, distant expression. They watched Maddison sweep his arm flamboyantly across the room towards the circular bed before drawing their gaze up to the mirrored ceiling.

'Get on with it, Maddison,' Adam demanded wearily.

'This is where the magic happens. Quite a lot of magic. There's a camera behind the mirror up there.'

Kitty thought her heart stopped.

Fuckerty fuck, fuck.

She glanced at Adam. He too looked in need of a defibrillator. Kitty had never regretted an orgasm more. Not even one that spectacular.

'There's a camera in the mirror above the bed?' she tried to ask casually.

'Above the red silk bed?' asked Shiraz, not sounding shocked. 'I'd like to see the footage from yesterday.'

Maddison was nodding enthusiastically.

Why is this happening to me? Why?

'I do hope it doesn't end up on the internet,' Shiraz said flirtatiously. 'I'd hate to break it.'

Adam's face was pale.

'Shiraz, please stop rolling. We need to cut all of this out. Stick to the script if you wouldn't mind, gentlemen.'

'Unfortunately, the last tenant to hire the place stole it.' Maddison turned to look at Shiraz. 'Shame. I've been told on several occasions that I have an unnaturally tantric constitution.' Shiraz giggled coyly.

'Haven't I, Kitty-cat?'

'From the top. ACTION!'

Kitty was fucking exhausted, and in that moment, bitterly regretted ever having been born. She watched as Adam yanked off his microphone and threw it on the ground, stomping away as Maddison barked with laughter. Wilf ran off to comfort Adam while Shiraz made a beeline for Maddison.

'Let's take a short break!' Kitty yelled, trying to act as though this unscheduled halting of progress was somehow her idea and everyone was following orders. She wandered over to the pool and flopped down on the sun lounger with her head in her hands. She needed a miracle.

Rebecca slowly lifted her sunglasses. 'Boys not playing nicely?'

Kitty took in Rebecca's long body glistening with oil and shook her head.

'You sure there's nothing going on between you and Adam?' she asked Kitty.

Kitty swallowed. Now was definitely not the time to be truthful. She shook her head again not trusting herself to lie out loud.

Rebecca regarded her for a second. 'Okay, leave it with me. Back in a sec.'

Kitty watched Rebecca float into the house and disappear. Then she came back out and floated over to Shiraz, whispering something in her ear and touching her hair gently before they both erupted into giggles. Next, she floated over to Wilf. Wilf appeared to be coming down from his mammoth high and was consuming his fourth bag of popcorn. Rebecca leaned over and whispered something in his ear that made his face light up.

She returned to her sunbed and swung her giraffe legs up onto the lounger. 'All done. You owe me one. So *don't* get in the way of me getting back with Adam. Deal?'

Kitty nodded.

Rebecca slid her sunglasses back over her eyes and swished Kitty away with a graceful, manicured hand. 'Right, time for my nap. Wake me when this shitshow is over.'

Wilf and Adam were the first to set up. Then Shiraz came tottering happily over. Next to appear was Maddison who'd undergone a costume change.

'For fuck's sake,' muttered Kitty, realising they'd now have to start all over again. She gave Maddison a look of incredulity.

'Just film the end sequence. No one will notice,' Maddison said smoothly, all smiles. 'I'm in a bit of a rush. Meetings. Things to do.'

He was incredibly upbeat and over-the-top friendly with Adam as though the last two hours had simply not happened. Before Kitty knew it, they were all shaking hands and parting ways. She was immediately suspicious.

'Can I take you all out to dinner tonight?' asked Maddison. 'Before I leave.'

At the same time as she and Adam rejected the offer, Wilf, Shiraz and Rebecca all said a resoundingly loud, 'YES!'.

Adam tutted.

'Excellent, that's settled then. See you at eight. Shall we say, Enrique's? They do a champagne and lobster bisque that is exquisite.'

'Then a club. A club with sexy dancers,' announced Shiraz much to Rebecca's delight. 'It's about time we had a decent staff night out. Isn't that right, Kitty?'

'Adam, you haven't taken me anywhere nice yet since I got here,' said Rebecca in a sulky tone. 'The least I deserve is some lobster.'

'Great. Adam, Kitty, you'll join us I'm sure. Now if you'll excuse me, I have an appointment with my waxologist.'

'I shouldn't have come,' Kitty was saying to no one in particular as she observed the throng of sweaty dancers. 'I really shouldn't have come.'

She'd spent the entire evening watching Wilf throw himself at Antonia, then Maddison then Adam in perpetual rotation. It was dizzying. Kitty felt for him. His two idols were sitting at the same table ignoring each other. He was like a child at Christmas caught between two divorced parents making him choose which one he loved best. Adam had been quite sullen during dinner, which was due mostly, Kitty had reasoned, to Maddison putting on the show of his life to charm the pants off Shiraz, Rebecca and Antonia and they were falling for it hook, line and sinker as far as Kitty could tell. They had been gyrating for him on the dancefloor like they were being paid in diamond bracelets.

She was about to sneak away, feeling that her work here was done, when Maddison came up behind her and pushed a glass of fizz in her hand.

'Come,' he said huskily, beckoning her with a hooked finger and pointing to a booth where the others were currently spilling drinks, laughing too loudly and gazing glassily around to see if anyone was watching them enviously.

'It's the least I can do after you so generously offered to pay for dinner.'

Kitty's mouth dropped open. 'I didn't offer. *You* offered to pay and then dodged out of it.'

'I would have gladly paid but you were all on a staff night out. A team bonding exercise. Surely that's a tab Harmonia films should be picking up?'

Kitty struggled to defend herself. Maddison had always been a slippery eel when it came to paying the bill. She should have known better especially when she'd seen the vast amounts of lobster and champagne being consumed. He'd had no intention of paying from the start. It was pointless even to try and get him to cough up. Perrie would be furious. They'd have next to no money to finish the remaining two episodes.

Kitty followed him over with the intention of saying her good-byes.

'I've ordered more champagne.'

And you can fuck off if you think I'm paying for it.

'Actually, I'm going to go, but you guys have a lovely evening.'

Maddison stuck out his lower lip as though to sulk.

'You're a big boy. I'm sure you'll cope.'

'Yes, he is a big boy. A very big boy,' laughed Shiraz and just like that, in an instant, Kitty became invisible.

She made her way outside to flag down a taxi. They all had to be up early the following day to film the episode three montage and greet the new house hunters later that afternoon. Luckily, the area that the couple for episode three wanted to search in was half an hour's drive from where they currently were, which meant that the crew could stay in their hotel, and they would not have to waste time packing up again and it would save on fuel costs.

'Do you mind if I join you?' Kitty spun round to see Adam hurrying towards her. 'I can't bear him any longer.'

Kitty looked about for Rebecca.

'She's not coming.'

'Oh.'

They walked to the taxi rank to find a queue forming. 'Listen,' Kitty said quietly. 'About yesterday. You know before... when we... while we were taking the photos.'

Adam leaned towards her.

'I hope you don't think that I... well, what I mean is...'

'Look, it happened. I don't regret it if that's what you mean.'

Kitty's stomach flipped. 'And did you tell Rebecca?'

'No.'

Kitty thought about how she'd lied to her earlier. 'Adam, she asked me out right if anything had happened between us and I lied to her. I feel terrible. I think she suspects something maybe did happen.'

Adam cocked his head. 'That must have nearly killed you.'

Kitty grinned back. 'I'll never be able to sleep at night with the guilt. You know I'm the worst liar. I'll feel guilty forever.'

'As long as you didn't regret it.'

Kitty would have loved to deny it, but her entire body was in wholehearted agreement. She chewed her lip. She felt an invisible sexual gravity pulling them towards each other.

'Rebecca thinks we have a chance of getting back together. Which is ridiculous by the way,' he said. 'We are well and truly over. But she seems to think that you and Maddison are a couple. Or soon will be. Are you?'

'No! I mean... what we had was... it's well and truly over, whatever we had.'

Adam nodded thoughtfully. 'You had a brief fling? A rebound thing?'

If only it had been a brief fling.

'Is that why you came out tonight? To see if Maddison and I...?' Kitty dared to ask.

Adam blinked slowly in response, causing a wave of excitement to roll through her. They threw themselves into a taxi, while Kitty tried not to act on the strong urge that was flaring up inside her. The atmosphere in the car had turned thick with desire. Every glance loaded with promise. As soon as the car pulled up to her hotel she gave Adam one last lingering glance, her heart thumping within her chest.

'I made a promise, and I must keep it.' Kitty could hear the longing in her voice. 'We shouldn't.'

It was more of a question but if he so much as inferred that actually 'Yes they bloody should', then she feared she would give in immediately.

'You're right. We shouldn't,' he said, while his eyes told an altogether different story.

Chapter 20

'Kitty, you are a genius!' squealed Perrie down the phone. She was ringing on loudspeaker from her office. 'I've just come from a meeting at the Network and guess what? They were doubled up. They kept asking if it was all a set up. It's so unbelievably hilarious Kitty. I mean how did you get Maddison O'Reilly to send himself up like that? That leopard print thong. He looks a complete idiot. And the costume change at the end? Like he's never heard of continuity. OMG. And Adam. He looked totally fucking furious throughout. Was he jealous? Do they hate each other or was it a put on? And don't get me started on those randy old twins.'

Kitty listened to Perrie crowing with delight. Apparently, episode two was an exponential hit. Who could have predicted that the bizarre carry on in Sierra Nevada with the old doggers who looked like they'd been birthed by the same woman and the surprise appearance of Britain's number two TV presenter revealing that he's blown his entire fortune on vulgar and tasteless artefacts, would have had them all roaring with laughter from start to finish?

Kitty waited for Perrie to finish explaining what had just happened in the meeting. The Network were very excited. The Network were talking of commissioning more episodes. The Network thought the crew made an excellent team. The Network were offering Kitty and Adam a huge pay rise to commit to another two series.

'This is it!' Perrie yelled to her friend. 'This is your moment to shine, Kitty. We'll get a huge contract, we can pay for Jake's treatment, we can get the banks off our backs for a bit longer and we'll even have some money for doggie wigs.' Perrie sounded full of joy. 'And I'd be amazed if we don't win the TV Lifestyle Award this year!'

Kitty let this information sink in.

'What do you think? Can you speak to Adam today? The Network are viewing you as a package. You both have to agree. They think that with you directing him, you make a great team. Obviously there were some questions raised about him being your ex-fiancé but that shouldn't be a problem though, should it? You seem to be handling it very well.'

Kitty remained silent.

'It shouldn't be a problem, right?' Perrie asked again, her voice ten decibels quieter. 'Kitty, honey, what's up? I thought you'd be ecstatic?'

Kitty took a moment. 'I'm sorry Perrie but I'm not sure I'll be able to take the offer. I'm really not sure if Adam and I can work together beyond finishing this series. They want him to be the joke of the presenting world and I won't hang him out to dry. He deserves better. I need to tell him the truth.'

'You're kidding me? What's going on? And just to be clear, we're talking about the fucker who left you high and dry, heartbroken for years afterwards and unable to maintain any sort of healthy romantic relationship ever since? Do I need to remind you of Maddison O'Reilly? Now, start from the beginning and don't leave anything out.'

When put like that, it sounded as though her ever-increasing feelings for Adam would lead to nothing but heartbreak and disaster. Perrie was spot on as usual.

'Okay, but it's a long story,' Kitty puffed out her cheeks, exhaling loudly.

Where to begin such a harrowing yet soulful and passionate account?

'Basically, we got stranded in the mountains... we drank too much, we had a deep and meaningful heart to heart where he apologised for everything and then somehow, we ended up sharing a...' *How to describe it?* '... not sex... it was more than that... it was a more of a *special* moment... in bed together.'

There were a few beats of silence while Perrie listened.

'That's not actually as long or romantic or as interesting as I thought it would be. To be honest, Alma's relationship with Ned is more complex than yours. So, you almost had break-up sex. A break-up fingering by the sounds of it. Show me a woman who hasn't. Kitty, this is our livelihood, our business at stake. For God's sake, don't throw it all away on a man who dumped you and never looked back.'

Kitty gulped.

She spent the rest of the morning, filming the montage with an upbeat Shiraz, in a bit of a daze. It was quite the quandary. She would love to accept the job offer. It was a dream offer. She might even be able to afford a better place for her and Alma, nearer to the centre of London. No more expensive uber taxis to work. Nicer parks for Alma to meet nicer doggies. And while Kitty wasn't going to encourage Alma to play the field, Perrie had given the impression that Alma was all but going steady with Ned. This needed to be nipped in the bud. Alma was far too young to be tied down.

A commotion at the reception alerted Kitty to the arrival of the new house hunters for episode three.

'THE GAYS ARE HERE!' shouted Shiraz, click-clacking over to them. 'THE GAYS ARE HERE!'

Kitty looked at Shiraz in alarm and half-whispered, half-squeaked, 'Please don't keep calling them The Gays. They have names.' Kitty suddenly regretted not having committed their names to memory as Shiraz eyed her expectantly. 'My point is you can't just trivialise their self-worth to a faceless group.'

'Well, whatever. I love The Gays,' Shiraz said proudly.

Kitty took in her new house hunters' amused faces. 'And it's *house hunters* Shiraz, not *The Gays*. Sorry. Hello, I'm Kitty. Pleased to meet you both.'

Kitty shook hands with two incredibly good-looking, young men and could tell immediately that the camera would love their expressive eyes, their high cheek bones, their well-toned legs in their fitted clothes. They oozed class and charm. They were also holding hands. Kitty was a huge fan of PDAs and hoped that they would feel as comfortable on camera as they appeared to be at that moment.

'Are you looking forward to finding your dream holiday home?'

'Totally,' grinned the shorter of the two. 'I'm Bibi, half-Nigerian, half-Scottish and this is my husband Henrik. He's originally from Norway.'

Kitty took in his tall athletic appearance. She'd put Bibi at six foot, so Henrik must be at least six foot four. Between these two and Adam, episode three was set to have men and women drooling. It wouldn't be a calamitous joke like the previous ones. This episode would ooze sex appeal and glamour. She wanted viewers to appreciate Adam as a resplendent sex-god, and to envy these house hunters and their adventurous lifestyle. She'd have them bareback horse riding, water skiing, cliff diving and soaping themselves extravagantly somewhere under a waterfall. She mentally ticked off a few suitable locations.

'We're especially excited to meet Adam Johnson. He's kind of Henrik's secret crush, isn't he?' said Bibi, elbowing his husband playfully.

Shite, thought Kitty. *Not again.*

'I'm not sure where to look,' exclaimed Shiraz, her eyes swivelling from one handsome face to another. She peered down through her camera lens to make adjustments. 'They are all so incredibly photogenic. It feels like a fashion shoot. And the clothes! Why are the gays so much better dressed than straight guys?'

Kitty heard Wilf harrumphing as he waved the mic boom across to the house hunters, to pick up the conversation they were having with Adam. They came across on camera as though they'd been friends for years. The atmosphere had been electric, turbo charged from the moment they had assembled at the town square. People had stopped to stare and admire them.

'The great thing about this place,' Adam was telling them, '... is that you not only have the cosmopolitan night life here and the café culture but all the traditional Spanish fiestas as well.' They were hanging off his every word.

Kitty was making a huge effort to ignore the escalating feelings of warmth and attraction she was experiencing towards Adam. With Perrie's warning ringing in her ears, she also reminded herself that he was not yet entirely available even if she did want to go there again. She had promised Rebecca that she wouldn't get in the way of her trying to win him back. She also needed to find the right moment to tell Adam the Network news. She couldn't very well make the important decision without him. The offer was to them both. The dual obstacles of one, the Network intended to hang him out to dry and two, the Network would hang her out to dry also if she was caught sleeping with the star of the show, were still considerations not to be taken lightly.

Kitty glanced over to him. He wouldn't like to be made a fool of simply to boost ratings, of course he wouldn't and for all she knew, once they slept together and he tired of her, he'd expect them to revert back to a platonic working relationship, just as Maddison had done. Perhaps Adam may decide that he possessed enough self-restraint to work with her under those conditions, but if Kitty was honest with herself, she wasn't at all sure if she could work with him if he rejected her for a second time. As soon as they took a break from the first two properties, she would ask to speak to him alone.

Everyone was in place. The sun was shining down, the trees looked greener, the sky a perfect blue and every single person looked happy. Kitty's heart lifted. This is when she loved her job.

'AND ACTION!'

After a few hours of successful filming, Kitty was relieved as the house hunters and Adam listened good-naturedly to her vision for the episode.

'We went bareback riding on our honeymoon,' Henrik was saying, his face lighting up. 'And Bibi is excellent at water skiing, so it's a yes from us.'

'I'm not sure what the exact point of us all showering together under a waterfall is, Kitty. Could you elaborate further please?' Adam said, trying to stifle a giggle. Reluctant to reveal the true sexual nature of the shot, Kitty held up her hands.

'To shine a spotlight on water conservation? And to show the viewers exactly what two hours a day in the gym can get you.'

'What are you three magnificent studs all guffawing about?' Rebecca demanded, as she strode towards them, her fiery copper mane swishing with each gigantic step. 'You must be The Gays I've heard all about.'

Kitty had no idea where she'd popped up from and assumed she must have been napping in the car between cigarettes. The smell of stale ciggies lingered in the air as she said a breathy hello to the house hunters. Kitty noticed Adam's eye twitch and his body language stiffen.

'This is Rebecca,' he said, before gently easing her away from the group. Kitty tried not to stare. She could do without Rebecca randomly turning up. Out of the corner of her eye she saw Rebecca glare at Adam, yank her arm away from him and stomp over to Shiraz to whisper something in her ear. Shiraz nodded enthusiastically as Rebecca gently slid a hand up and down her arm. BFFs already.

'See you later,' Rebecca called out to everyone.

Kitty half-smiled and waved politely. *Not if I can help it,* she thought, gathering everyone round. 'We're off to Nerja to film the water sports and horse riding. Wilf take the kit and Shiraz you're with me, we can discuss the schedule for tomorrow. Adam, would you mind taking Bibi and Henrik with you?'

Once they were all settled in their cars, Kitty felt light-headed. With both Rebecca and Maddison out of the way, for once everything was running perfectly. The house hunters were behaving themselves. Adam looked mostly relaxed and engaged with what he was doing. He'd even been a little self-deprecating which had come across enormously well on camera. He was easy and charming and between the three of them, they'd oozed sophistication. Even Wilf, had turned up bright-eyed and bushy-tailed and on time for work.

It was Shiraz who was the only blot on the landscape as far as Kitty could make out. Shiraz had been uncharacteristically friendly towards her all morning. Kitty had not had to ask her to help load up or unload the cars, nor had she needed to remind her not to flirt with the house hunters or Adam. She had been immediately suspicious, but chose to bat away the creeping feeling that Shiraz was up to something, in favour of having a wonderful, productive happy day filming her potentially award-winning show. She beamed at Shiraz in the passenger seat.

'The Network are loving the quality of your work in post-production. You really are excellent at what you do, Shiraz.'

'I know I am. By the way, Maddison is going to meet us in Nerja. He's going to keep Rebecca company while we film,' Shiraz said. 'So, I won't need a lift back.'

Kitty bit her tongue. She should have known it would be too good to be true. They were adults. Consenting adults. What Maddison got up to, was no concern of hers. What Shiraz got up to outside of work was no concern of hers either. How Adam felt about Rebecca hanging out with his smarmy, misogynistic nemesis, wasn't either. She jabbed at the ignition with the car keys, firing up the engine with a loud roar. 'Fine. But in future, don't invite people to the set without clearing it with me first.'

The journey continued to be unpleasant, with Shiraz describing Maddison in great detail as though Kitty had never met him.

'He's such a character. So interesting, so deep.'

'I hadn't noticed.'

'He's very charming. Those eyes. I could get lost in those eyes.'

'He wears mascara.'

'Does he?' gasped Wilf.

Kitty was disappointed in herself. This sort of white lie was beneath her.

'He's got such excellent taste,' Wilf said.

'He's extremely sexy. He's got extraordinary stamina for a man his age,' Shiraz was gushing.

Kitty could not stand another moment hearing about Maddison this and Maddison that. She was sick of Maddison O'Reilly.

'He once sat on a kitten, and killed it.'

Chapter 21

Kitty pulled up at the main beach carpark, near to the Dive Centre where they'd be hiring the water skis and got out of the car. 'Shiraz, can you go in and let them know we have arrived please, while I unload? Thanks.'

Kitty watched her sashay into the Dive Centre and opened the boot to lug the kit out.

'Hey there gorgeous.'

Kitty's heart sank. Maddison O'Reilly was standing right in front of her with a huge grin on his face.

'Surprise.'

'Maddison. I'm trying to work here. I really don't need you hanging around and distracting all of my staff.'

Maddison looked mock-affronted. 'Who moi?'

'Yes. Please leave.'

'Most women beg me to stay.'

His face fell a fraction. Kitty shrugged. What did he expect her to say? He'd dumped her without a thought for how she'd take it and now that she'd finished filming episode two, she had no further reason to have anything to do with him.

'You could at least pretend you're pleased to see me.'

'Maddison. I simply don't have time to entertain your huge ego. I'm working. Look around. The world is full of women lusting after you. Go pick one and let me get on with my job.'

'Okay. Yes. I'll get out of your hair.' He looked genuinely hurt. 'Listen. About us. I am truly sorry you know.'

'Sorry for what exactly?' The list was incredibly long. There weren't enough hours in the day to even scratch the surface.

'I'm sorry I broke up with you the way I did. It was very disrespectful and must have been very hurtful.' He was hovering an inch from her.

She took in his signature, doe-eyed expression and felt an unexpected rush of relief. She'd waited twelve long months for that apology.

'Yes, you behaved really badly. And not just at the end. All the way through. I should never have allowed myself to be treated like that.'

Maddison became immediately defensive. 'It wasn't that bad. You did get an expensive puppy out of it I seem to recall.'

This was very typical of him. He'd have already rewritten history in his own head. Kitty sensed she was being watched. Across the carpark, Adam was staring at her.

Maddison followed her gaze. 'He's bad news, Kitty. Don't fall for that prick. He only wants what he can't have. The things I could tell you about him.' Maddison put his hand possessively on Kitty's back. 'Leave well alone, Kitty-cat.'

Talk about the pot calling the kettle black, thought Kitty, stepping out of his embrace. 'Listen, thank you for allowing us to use your villa. I'm sure you'll get loads of offers from people interested in buying it. But now that it's over, we have no need to be in contact. My life is of no concern to you Maddison. It hasn't been for the last year.'

'But it could be. It could be.'

Kitty shook her head at the audacity of the man standing before her, and hurried away towards the Dive Centre. He was such a prick.

Half an hour later, Kitty, Wilf and Shiraz were crammed at the back of a boat hurtling out to sea. Water was spraying everywhere as they jostled up and down every time the boat bumped over a wave. Adam was eyeing her intently. She turned away not wanting to ogle at him in the tight-fitting wet suit that he was wearing. He looked magnificent.

'CHRIST, WHY DO MARRIED GAYS ALWAYS LOOK SO HOT AND SEXY?' shouted Shiraz above the roar of the engine.

Wilf rolled his eyes. Kitty made a mental note to include him in some of the manly heroics she'd scheduled for later that day, as well as having another word with Shiraz about her free and easy usage of adjectives describing people's sexuality. Once the boat had come to a stop nearby some coves, the instructor set about explaining to Adam and the house hunters the order in which they'd dive. He gave Bibi some dive goggles to put on and took him to sit at the ledge on the side of the boat.

Adam stood up and stretched. 'How do you feel?' he asked warmly. Kitty was immediately touched that Adam had remembered that she was not great on speedboats. 'I wanted to make sure you weren't going to be sick on my face.'

Kitty burst out laughing. 'I don't think I'll ever stop apologising for that. Ever. But to be clear. It was near your face. Not on it. There was a car windscreen protecting you.'

Adam laughed. 'Well, you got an ear and most of my hair, but I like the idea that you'll be forever in my debt.'

Kitty was hugely pleased that there seemed to be no ill-feeling over Maddison turning up out of the blue.

'Listen, Adam. Is there any chance you'd be free tonight to discuss something with me?' She was aware that Shiraz and Wilf were listening to every word. 'Perrie rang earlier with an update from the Network. They have,' Kitty paused. '... a proposal they want us to consider.'

'Sure,' Adam said quickly. 'I have no plans. Rebecca is going out to dinner with Wilf and Shiraz tonight apparently. Just the *three* of them.'

Shiraz and Wilf both suddenly became very interested in a piece of rope lying at their feet.

'Great, thanks,' said Kitty, beaming. 'Well good luck with the diving. You're up next after Bibi. I'll take some pics for your Instagram, shall I?'

Kitty felt deliriously high. She ordered Shiraz to move over to the side of the boat to get a clear shot of Bibi. She directed Wilf to balance himself on the opposite side with the boom, to capture Adam laughing along with Henrick as they cheered him on.

'I'll get an arial shot with the Steadicam,' she said, climbing onto the flimsy roof covering the helm. She felt spontaneous and reckless. 'Adam if you can say your line then look up into camera, please.'

After the dive shots, they sailed further out to sea for the water sports segment. Kitty took a great many shots of Adam water skiing like he'd come out of the womb doing it. Adam chatting to the house hunters. Adam closing his eyes to allow his skin to take in vitamin D from the sunshine. Adam staring thoughtfully out to sea as he perched on a crop of rocks while he waited for the house hunters. Adam back in the marina helping tie the boat up as though he'd been a sea mariner all his life. Adam peeling down his wetsuit to dry off. Adam handing over the wetsuit and goggles dressed in nothing but wet swimming shorts that clung to his muscular thighs like clingfilm. Adam smiling at camera as he towel-dried his hair. Adam grinning to camera as he dabbed at his bare torso.

They gathered in the carpark once all the diving equipment and wetsuits had been returned.

'Okay if that's us done, then I'm going,' announced Shiraz, skipping off to join Rebecca and Maddison as though she was three years old.

'Wait for me,' yelled Wilf, running to catch her up. 'Wait for me!'

It's all very school yard, Kitty inwardly sighed to herself.

'Looks like me and you driving again?' she said to Adam. The sun was shining behind him. Even his silhouette was God-like. 'I'll take the kit and the house hunters back with me. Where do you want to meet later for the talk?'

'Could we talk over dinner?' Adam asked almost shyly. Kitty was taken aback. There was no way she should accept. It could only lead to trouble, yet she found herself nodding. Her heart began its now familiar thumpity thump.

'Cool,' Adam said, lowering his head as he dragged his foot along the sand. 'I'll pick you up at eight?'

Back at the hotel, Kitty had never been so nervous in all her life. *This is not a date. Not a date,* she kept repeating as she checked out her reflection in the mirror. She had gone for sexy but casual. She'd piled her hair up on her head. She had let it down again. She had decided to straighten it before realising what it needed was a curl. Then on seeing there was perhaps too much curl to it, she had straightened it again. Then in a panic she had piled it back up into

234

a top knot. She had applied light but effective make-up. She had on a pretty, floaty almost see-through summer dress. Her mind pinged back to the scene at the mansion when Adam had stared at her body as though it was an ice-cream sundae. She shivered. She couldn't remember a time when she had experienced so much rummaging around in her lady garden during a work trip.

She went down to reception ten minutes early to allow her nerves to settle, and to stop herself reapplying her Raspberry Fool lipstick yet another time. Her lips were plump and luscious. She didn't need them to look like two red bananas stuck to her face.

'Kitty!' bellowed Wilf from the bar and ran over. He had the eyes of a spooked cat.

'What's wrong?' she asked, adding silently, *please don't tell me.*

Wilf held the back of his hand to his lips to prevent a sob escaping and grabbed Kitty with the other. He led her to the bar and plonked himself down at a table. His eyes were rimmed with red. He'd been crying again.

With time very much of the essence, she begrudgingly allowed Wilf to babble at her in a voice two octaves higher than the one he'd usually use, before she felt she had to intervene.

'Wilf, calm down and start from the beginning. I thought you were out to dinner with the others,' Kitty said, not wanting to mention Maddison by name and taint the wonderful feeling of excitement currently flooding her body. Adam would be arriving at any moment.

'But that's what I'm trying to tell you. Shiraz refused to let me join in. She just wants to keep them all to herself.'

Precious minutes were ticking by, and Kitty felt no further forward.

'Antonia,' he said sadly. 'Antonia came here before we left to meet the others.'

'But I thought she was the love of your life?'

Wilf, with his watery, sad eyes, dug around in his pocket. 'So did I until she showed me this.'

Confused Kitty looked down at his phone. She could make out a tangle of naked bodies on camera. They were touching and caressing, stroking each other erotically. The camera zoomed in on two women. Their lips and tongues feasting enthusiastically on each other's mouths. The camera swivelled downwards to reveal their fingers engaged in hedonistic play. These women were indulging in consensual lovemaking.

'Why are you showing me lesbian porn, Wilf?' Kitty worried her management style had become too relaxed. When had she given any indication that crew members were encouraged to share this level of detail about their hobbies outside of work?

'Keep watching,' Wilf pleaded.

Kitty watched as three sets of hands and fingers continued to give pleasure. Threesomes had never been her thing, although Maddison had often hinted enough throughout the entirety of their time together. Then the penny dropped. Those hands. Those well-manicured, pampered hands.

Maddison's leering face came into view at the same time as his impressive arousal. As far as Kitty could see, no erogenous zone was being left untouched. He was mesmerised by the two women worshipping each other, their sumptuous, succulent, yielding flesh being teased by what looked like a giant vibrator. Kitty recognised it as the lava lamp she'd seen on his coffee table. Kitty watched as they satisfied every urge. She couldn't drag her eyes away as the camera panned out to reveal Shiraz and Rebecca taking turns to kiss and caress from all angles while Maddison pleasured himself between them. Then as the camera drew in close, a fourth lover settled between Shiraz's splayed thighs to deliver sensual oral pleasure with the delicate tip of her tongue. From the mountain of sleek white-blonde hair, Kitty could tell exactly who it was. No wonder Wilf had been upset.

'Okay, here's what could have happened,' Kitty said in a business-like manner. She checked that Adam was not walking through the door. 'Maybe she tripped and sort of... fell. It looks like she fell, yes, fell.'

'Nose first?' Wilf sounded wounded and sceptical. 'How many times have you fallen nose first into someone's vagina?'

'It happens. It could happen. That totally looks accidental to me.' Kitty was categorically bad at lying and could feel her excitement over the imminent arrival of Adam over-riding any feelings of sympathy for this latest drama. 'Antonia knows you really like her.'

But just as Shiraz was being brought to a squawking climax, Maddison boomed, 'Antonia honey, me next. Do that thing I like.'

Kitty was quite breathless by the time the four-minute video had finished. A few weeks ago, seeing Maddison with another woman, never mind three naked ones, one of whom was sucking on him like a lollipop, would have torn at her heart, it would have certainly broken her spirit, but as Kitty stared at the frozen screen, she realised that she felt numb towards him. Those dreams over the last twelve months where he came back full of apologies, begging to get back together were now no longer what she wanted. Strangely, Kitty felt contentment. She was ready to truly move on from him. He could indulge in as many lesbian orgies as he wanted as far as she was concerned.

'They didn't even invite me to join in.' Downcast, Wilf did not appear to be having the same epiphany as she was. 'I feel so left out. I didn't even know anything about it.'

Kitty put her arm round his shoulders as the tears slid down his face.

'Didn't know anything about what?'

Before she could act, Adam pulled out a chair and asked Wilf what was wrong.

Fuck.

Chapter 22

Adam looked devastatingly handsome. Like herself, he'd obviously gone to some effort for their meeting that evening. They would seem like two people on a date. Kitty experienced a pang of guilt. She desperately wanted to grab Adam's hand and pull him away so that he would not have to see what she'd just seen. Partly because she had convinced herself that between them, they could manage the Network's expectations without ruining his reputation and it would not be a barrier to working together for another two series. She had hoped that the potential for winning a prestigious award, that would catapult both of their careers into the stratosphere, would sway him. But mostly, she felt guilty because the video had made her so horny, she was eyeballing Adam with a wanton, lustful gaze.

He watched the video behind a stony-faced mask. To her horror, Kitty found watching it again just as erotic as the first time. It was all she could do to stem the fluttering and tingling rising from her nethers. This was entirely inappropriate on so many levels, particularly as she knew three of the lovers in a professional capacity.

Nonetheless, Kitty found herself wishing that Adam would satisfy her every urge right that instant. She tried not to observe Adam through the eyes of a sexual predator and switched her attention to Wilf who was now openly sobbing that he'd been robbed of his one and only dream in life.

'How many times have you watched it?' Kitty asked.

'Twenty-seven,' Wilf said miserably.

'Maybe you should think about deleting it, and moving on from Antonia?'

'Where am I going to meet someone as sexually free and obliging as her?' Wilf said in a horrified tone. 'No, Kitty. She's the one. I love her.'

Kitty traded glances with Adam. She still couldn't read his face or what was going through his mind. He stood up to leave.

'Sorry, Kitty. I'll have to take a rain check on our meeting tonight. I hope that's okay. There's someone I need to see and something I need to do. I should have done it sooner.'

Kitty nodded, disappointment flooding her bones.

'Wilf, mate,' he said. 'You can do better. At least find someone that'll let you join in.'

Wilf sniffed and nodded. 'Maybe.'

Kitty watched Adam walk away. The conversation would have to wait until another time.

·❤·❤·❤·❤·❤·

The following morning, Kitty met Shiraz and Wilf in the restaurant for breakfast. As soon as she walked into the room, she knew something was off. Wilf was sitting scowling at one table. His face pale, hungover and angry. Shiraz was sitting at a table far away from him looking like the cat that got the cream.

Kitty had a tough decision to make. Being a good leader and manager of people on this trip was turning out to be more of a minefield than she'd expected. Luckily the house hunters were also enjoying breakfast at a table between the two. They were impeccably dressed and called out to her. Kitty, relieved at not having to choose between her camera operator and her sound engineer, sat gratefully down to join Bibi and Henrick.

'We wondered if for the bareback horse-riding segment, we could go topless. It's always been a fantasy of ours, hasn't it?'

Kitty willingly agreed. She wasn't going to have to try hard to make this episode sexy. Episode three, it would appear, was taking on a life of its own, in front of *and* behind camera.

While she munched her way heartily through breakfast, half listening to the men chatting about the previous day's properties, Kitty's mind wandered to Adam. She wondered how he would be on set today. She wondered if he'd had it out with Rebecca last night. She wondered if he'd sent her packing or whether Rebecca had turned her sexual charms to her advantage and pleasured Adam

241

all night long until, in the throes of passion, he'd been unable to do anything but get back with her.

Kitty had a clear visual of Adam's face, the distant memory of how he used to look at her when they made love. She felt a pang of loss. Then a jealous thought pinged into her brain. She wondered if Adam was annoyed, like Wilf, at not being asked by the women to take part in an orgy. She shook that thought away. Adam had been made all kinds of saucy offers during their time together and he'd always told her about them saying he never did see the appeal.

Lost in thought, Kitty was only just aware that the waiter hovering around their table was asking if she'd like her coffee cup refilled. Snapping to attention, Kitty realised all the tables around were empty. The crew and the house hunters gone.

'What time is it?' she asked, wondering how long she'd zoned out for. They were behind schedule. She'd been sat there daydreaming and now they were going to be late to the next property. She still needed to arrange picnic hampers for their al fresco lunch and load the kit bags into the car.

She must get a grip. She had to stop obsessing over Adam. There would be no more being distracted by the crew and their sexual triangle that was more of a square really. They still had two episodes left to film. Kitty gave herself a sharp mental slap. She was better than this.

·♥·♥·♥·♥·♥·

Kitty drove Wilf and the kit to the next property. Shiraz drove the house hunters. She was still smiling from ear to ear, giggling at whatever they said and generally glowing like a woman who'd recently had an orgasm from every conceivable hole.

Kitty barked out instructions to Shiraz and Wilf, who still weren't speaking to one another and tried to give the impression that her head was one hundred percent in the game. She would take no nonsense today. She had an award-winning episode to film and that's all she would focus on.

She marched over to the house hunters to apologise for her earlier lack of courtesy and to make up some lies to explain why the atmosphere was so awkward between Wilf and Shiraz and why Adam would be late or even a no-show. In short, Kitty had no effing idea how the day would go. But the main thing was to keep the house hunters happy and very much in the dark as to the murky truth of what really happens behind the scenes of a successful lifestyle-themed TV programme. Sometimes with on-set gossip, before you knew what was happening it could be all over the internet. She needed to keep the goings-on well and truly under wraps.

'Don't worry about breakfast. We hear you've a lot on your plate,' Bibi said sympathetically.

Kitty nodded, not liking where this was going.

243

'Poor Adam,' Henrick added. 'Rebecca should have at least mentioned it was being filmed. I hope she's signed a confidentiality agreement. You don't know where shit like that will end up. She's in a stage play, isn't she?'

Kitty's heart drooped. 'Yes. Thrush, the Musical.'

This was beneath her, but Kitty simply couldn't help herself.

Bibi sniggered with delight. 'It could go viral, with someone like Maddison being chomped off on it by Adam's fiancée. I mean, we watched it quite a few times, didn't we?'

'I wonder if they'll still get married.'

Kitty opened her mouth to correct them, but the words got stuck in her throat at the thought of Adam marrying someone who wasn't her. *Had things been that serious between him and Rebecca?*

'And poor Wilf,' Henrick agreed. 'They should have at least invited him.'

Shitting hell, thought Kitty, throwing a disgruntled glance over to Shiraz. She felt very sure that Adam would be mortified to find out that everyone knew his private business.

'No wonder Adam and Wilf were up early to do cuddle buddy exercises. He's very in touch with his emotions. I would very much like to be his cuddle buddy for a shoulder to cry on. Wilf is a lucky man.'

'You would be so good at that,' said Bibi, looking fondly at his husband.

Kitty had not thought to check Adam's Instagram but now was not the time. They were running late, and she needed to get some footage in the can. Kitty directed Shiraz to set up in the property so that they could take some shots of Bibi and Henrick viewing this property on their own.

'We'll add Adam saying his lines about the couple knowing what they're doing and trusting them to view the property without him, later when he gets here.' *If he gets here,* she added silently. 'Wilf, we'll need you to track sound in every room to make sure they don't echo, Shiraz, you're on the steadicam and I'll squeeze in behind with the light reflectors.'

As Wilf jogged away to get his kit ready, Kitty turned to the house hunters. 'House hunters, remember body language facing camera. Never look into camera and always, always start with a positive comment before any negatives. Try to point out unique features like storage, high ceilings, the amount of light and whether you'd get a double bed in any of the spare rooms for visiting friends and family at Christmas.'

'Got it,' said Bibi. 'And we'll probably just say that it will be perfect for *someone* but just not for us. I like it when they say that on A Place in the–'

'Do your best to like it though and Henrik if you could disagree with him over the outside space, that would be great.'

After an hour, the house hunters had seen enough, and Kitty called for a quick break. She went over the details for the horse-riding and trip to the waterfall scheduled for later in the day. Kitty found a spot away from Wilf to message Antonia who had agreed to set up the riding for them yesterday and she had also located a waterfall where the men could soap themselves in private. Wilf might not be happy, but Kitty had asked Antonia before she had realised that she was so obliging. It would seem that no request was beyond her. It showed an immense resourcefulness and initiative that Kitty couldn't help but admire. Yes, Antonia was a strong independent woman with a runaway libido, answerable to no one but herself. There should be no shame in it.

Kitty's phone pinged. It was Adam saying he would meet them at the riding centre shortly and apologising profusely for his absence that morning. Kitty felt a flutter in her stomach. She checked about to ensure no one was nearby and swiped onto his Instagram page.

Images appeared of Adam at sunrise, his arm slung casually over Wilf's shoulders #mantime #cuddlytherapy #friendinneed. Adam was gazing thoughtfully out to sea while Wilf looked despondently into camera. It was in black and white, and Kitty had to admit it made a very striking image. She peered closely at Adam's serene face. The next photo showed him and Wilf sitting snuggled up, eyes closed. Wilf was relaxing backwards into Adam's embrace. Wilf's arms were folded in front of his chest while Adam held them secure, cradling Wilf's forehead. It was like a headlock, as far as Kitty could make out, but more comforting. She made a mental note to try cuddle therapy in future. Maybe it wasn't as bonkers as it looked.

Once they arrived at the riding centre, Kitty strode up to the stables to find someone in charge. She'd decided that if Adam was too upset or not inclined to ride or indeed afraid of horses then the two house hunters could go by themselves. Kitty had a vague recollection of horses being very intuitive. They may pick up on Adam's inner turmoil and be spooked by it.

'Harmonia Films? Cuatro personas?' a man was saying, coming up to her.

'Non.' Kitty looked briefly down at her notes. 'Tres personas.'

She pointed to the house hunters who were already trying on riding hats and stripping to the waist. The man handed Kitty a hat. She politely declined but found him very persistent.

'Big man say yes.'

As she was wondering which big man he was referring to, Adam rode into the yard looking for all the world like he'd ridden off the page of a Jilly Cooper novel. Kitty's heart clip clopped. Time slowed as Adam's floppy mane of hair swished with each rise and fall out of the saddle. He brought the powerful beast to a stop beside her.

Kitty was not the only one to gasp. Adam looked resplendent in tight-fitting jodhpurs, ab-skimming T-shirt and riding boots. He flashed his brilliant white smile at them all.

'I'll explain as we ride.'

Chapter 23

Without thinking, Kitty allowed herself to be measured for a horse, and before she could blink was plonked atop of a wonderful beast called Pepper. In the space of a few short weeks, she'd been out of her comfort zone more times than she had in the last few years. It was quite a thrilling personal achievement.

'Let's get a shot of the house hunters riding into the forest. Then if you two,' she said to Wilf and Shiraz as they stood sulking, 'can manage to sort out your differences while we are on the trek, you can get some shots of the local scenery before you film us returning. We'll be back in an hour.'

While not one hundred percent confident about riding, Kitty felt she'd rather brave a fall than listen to Wilf and Shiraz discuss the mechanics of how the orgy of the previous evening had come about.

The Spanish instructor mounted his steed and they set off in a line. Kitty was dismayed to find herself wedged behind Bibi and in front of Adam who would have a clear view of her backside and thighs, now liberally spread out over the wide, heavy leather saddle.

Thankfully the trail widened out to enable Bibi and Henrick to ride alongside one another. They were clearly enjoying the trek. Adam came up alongside Kitty and immediately began apologising.

'You don't have to apologise to me,' said Kitty. 'I'd rather know if you're okay. That video must have come as quite a shock.'

Adam nodded. 'I guess it was quite a shock for you too? I figured that you and he...' He looked briefly away before continuing. 'That you and he... were an item for quite a while. More than just a brief fling?'

Kitty blew out her cheeks as they shared a private moment. 'What can I say? I have terrible taste in rebounds.'

She hadn't meant to draw attention to the 'jilting' and wasn't sure how she felt about referencing it, even as she was telling him. It seemed so long ago, yet still as fresh in her mind as though it happened yesterday.

Adam's face fell, as though reading her thoughts.

'Bit weird don't you think?' he said.

She nodded. Both of their ex-lovers shacking up together didn't sit well.

'It's not that I want Rebecca back or anything. Not at all. It's just that I don't trust either of them. I hate that they know us so... erm, personally.'

Kitty had seen her fair share of 'kiss n tells' about Maddison throughout their relationship and he'd always denied them, blaming the women. In retrospect, she doubted he was telling the truth. She also doubted whether it would have been the women selling the stories. Maddison may well have engineered those himself. Maybe even to pay for this luxury brothel he'd bought in Spain but had never once mentioned to her. The more she was finding out about him, the more emotional distance it was giving her.

'I could never really trust Maddison. It was as though I purposefully kept myself in a state of denial,' Kitty said, unsure as to why she was opening up to Adam in this way. Maybe it was something about the steady rocking of the horse, the comfort of gently stroking its neck, the loud snorting. It was a very mindful experience and Kitty could feel herself being relieved of pressure the more they rode on.

'Things with Rebecca were never really serious. I'm not sure I could trust her either.'

'To be fair to her, we haven't exactly made that easy.'

The house hunters were quite far in front with the instructor. They were clip-clopping along alone.

'There's never been anyone serious since you, Kitty.'

Kitty's heart thumped against her ribcage. She was in danger of falling off. She tightened her grip on the reins but Pepper, sensing a shift in mood, suddenly took this as a sign to canter off with a squealing Kitty in the saddle. Within seconds Adam had cantered up beside her and leaning over pulled back on her reins, slowing Pepper back to a plod.

'I guess you didn't like what I said?' Adam asked, still facing her. His piercing eyes were brimming with honesty. 'I didn't mean to make you uncomfortable.'

'You didn't.' Kitty looked away, Perrie's words echoing in her mind. Theirs was destined to be a professional relationship. Her career depended on it. She would be a fool to jeopardise that for a relationship that had already failed once. 'Adam, I have something to tell you.'

Adam listened as Kitty outlined the Network's plan, their generous offer to sign them both for two more series and the hope that they'd be shortlisted for the national TV awards.

'That's fantastic news. How do you feel about it?' he asked her.

'I'd love to work with you on another two series,' she said honestly. 'It's just...' She felt her cheeks redden.

'Ah, I see,' Adam said. 'So, if we sign this contract, we'd have a professional working relationship only. Is that what you're saying?'

Kitty nodded. It was practically an unwritten rule that crew members were not allowed to bonk while away working. Adam would know this too, she was certain. It had ended in disaster one too many times for almost any film company Kitty cared to name. Besides, she had more than enough personal experience to know better than to keep repeating the same mistakes over and over.

'Okay.' Adam's face fell slightly. 'Leave it with me. How long have we got to think it over?'

'Forty-eight hours. But there's something else to consider. It's about how the Network want to portray the series and, well, you. You're not going to like it.'

Kitty was one hundred percent sure Adam would hit the roof once he heard about how well he'd gone down with the pilot audience and why.

'I'm sure I've heard worse. You didn't see '*You're a Lousy Cook*'. I left that show without an ounce of dignity.'

Adam was smiling. She found this self-deprecation immensely appealing. This was the first glimpse she'd had of the Adam she'd fallen for over a decade ago. Confident enough to have a laugh at his own expense, not taking himself too seriously.

They returned to the yard to find Shiraz spitting feathers and this time it was Wilf who looked like the cat who got the cream. Once the filming of the sliding dismount, the close up of tight buttocks, the sweat being wiped from foreheads, the naked torsos glistening in the hot midday sun and the friendly nuzzling into the horses was done, Kitty announced that she'd organised a picnic lunch at the waterfall up in the foothills of the Sierra Nevada.

'Antonia is meeting us there,' Kitty announced. 'Wilf, you okay with that?'

Wilf beamed back. 'More than okay, boss. Me and Antonia are officially back together.'

'Only because she's narked that Rebecca has moved in with Maddison and he didn't invite either of us to join them. It's sickening. Who does that? I got with him first. It's the height of bad manners,' Shiraz yelled to no one in particular. She threw up her hands in annoyance before packing away her tripod and camera.

Kitty laid out the picnic blankets at the next location as Wilf and Shiraz set up with the help of Antonia. The house hunters stripped down to their swimming shorts, dived into the small lake and swam over to the waterfall. Kitty admired the view. It was the most idyllic spot she'd ever seen. It was breath-takingly beautiful, tranquil, unspoilt, bursting with greenery and flowers. Adam strode over to help her with the food hampers the hotel had provided for them.

'Well, isn't this romantic? It reminds me of that time we went on holiday to Greece.'

Kitty's head snapped up.

'Sorry. That's inconsiderate of me.'

She could remember only too well the moment that Adam had proposed to her. It had been the most romantic moment of her life. She shook her head. 'No need to apologise.'

They took a beat to stare at each other, lost in the same moment. That glorious moment years ago when they had been lying on the picnic blanket, kissing and rolling around. They were surrounded by nothing but nature. Their bodies were wet from having showered under the waterfall. Adam had taken her face in his hands, looked deeply into her eyes and asked her to be his friend, his lover, his soulmate for the rest of his life. She had kissed him in response and had felt such peace, such agonizingly sweet, all-encompassing joy that she barely heard him whisper 'marry me'. They had made slow, tender love outside in the warm breeze as it

253

caressed their naked skin, with the smell of blossoms filling the air, the sound of the waterfall gently splashing into the lake and the hum of wildlife in the trees. She could still remember the way her body had responded to his touch as he had grazed her nipples with his lips. The way his quivering body had responded to hers as she took him inside her, straddling him. She remembered squeezing her Cupid's tunnel tightly around him as she undulated up and down, sending him wild with desire. His orgasm coming in waves as he deliberately, slowly came to a climax. She could feel him shuddering inside her, never once taking his eyes from hers. They were connected, physically and spiritually. It was the most soulful, magical and thrilling moment she'd ever experienced.

Kitty was snatched from the memory by her phone ringing. It was Perrie.

'She'll want to know if I've talked to you yet. About the contract and the TV Lifestyle Award,' she said, slightly breathless, her heart hammering at the close proximity of Adam and the vivid images of him writhing beneath her, still fresh in her mind.

'I don't need to think about it,' said Adam squarely. 'Tell her it's a definite yes. Even if we can't be together, I still want to be in your company.'

Kitty gulped, taking her phone with trembling fingers to press accept.

·♥·♥·♥·♥·♥·

'So, Kitty, or should I call you yummy mummy?' Adam broke into a giggle. He'd overheard her entire conversation. 'You never had kissy wissies for me when we were together. And what on Earth was all of that about doggy wigs? Surely you and Perrie don't dress that poor creature up in clothes and fake hair? Please tell me you're not one of those people who takes their dogs for a walk in a pram. Or sends them cards on their birthday and buys them Christmas presents?'

'Of course not,' she lied, thinking about the doggy cupcakes she would bake religiously every weekend. 'Anyway, Alma has only got little legs. She gets tired, so of course I've got a pram. Plus, she's not keen on the rain. Or the wind. Or walking, so it makes sense.'

Adam laughed. 'It makes no sense! Come here and let me see what you've done to this poor baby of yours.'

Kitty and Adam shared a few minutes scrolling through photos of Alma in various doggy wigs and outfits.

'Has she given any thought to having her own Instagram account? I think she really suits the blonde ponytail with the pink tutu and leg warmers.'

'Me too,' said Kitty, unsure as to whether he was being serious. 'Want to know what else the Network said?'

Adam nodded, lounging comfortably beside her.

'They think that we'll definitely get nominated for an award, and the fact that we'll be continuing with a second series and on air at

255

the time of public voting, it'll put us right up there with a chance of winning. And if we do win, they reckon that's two more years at least, of guaranteed shows plus... the possibility of your own show. They'd be interested in a pitch from us. It could be your chance to cover more serious topics?' Kitty smirked. 'But please, anything but that political conceptual juxtapose idea.'

Adam's jaw dropped. He sat bolt upright. Stared at her for a few seconds and before she could react, he planted a light kiss on her lips. 'Thank you. That's amazing.'

'What's amazing?' asked Antonia, coming over to pick at some of the food Kitty had laid out.

'Oh nothing. Just some news about work.'

'This award for television I hear you mention?' Antonia beamed. 'And your own show? You'll be very famous Adam, no? More famous than Maddison, I think. And you best friends with my boyfriend, Wilf. This is very good. Very good.'

'Well, it's very hush hush at the moment. It's a secret Antonia, so please don't tell anyone. Not even Wilf.' Kitty was keen to stop any gossip leaking out. 'Don't say a word. It's not final yet.'

Antonia nodded, picked up a slice of tortilla and wandered off to dangle her feet in the water. As if the scene was playing out in slow motion, Kitty and Adam watched as Wilf went over to join Antonia. She whispered something in his ear. He turned towards them before receiving a sharp dig in the ribs from Antonia. Wilf then got up and casually sidled over to Shiraz who was filming the house hunters horsing around in the waterfall. Wilf leaned in to say something to her, her face registering surprise. She too turned to look before Wilf tugged at her elbow.

'I guess that's the secret out then,' Adam mumbled.

Kitty was appalled at the lack of professionalism they were currently exhibiting. It was almost as though no one had a shred of respect for her authority.

'Food's ready!' she called, very disappointed in the lot of them. As they trundled over to sit down, they all stared at Kitty and Adam expectantly.

'Do not, under ANY circumstances repeat what you may or may not have just heard from any unreliable and unsubstantiated source. Is that clear?'

It wasn't clear, but it was the best that Kitty could do under the circumstances. She was fighting the urge of excitement firing through her body as it was, but Perrie had told her not to tell anyone of the Network's plans. They all grinned, nodding agreement before tucking in enthusiastically.

'Henrick, tell me what you'd like to see this afternoon for the last property. I know Bibi you have a clear favourite so we really need to get one for Henrick so you can battle it out as to which one you choose,' Adam said, diverting attention successfully away from Kitty.

Shiraz had perked up considerably and had made her way stealthily towards Adam, in order to hang off his every word and laugh at his every comment.

Kitty could only wonder at her fickle nature.

Looking at him with big cow eyes, Shiraz asked, 'Adam, would you like me to take some video in slow mo' of you soaping yourself extravagantly under the waterfall for your Instagram? I think your followers would really appreciate that.'

Adam gave Kitty a sheepish look before turning back to Shiraz. 'I'm not sure that's what they...'

'Yes,' said Henrick excitedly. 'We would. We really would.'

Chapter 24

After a very successful house hunt, Kitty was sure episode three would be a sizzling hit. The chemistry between Adam and the house hunters had been undeniably charged. On camera the electricity between the three men crackled. They shared laughs, jokes, banter. There had been happy tears. There had been group hugging. There had been lingering looks, hand holding, shoulder squeezes and best of all, Bibi had gotten down on one knee and declared his undying love for Henrick and insisted they buy the house of his husband's dreams, because all Bibi wanted in this world was for Henrick to be happy. Even Adam had happy tears rolling down his cheeks and by the time Kitty had called 'CUT!', they all knew that they were creating something very special.

It was the last night for the house hunters before they left the following day and they'd invited the whole crew out with them to celebrate.

'They put a cheeky offer in on a stunning two-bed, two-bath, lake view apartment at the foothills of the Sierra Nevada,' Kitty was gushing to Perrie. 'On the outskirts of a bustling town called Velez de Benaudalla. It's perfect for them. Adam worked his magic and charmed the seller into not only accepting the offer but throwing in all of the furniture and the hot tub too, can you believe it?'

'I can, and I think because they're both so loved up and hot-looking nobody would want to see them argue over the properties anyway. It's been a real scorcher of an episode. The chemistry sizzles off the screen. Well done, babe.'

Kitty had been delighted. With a second commissioned series riding on the back of a successful first series, and a potential award nomination and with the charismatic house hunters being such fun to be around, the whole crew were in high spirits as they met at the hotel bar before dinner. Adam had ordered champagne and was declaring that dinner was on him tonight as they clambered into taxis, dressed up to the nines.

Kitty was relieved. She had checked her bank account to see that she was at the end of her overdraft and the bank wouldn't issue any more extensions. The one company credit card had limited funds thanks to Maddison's extravagant lobster night.

'Wait. You don't think this is a team building experience, do you? This is you taking us out for dinner out of your own pocket?' she couldn't help checking. 'And it's not a freebie either, is it?'

'Absolutely not.' Adam looked amused. 'I'd just like one night out that doesn't end in disaster.'

'Famous last words, Adam. Famous last words.'

·♥·♥·♥·♥·♥·

They arrived at the restaurant to find it packed out. Glad she'd dressed up, Kitty noticed the clientele had gone to great lengths to look glamourous for their evening of fine dining. Adam had chosen very well, and they were seated at the best table in the place with a view across the twinkling night lights of the yachts out at sea. On her way back from reapplying her lipstick, Kitty paused to watch the restaurant scene from a distance. Shiraz was radiantly snapping away on her phone, taking selfies of herself, the champagne and an obscene number of photos of her and Adam. Wilf was chatting animatedly to the house hunters, seeming immensely cheered after his traumatic romantic rollercoaster ride. Adam was laughing at something Bibi was telling him. Kitty felt light. She had the crew back on track. She was pleased at how well she was getting on with Adam and, although she kept trying to deny it, she was ecstatic at the prospect of working with him for another year at least.

'Top up?' said Adam, clearing his throat while discreetly casting an appreciative eye as she sat back down. Kitty was wearing a dress Perrie had sneaked into her case. It flowed gently around her curves, it was criminally thin, almost see-through enough to show a glimpse of her thong at the back and too low at the front, which meant that Kitty made sure her hair and make-up looked fabulous enough to draw the eye away from her bounteous cleavage and her plentiful rear end.

It wasn't until the raucous dinner was almost at an end that they were interrupted by a couple approaching their table. Kitty looked up into the piercing, lavender eyes of Maddison O'Reilly. Rebecca was hanging from his arm with an almost bored expression, unable to make eye contact with any of them.

'Good evening,' he said, in his charming manner. He beamed a toothy smile around the table. Kitty could tell he was hiding his annoyance at the happy group. Maddison liked to be the centre of attention. He liked to be where the party was at. He also liked women who ate food but looked like they didn't. He wasn't going to have any fun with Rebecca at a restaurant, Kitty felt sure about that. She would most likely need to nap between courses.

The house hunters were quick to get up and shake his hand enthusiastically, gushing how excited they were to meet Britain's number two TV personality. Maddison bristled, before his eyes widened as though an idea was forming.

'That's so kind of you,' he was saying to them. 'Have you watched my new show? I could tell you hundreds of hilarious stories about what goes on behind the scenes. Honestly, you wouldn't believe half of them. You gays adore pets, don't you? In fact, if there's room, we...'

Kitty suddenly realised that Maddison was about to invite himself to sit at their table. She couldn't think of anything worse for herself or Adam or Shiraz for that matter.

'We would invite you to join us but we're just about to leave. Enjoy your evening though,' she said briskly.

Maddison and Rebecca tutted loudly before strutting off to a table at the far end of the restaurant. Shiraz gave her a grateful look. Adam squeezed her hand under the table and mouthed 'Thank you.'

Kitty felt her stomach do a flip at the touch of his fingers on hers. It was such an intimate gesture. She stared into his eyes for a second too long as he gently rubbed his thumb over her palm before releasing it. It sent tingles through her body. He picked up his glass to make a toast.

'To Kitty,' he said. 'This show is nothing without you. You find all the properties, organise absolutely everything and make sure we are all so well looked after.'

Kitty blushed. Never in her wildest dreams had she ever thought managing a team would be this rewarding. As the crew and house hunters cheered, she felt Adam's fingers wander lightly up and down her leg beneath the table.

He leaned in close to whisper in her ear. 'Here's to 'working' together on a second series.' He managed to make the word sound filthy.

She struggled to follow the conversation as Wilf and Shiraz explained just how very important their own contributions were to the show. She tried not to gasp when Adam's fingers began to make delicious circles around her inner thigh. She gulped down some champagne.

'Here's to my brilliant crew!'

The more he teased, the more she tingled. And the more she tingled, the more convinced she became that it would be entirely possible that theirs might be one of those relationships that can become quite physically sexual behind closed doors, yet still retain a certain modicum of professional distance on set.

Her revelry was broken by Rebecca thumping past. She stopped briefly to shout at Adam. 'Didn't take you long to move on, did it?'

Adam whipped his hand away. Everyone took a moment to stare at Rebecca, staring at Adam. Then she shifted her furious glare to Shiraz sitting next to him. 'And you. You're just as bad!'

Kitty was almost relieved. She'd hate to be caught in the crossfire between these two. Rebecca might look the sort to stab someone with a fork out of jealousy, but Shiraz had it in her to play the long game. She'd crucify you slowly upside down over a burning spit. The two women flicked their hair and screwed up their eyes. Both remained expressionless, due to the overindulgence of Botox, but the fury emanating from them was palpable. The atmosphere suddenly tense.

'You weren't interested in him until five minutes ago when you found out he'd be getting a second series, his own show and an award. You're so shallow,' Rebecca spat.

'I'm shallow?' Shiraz retorted. 'You're the one who dumped me to run off with that orange-faced prick over there.'

'That's no reason to throw yourself at my very recent ex.'

Adam intervened. 'Not that recent. It's been at least a month. And there's nothing going on between me and Shiraz.'

'Fuck off, Adam. It's not all about you,' both women managed to say in perfect unison. They took a beat to let this land as Rebecca huffed, shifting her weight to the other stiletto. The two women seemed locked in a furious staring competition. It was hard to imagine that only a day ago they were eating each other's pussies and tweaking each other's nipples like they were trying to change channels on a car radio.

Eventually, the squabble over TV presenters seemed to be drawing to a close.

'What did you expect? I'm hardly going to shag Wilf, am I?' Shiraz said to Rebecca, her tone slightly softer. 'No offence, Wilf darling, but all you young men go at it like you're drilling for oil.'

Yeah,' joined in Rebecca. 'Like they don't know the hole is already there!'

Both women had finally found some common ground and began to go into depth about the inadequacies of men in their twenties at lovemaking.

'That's what I love about Maddison,' said Rebecca. And just like that, Shiraz looked about to explode. And even though Kitty was aghast that the news of the second series and the potential award had been further leaked, she was thankful that there seemed to be no implication of herself in this unfolding drama. It was time to nip this conversation in the bud, for the sake of her team.

'Rebecca, kindly leave, please,' said Kitty sternly. The exchange had taken the wind out of her sails, and she'd had quite enough. It was important for a leader to stand up for the little people. 'You've nothing to complain about. Leave Shiraz and Wilf alone and go back to Maddison and your evening. We don't want any trouble.' Kitty thought she sounded firm but fair.

Rebecca, however, did not.

'How dare you!' she roared at Kitty. 'I wouldn't be here if I hadn't caught you in bed with MY fucking boyfriend in the first place!' Everyone in the entire restaurant stopped what they were doing. 'Is there anyone around this table that you AREN'T currently fucking?' Rebecca yelled at Adam, her voice full of hurt and venom.

To be fair to her, Kitty thought, *she does have a tiny point.* The house hunters were positively beaming at the prospect. Maddison was at Rebecca's side in seconds. He was glaring at Kitty.

'YOU AND HIM?' he bellowed, pointing at Adam. 'How could you? How could you sleep with a man that has no sense of PRIDE OR LOYALTY? A man who USED you to advance his career and then JILTED you at the altar! He doesn't deserve to win the TV Lifestyle Award or the PUBLIC VOTE.' Maddison darted his gaze around the restaurant as though he was the guest of honour making a rousing speech. 'The public DESERVE better.'

With the atmosphere now well and truly popped like a party balloon, they watched Maddison and Rebecca stomp out of the restaurant.

'I KNEW IT! SHE'S RIGHT! HOW COULD YOU?' Shiraz yelled at Kitty before getting up herself and marching towards the door. 'Wilf, come on! It's your lucky night!'

Wilf scrabbled to his feet. 'Coming. Shall I ring Antonia?'

The house hunters were quick to follow suit. 'We have an early flight in the morning,' Bibi said, yanking Henrick up from the table. 'Thank you for the meal, it was delightful. And thanks for finding our dream holiday home. You're both invited any time of course.'

Kitty and Adam sat staring at the empty chairs around them. Less than three minutes ago they were all toasting Kitty's success, Adam was making her feel all horny and she was looking forward to the rest of the evening partying with her team.

'So that went well I think,' Kitty said, folding her napkin.

'Yes, I agree. Both of our ex-lovers hate us. Shiraz and Wilf are probably no longer speaking to us because they'll regret banging each other tonight and will blame us in the morning. Our house hunters couldn't wait to get away. The big secret we were supposed to be keeping for the Network is well and truly out in the open and therefore unlikely to happen now, if history has taught me anything, and,' Adam paused, 'everyone thinks we slept together even though technically we didn't.'

'Yes, but apart from that though, it was a lovely evening, wasn't it?'

Adam's eyes were full of mischief. 'I suppose we could use this time alone to discuss potential pitches for our new programme. Is it the Middle East you're interested in? Climate change? Poverty? Doggie wigs? That kind of thing?' Kitty was having difficulty concentrating. Adam's hand was on the move. 'How would you feel about me getting the bill and taking you back to my hotel?'

Kitty's heart was thumping and her body tingling. This was finally happening. Against her better judgement and not remotely how she imagined, but it was happening. Kitty allowed her eyes to wander down to Adam's crotch. She picked up her spoon and suggestively licked it with the tip of her tongue as she made eye contact with him. She heard a small groan escape from his lips.

He stood up abruptly. 'Come on. I'll pay on the way out.'

Kitty couldn't believe the turn the evening was taking. They ran out of the restaurant, jumped into a waiting taxi and were kissing like teenagers on the back seat while it hurtled them to his hotel.

'I want you so much,' Adam was murmuring into her neck, sending shivers down her spine and causing sparkles to swim in front of her eyes.

'Wait,' Kitty said. 'Is this just like a casual, empty, rampant work fling?'

'It's not casual, Kitty, come on. It's me and you. You and me.'

Kitty felt a moment of sobriety. 'What if this changes things between us?'

Kitty held her breath, not entirely sure why she was pursuing this passion-dampening line of conversation right in the middle of heavy petting in the back of a taxi. Adam surveyed her, his face becoming a fraction serious.

'Good. That's a good thing.'

Chapter 25

The next morning, Kitty's phone pinged with a notification. It was a text from Perrie to say call urgently. Kitty sat bolt upright in bed. She knew Perrie very well. This sort of text would not be good news. Before she could get up and mull it over with a few strong black coffees inside her, the phone sprang to life, and before she knew what had happened, she'd accidently accepted the call.

Perrie was annoyed. 'Well?'

Kitty squinted her eyes and tried to pull her hand through her hair. It was unusually tatty. Her throat felt dry. She had no idea what Perrie could mean.

'Last night? The video?' Perrie demanded.

Kitty frowned. 'What video?'

Shitting hell, she thought. *Had someone videoed her and Adam last night?*

'Not the... do you mean... Perrie, does it take place in a jacuzzi?'

Her mind flew back to the antics of the previous evening. No, it couldn't be. They had been in Adam's room. The private jacuzzi was on the balcony and hidden from view by strategically placed potted trees. It wasn't overlooked by any other apartments. God forbid anyone had spied her being taken from behind against a backdrop of twinkling Sierra Nevada lights, her bongos being thoroughly massaged by each of his hands or the way she'd ever so enthusiastically taken Adam in her mouth, cupping his smooth balls lightly while inserting a bit of pressure in the spot that, she remembered only too well, would guarantee to drive him over the edge. She'd also spent a great deal of time waving her fanny in his face, as he lay relaxing in the hot tub, his tongue lazily lapping at her as she came very loudly, over and over and over.

'Kitty, stop zoning out. Jacuzzi? No. You haven't seen the video, have you?' barked Perrie, eyebrows poised.

She had no idea what Perrie was talking about. Then an awful thought struck her.

'It's not the orgy video, is it?' Kitty said nervously. The Network would probably not like a member of the crew involved in a salacious scandal.

'What orgy? Jesus Christ, what is going on over there?'

'Erm, sorry, not orgy. Do you mean the video of Adam being soaped by the house hunters? That probably went a little too far, but to be fair they were very excited.'

'Kitty! What is wrong with you? We are trying to impress the Network with how professional our film company is, not give them the impression that... wait, who the fuck's that?'

Kitty froze. There was a movement to her left. She discreetly slid her eyes over to investigate.

'ADAM! ADAM IS THAT YOU?' Perrie yelled. 'FOR FUCK'S SAKE. AREN'T ANY OF YOU TAKING THIS FUCKING SERIOUSLY?'

Kitty watched Adam wince as Perrie yelled angrily at them both. He gave her a sheepish wave.

'GOOGLE MADDISON EFFING O'REILLY AND WATCH THE VIDEO. YOU'RE BOTH A PAIR OF PRICKS,' she roared.

Kitty nodded.

'Oh, and by the way, Alma had a date last night and it went very well. She's in love with Ned and now she won't eat her gourmet puppy brain food unless he comes and eats it with her. I thought you should know, but you're obviously too busy bonking to care,' she fumed through tight lips.

Adam and Kitty took a moment to stare shamefully at the blank screen after Perrie abruptly hung up. She was furious with the pair of them. Adam flopped back onto the sumptuous pillows.

'Best night of my entire life. Ever.'

Kitty felt giddy as Adam turned to kiss her.

'Let's see what the hell is going on, shall we?' she asked him.

'Let's not.' He took the phone from her hand and flung it onto the floor.

'Okay,' she said. 'But this has to be the last time. We can't fool around like this until we have successfully delivered on all the episodes. Agreed?'

'No,' said Adam, lifting the covers to eye her naked body. 'Absolutely not.'

'I'm serious, Adam. This job means a lot to me. It's my career on the line here.' Kitty was unable to ruminate further, mainly due to Adam sliding under the covers to deftly part her legs and settle himself between her thighs. Two licks in and she'd forgotten her own name.

'Well, it wasn't me,' said Shiraz as Kitty raced over to their table to have breakfast with them an hour later. She'd just had time to get back to her room to shower and throw on some clean clothes.

'And it wasn't me either,' said Wilf. 'Whatever it is. I haven't actually seen it.'

Kitty pulled out her phone to show him the video someone made of them all arguing round the table the previous evening at the restaurant. You could make out Maddison and Adam very clearly and hear the rest of the diners round the table all squabbling and accusing each other of sleeping with one another. If it hadn't involved herself, Kitty would have normally loved this type of thing. The fact that it involved two famous TV presenters made it news, however. Big news. Especially because one of them was alleging the other of letting down the entire British population. Perrie had every right to be angry. It made Kitty look like she'd lost entire control of the production team, which in all honesty she had, and it made the crew look like nymphomaniacs, which to be fair they sort of were.

Perrie had messaged Kitty to tell her to get a grip, to stop fooling around with the star of the show and to get episode four organised and underway, while Perrie attempted to get the Network back on side by spinning the media catastrophe in a better light. Kitty closed the video. Shiraz and Wilf had bloodshot eyes and that awkward look of two people who had more intimate carnal knowledge of one another than they'd ideally like.

Wilf and Shiraz hung their heads, mutely picking at their breakfast cereal. You could cut the atmosphere with a spoon.

'We have today to shoot the location scenes for episode four. It's a young couple. They want to be on the south coast where she holidayed as a child with her parents. It's a happy memories episode. They have a really healthy budget, so we'll cast the net wide and because they're young we'll do nightlife, beach scenes, water parks. Anything that carefree, childless, financially solvent young couples might do before they get pregnant, and it all becomes a distant dream.'

'So we're not checking out today? Good. When do they arrive?' Shiraz asked, still unable to meet anyone's eyes.

'Not until tomorrow so we have plenty of time today to sort out this mess with the video leak and get all of the footage we need. But listen you two. This is the last episode. Nothing can go wrong. We're staying in this hotel until the end of the week, but you'll have to stop...' Kitty paused. 'You'll have to stop sleeping around and messing about with people you shouldn't be messing about with. I need you both to act professionally. Okay?'

They stared long and hard at her.

'We will, if you will.'

Shiraz was making a very valid point.

'Understood. Let's go and pick up Adam. Wilf, you're in the car with me.'

Kitty managed to avoid close contact with Adam for almost the entire day, preferring to let Shiraz and Wilf fuss over him. She made sure the crew were kept busy, focussed, and on the road at all times, stopping only for a brief bite to eat at a roadside diner between Malaga and Almuñécar. Even the millionaire property was organised remotely via Antonia, to ensure she did not do anything sexually inappropriate with any crew members during the shoot. It was a jaw-dropping £4 million mega-mansion overlooking a canopy of trees and boasting spectacular sea views. They all took a beat to stare open-mouthed at the infinity pool. It was opulence of the highest order. A far cry from the over-the-top ostentation of Maddison's holiday home. Adam had sidled up to Kitty to drop a kiss on her bare shoulder.

'I can just imagine you and me here,' he'd whispered. Kitty had glared at him in warning and swivelled her eyes around to make sure they hadn't been caught.

Adam chuckled. 'Please tell me you are not serious about the 'no messing around' rule.' Adam trailed a leisurely finger down her back causing her to shiver. He had always had the ability to reduce her to a delicious mess and for a split second she leaned against him, before coming to her senses.

'Deadly serious,' Kitty told him, watching as he good-naturedly wandered off.

To make matters worse, Kitty received a text from Maddison requesting she meet him alone, later in the day.

She read the message. He needed to discuss the PR disaster with her urgently. Kitty was conflicted as to whether to tell the crew or Adam about it. She decided it would be best not to until she had heard what Maddison had to say. She assumed he would be furious about the leak. Namely, because he was also up for the same award and also because he would have hated to have been shown to be jealous of Adam. Especially as Adam came out of it looking like a total fanny magnet. Having watched the video several times, Maddison did not come out of it looking anything but petty, jealous and philandering. Kitty wasn't sure what he expected her to do about it. The damage had very clearly been done.

'I have meetings and things to work on tonight, so you'll be dining without me,' Kitty told the crew as they unloaded the cars at the end of the day. She avoided eye contact with Adam, feeling in some way that by agreeing to meet with Maddison, she was sneaking around behind his back. She simply didn't have time to add his objections to the growing list of complications.

'Need some help?' Adam asked, trying to catch her eye.

275

'No. No, thank you,' Kitty answered with barely an acknowledgment. She hurried away before he could ask any more questions.

·♥·♥·♥·♥·♥·

Once back at her room, she checked her phone to see that Maddison had texted again to say he would meet her at his house, rather than the nearby restaurant that they'd originally agreed. Smelling a rat, Kitty dashed back a text to say she would rather not. Her phone rang instantaneously.

'Kitty-cat, it's me.'

Kitty froze. It was still somewhat unnerving to hear him say her name and to say it in the way that he did when they were together. She would not get pulled into that again.

'Listen,' he continued. 'I'm not trying to pull a fast one here. I just want to make sure that we're not seen. I have something very important to discuss with you and I'd rather it not be in public. Not after last night.'

'So, me, you and Rebecca? How do you know you can trust her? You've known her for less than a week. And by the way, I won't be joining you for any funny business if that's what you're thinking.' Kitty could hear Maddison snigger down the phone.

'That girl is quite talented I can assure you, Kitty-cat. I'm sure she'd have you purring in no time.'

'Right, that's it. Forget it. I'm not meeting you.'

'Oh, come on. I'm only teasing. Besides, we broke up.'

'Broke up? You were barely together.'

'She's met someone else. Besides, she spent the whole time napping. No bloody wonder. She doesn't eat for Christ's sakes! So what do you say? Dinner at mine? I'll send a car for you. I've ordered in. I have some news regarding this PR disaster that might get us all off the hook. Even that prick you're shagging will come out of it looking good.'

Kitty perked up. 'Why can't you simply tell me over the phone?'

'See you at eight-thirty, Kitty-cat.'

'Stop calling me –'

Maddison hung up. He'd always been a bit impossible to handle.

Kitty suspected Maddison was going to be trouble. And she was right. She knew she was walking straight into a trap as soon as she got out of the car and twinkling lights lit the way to the grand entrance. On the journey up, Kitty realised just how isolated this place was, and in the darkness the villa looked imposing. Having an immediate change of heart, she called out to the driver, chasing it up the drive only to see the car disappear swiftly through the gates and into a wall of darkness.

She whipped out her phone to book a taxi. No mobile signal. *Of course there bloody isn't.* Out of options, she gingerly made her way back along the dark pathway to the villa. She rang the doorbell and listened to the lady have a long and deeply satisfying orgasm before Maddison eventually answered the door, barefoot, loosely clothed, towelling his wet hair, his body billowing expensive, fragrant fumes. The lights were low, music was playing softly, and the intoxicating smell of Spanish cooking filled the air. He fixed his lavender eyes on her and waggled his eyebrows.

'Come in.'

'What, no harpist?' Kitty huffed sarcastically. 'I'm not here to be seduced.'

Maddison held up his palms. 'I promise, I'll be on my best behaviour.'

Kitty hesitated and despite her numerous misgivings, stepped through the door. She might have been unsure as to how this evening was going to go, but there was one thing that she was absolutely certain of - Maddison O'Reilly did not know the meaning of best behaviour.

Chapter 26

'Maddison,' Kitty said, detecting a slight slur in her voice. They had been talking for what seemed like an eternity. 'Can we please get back to this PR disaster? I don't want to hear any more about 'Britain's Got Pets'. I'm sure it's a fantastic show and in the right hands I'm certain you'll improve ratings. Sometimes these things take time to catch on.'

'That's just it, Kitty. That's what I'm trying to say. We don't have time.'

Maddison was sitting across from her. They were well into their second bottle of wine even though she'd initially refused a glass, but he'd insisted she couldn't properly appreciate the succulence of the meats and cheeses without the accompanying fine wine. He'd been right of course. The wafer-thin slivers of meat had been melt-in-your-mouth. The cheese, out of this world and the pasta just the right side of *al dente*. Maddison had persuaded her it was more of a Spanish experience than a meal. However, Kitty was dismayed that part of the experience was Maddison pulling out all the stops to make sure she felt flattered. Against her own gut feelings, she softened towards him.

'Why don't you have time?'

'We're up for the TV Lifestyle Award. We need ratings to be high. That's where you come in. And the video.'

'Me? I don't follow. What's this got to do with the video leak?'

Maddison reached for her hands across the table and grabbed them before she could pull away. 'It's *you* we need. We're going to use the video to create a huge media storm. A battle between *Your Place or Mine?* and *Britain's Got Pets*. We'll go head-to-head and eliminate all the other competition. We'll make it a two-horse race. We'll be the only two programmes everybody is talking about.'

Kitty took a second to digest what he was saying. The wine had loosened her tongue. 'That makes sense. But we'll win. My programme is way better than yours.'

'I know.'

Realisation dawned. 'You've lured me here under false pretences.'

'I know.'

'You want me to jump ship?'

Maddison nodded his head slowly, not taking those striking eyes from hers. 'I don't want you to feel under pressure, but Adam is only using you to advance his career, you know that, don't you?' He began to rub his fingers seductively across her wrists and palms.

Kitty pulled her hands free. 'No. The answer's no.'

'You don't know what they're offering you yet.'

'The answer is still no.'

'They'll make you director. Full control. Your own crew. A proper crew. Not those two idiots you've brought along. A huge pay rise and Kitty,' he said. 'It'll be like old times. Me and you. Back together. A proper couple this time. We were always so good in bed together.' Maddison waggled his eyebrows again. 'What do you say?'

Kitty's head was swimming. She wasn't sure if it was the wine or the seductive offer. She gulped as she stared into his lavender eyes.

'So just to be clear. You're offering me a massive promotion... but I also have to sleep with you?'

'Yes.'

'Or the deal's off?'

'Yes. Try not to make it sound so... depraved.'

'Which it is.'

'More wine?'

'I can't believe that you're actually saying you want me to *sleep* with you in order to get the job.'

'You keep bringing it up like it's some sort of moral crime. Manchego?'

God, he was infuriating.

'I'm not interested. Sexually or otherwise. How have you not been sued by now?'

'Think about it. You have until tomorrow evening,' Maddison said gently, caressing her with that silky smooth voice of his. 'Now, why don't we go relax in the hot tub?'

'Not a chance,' said Kitty, desperate to regain her senses. She was finding Maddison's voice increasingly hypnotic.

'I've missed you Kitty-cat,' he purred, topping up her glass before sliding his eyes deliberately slowly from her lips down to her breasts.

The next morning, Kitty hid a raging hangover from Wilf and Shiraz as they sat together at breakfast. She laid out the schedule for the day on the table.

'Your hands are shaking. Why are they shaking?' asked Shiraz. 'You must have been unbelievably shitfaced last night. Who were you out with?'

Kitty stared at them both, unsure of what to say.

Wilf gasped. His eyes wide with pain. 'Not Antonia? I knew it! I knew she wasn't at her cousin's Tupperware party. Why? Why does this keep happening to me?'

'It doesn't,' said Adam approaching. 'It wasn't Antonia.'

Kitty stared at him and shook her head, wincing with the effort.

'There's only one person hanging around this area like a bad smell and I think we all know who that is. And crucially,' Adam said as though giving evidence in court, 'we all know why.'

Kitty massaged her temples. 'It's not what you think.'

'Do enlighten me. Were you with Maddison last night? Did you have dinner together? Yes or no.'

282

Kitty continued to sit open-mouthed. She really hadn't had time to think this through. 'Yes, but...'

'He's posted up pics of you both together on his Instagram,' spat Shiraz, showing the incriminating photos to Adam. 'You look pretty cosy to me.'

'You must think I'm an idiot,' Adam said in a hurt tone as he walked off.

Kitty spent the next hour loading up the car and trying to think of how to explain her decidedly poor choices to Adam and the rest of the crew. The evidence went against her. She was dismayed to see Maddison had posted up photos of her looking worse for wear, shovelling food into her mouth in quite an unattractively enthusiastic manner and clinking cocktails across the table. Her brain hurt. Whatever impression the photos gave, she was one hundred percent sure that nothing happened. It took immense persuasion to convince Wilf and Shiraz she wasn't abandoning ship.

'Did Maddison at least ask after me?' Shiraz asked her huffily as they got into the car.

Kitty shook her head.

'TV presenters,' she huffed. 'They're all the bloody same.'

Kitty nodded.

When they arrived at the designated 'meet n greet', Kitty slapped on a huge smile for the new house hunters and introduced them to Adam.

'Hi,' said Jess. 'This is my husband-to-be, Ben.'

'Congratulations,' said Adam warmly, shaking their hands. 'When's the big day?'

The young couple looked at one another and Kitty sensed a shift in mood. 'Oh er, we haven't set a date yet. We were going to... but then we... well, we're not sure. We'll see.'

'No harm in waiting, is there? As long as you know you're with the right person, that's the main thing. Isn't it, Kitty?'

'SET UP FOR INTRO!' she barked, instructing Adam and the house hunters to walk over to the beach for the 'walking hand in hand' and 'welcome to the Costa del Sol, what brings you here?' segments.

The awkwardness continued as Adam struggled to get any sense of enjoyment out of them.

'It's almost as though they aren't bothered,' Adam reluctantly confided to Kitty during a break. 'They haven't even asked me for a selfie.'

'This is going to be so fucking boring,' complained Shiraz. Kitty ignored her. She was having enough trouble fighting the sinking feeling as it was. This episode seemed doomed. She needed to inject a boost to team morale and she wasn't sure how.

It wasn't until they began to film the seated tear-jerker that Kitty felt her hangover recede. In a moment of clarity, she changed her mind about where to have them sitting.

'We're not going to do it on the beach anymore,' she announced. 'We've seen tables perched by the surf a million times before. Follow me.'

To much grumbling, the crew and house hunters followed Kitty off the beach, across the busy promenade, down a quiet side street and into an old village square. There was nothing much in it but a glorious, stone chapel with huge, dusty, wooden doors.

'Wait here.'

Kitty pushed at the door as it creaked open. She slipped inside. The place was beautiful. It would provide the calm, atmospheric, peaceful, soulful moment she was after. Something about the place felt right. The couple were young, and this was the last place you'd expect to see them, but Kitty was following a hunch. A movement at the front caught her attention.

Kitty made her way over to a clergyman kneeling in one of the pews. After a quick word, he spoke surprisingly good English, and the promise of a large sum of euros towards the coffers, he happily granted permission to film in there for a few hours.

In her mind she would overlay gentle, soothing choir music to a montage of stain-glassed windows, the sunlight shining down onto old wooden benches, carved stone statues, dusty old books and a blurry shot that would reveal Adam coming into focus as he skilfully reduced the house hunters to a weeping mess.

'Action,' she called, hoping this gamble would pay off. The couple smiled blandly. Adam looked pleadingly to camera.

'Tell me why this move is so important to you both?'

The couple shrugged.

'Are you after lots of walking, plenty of outside living, a healthy lifestyle?'

Adam was filling all the silences.

'You seem like a couple who should drink a lot... I mean a couple who could socialise more. Do you enjoy the Spanish culture?'

Kitty knew she'd have to cut all of this painstaking drivel out but encouraged him to keep going.

'I suppose you want,' he turned back to face them, 'more bang for your buck? Somewhere to have Christmas with the whole family? A bolt hole to escape the rat race?'

Jess looked nervously to her fiancé. Something wasn't right. The atmosphere was tense. Kitty wasn't sure what was going on, then it hit her. She stealthily indicated to Shiraz and Wilf to go close up with the lens and boom. Her heart sank with apprehension.

'You've had a really hard time lately, haven't you?' Adam intuited in almost a whisper.

Jess nodded. Ben put his arm protectively round her shoulders.

'It must have been very difficult for you.'

After a few beats, Adam's speculation had paid off and Jess answered him. They all watched as a single tear fell down the house hunter's cheek. Her eyes glistening with pain. Kitty could spot a true survivor a mile off. This woman was hiding a huge sadness.

Jess sniffed up her tears. 'We came here as children on holiday. Always to the same spot every year for a week. It was my parent's dream to own a holiday home but,' Jess wiped at her face, '... but like most people, when you most want it, you can't afford it, can you?'

Adam nodded his head in agreement, not taking his eyes from hers. His face a picture of empathy.

'When we found out my dad had pancreatic cancer a month before our wedding, being here was the only thing he'd talk about. How he wished he'd spent more time with us. How he wished he'd bought an apartment so we could have had more family holidays. How he wanted to see me married. How he wanted to play with his future grandchildren on the beach. It's not much to ask, is it?' Jess's face streamed with tears. 'Instead, we buried him on the day of what would have been our wedding. In the same church, with the same guests.'

Jess was sobbing, Ben was sobbing, Adam was barely keeping it together. They all had wet faces.

'Sorry,' Jess kept repeating, wiping her cheeks. 'If it's possible, I was wondering if I could do a shout out on his behalf to all the men out there to get themselves checked as soon as they think something's not quite right.' A fresh burst of tears fell from Jess's eyes. 'Dad left it too late.'

'Now that's a cause that *Your Place or Mine?* can get firmly behind, can't we?' Adam asked into camera. His eyes brimming, his face melting with compassion.

Kitty's eyes popped wide. She wasn't sure how well this impromptu call to action would go down with a blood-sucking TV network, but she admired Adam for trying. If he managed to keep talking, they wouldn't be able to cut it out. She signalled to Adam to keep going.

When he'd finished, Kitty could barely get the words out to call for filming to stop. She flew over, wrapped her arm around Jess who was still full of apologies and told her not to worry. She told everyone to take a break.

'I'm the one who is sorry,' Kitty told the couple. 'I thought this place would be soothing but I got it wrong. We can do it again, later, tomorrow, whenever you feel ready.'

'No, it's a lovely church. I haven't been able to face going into one since the funeral. It's why we'll never be able to get married,' said Jess, her voice full of pain.

Kitty watched Ben pull her in close and kiss the top of her head tenderly. Her pain, clearly his pain.

'Kitty, I was wondering, if it is okay, could we take some time in here... to say a few prayers? I think it might help.'

'Of course. Take as much time as you need.'

Kitty mouthed to the crew to follow her out of the door. Once outside, she spied a few parasols and tables at a cafe across the square. 'Let's go for a coffee and give them half an hour.'

She sat opposite Adam, Shiraz and Wilf as they sipped their drinks. They all looked drained.

'You just never know what's going on in a person's life, do you? A smile can mask a multitude of things,' said Kitty heavily. She could barely look Adam in the eye. Ever since Adam had jilted her, Kitty had basically smiled through three years of pain, pretending it wasn't there, papering over the cracks when they showed.

'We all have undealt with shit hidden away, don't we?' said Shiraz unexpectedly. Her eyes glassy with tears. Kitty nervously reached for her hand under the table and gave it a light squeeze.

She glanced over at Wilf, his mouth turned downwards, and suspected he was on the brink of offloading too. She had unwittingly opened the floodgates and must find a way to bolt them shut again until the episode was in the can.

'My dog died when I was eight. I've never really gotten over it,' Wilf said, his voice croaking. 'And we had four cats. They all died too. And two hamsters. All dead.'

Kitty suddenly found she had no words. Wilf was incredibly immature and thoughtless. But broaching the subject now might ruin this tender managerial moment she was having. She reached out to squeeze Wilf's hand. They sat hugging their drinks and watching the square come to life with people bustling around them. Kitty sneaked a glance over at Adam. He was deep in thought.

It wasn't until a little later, while she was fiddling with the mobile camera as they sat waiting, that Kitty had an epiphany about the previous night. Something about the whole evening had been off and she suddenly knew why.

'Look at these photos and tell me what's fishy,' Kitty asked them.

'What do you mean?' Shiraz asked her.

'You're the selfie experts. You tell me,' Kitty said, thrusting out her phone to show them Maddison's Instagram account. 'We were at his house dining alone.'

'You couldn't have been. That camera angle of the two of you is not a selfie.'

'Exactly. It was a honey trap. I didn't notice him take one single photo while we were eating. There had to be a third person taking these photos. He lured me there under false pretences. I should have been honest with you all, but I wasn't sure how you'd take it. He said he had a way out of the PR disaster. A way to save our team and its star,' Kitty said, training her eyes on her coffee cup, 'from further public embarrassment. But instead –'

'But instead, he seduced you and lured you away with a tempting job offer?' Adam finished for her.

'Almost,' said Kitty. 'It didn't work. I didn't take the job offer. Besides, I like working with you guys. You're like the ultimate challenge. I have no idea what each day will throw up.'

'Or who will throw up.' Shiraz elbowed Wilf playfully.

'I'm convinced Maddison set the photos up and the video in the restaurant to make us look bad just to get himself in the public eye, using our show as a springboard. Can't you remember the way he kept yelling about the British public deserving better? I mean, who talks like that? Apart from TV presenters, obviously. You're all a bit... well, whatever. He has no reason to contact me again so that should be the end of it. With any luck, he'll be on the next flight back to London and out of our lives for good.'

Adam remained unconvinced.

As if Kitty had planned it, her phone lit up, Maddison's smiling face covering her screen to let them all know he was incoming. Adam looked disappointedly at Kitty and screwed his eyes. Kitty gingerly accepted the call and shuffled her body sideways. This was awkward on so many levels, not least that she was finally making some headway with her team-bonding. And now she'd have to speak to her ex-lover on the phone while *his* ex-lover was sat beside her and *her* recent ex-lover was sat to the other side, with her own ex-lover sitting in front of her. The team dynamics had been well and truly shot to bits.

'No Maddison, I don't think that's a good idea. Hold on a second.' Kitty stopped talking and held the phone to her chest before gingerly putting the phone on loudspeaker so that they could all hear it. She wanted to convince them that she was telling the truth.

'Kitty-cat, come on. One more dinner. Let me at least try to persuade you to leave that useless crew of yours and to come work for me. You'll find we have a very professional set up at '*Britain's*

Got Pets'. Honestly, I don't know how you work with that pair of booze-hound coke-heads. I'll make it worth your while. Very worth your while.'

Adam rolled his eyes. Maddison was putting on his smarmy voice. Kitty found it stomach-churning. She wondered once again how and why she'd ever been attracted to him. Shiraz and Wilf were staring at her phone looking bereft, like Maddison had destroyed their confidence in one cruel blow. She was more than familiar with how that felt.

'No thank you Maddison. I made it very clear last night that I'm not interested in the job offer... or anything else for that matter,' she added for Adam's benefit. 'And as for my crew. We make a great team. We might be slightly left field at times, but we produce unique quality television. I wouldn't swap them for anyone.'

'Yeah, right. Don't play hard to get Kitty. Just take the offer,' Maddison growled impatiently, his tone changing. 'Since when did you grow a pair? I remember not so long ago you'd be only too happy to do literally anything I told you to.'

'That's not how I remember it,' Kitty said, mortified that Adam was seeing this side to her. 'I remember you being quite controlling actually. But that didn't work last night, and it won't work now.' Kitty wasn't sure where any of this was coming from or whether it was truly painting her in any better light. Her cheeks flamed. She went to undo the loudspeaker, but Adam caught her wrist.

'Leave it.'

'That's him, isn't it? You're trying to make me jealous,' Maddison's voice suddenly dropped an octave. 'Don't be a fool Kitty. Get over here. Sign the bloody contracts and then you can show me just how effing grateful you are. Jesus! Most women would die to be in your position right now.'

Kitty had had enough of this conversation. She flicked her gaze to Adam and feeling brave, continued. 'Do whatever you want with the video, we all know it was a set-up, but you know what, Maddison? No one will care because your show is *boring*. Because you make it all about yourself instead of the pets. Adam's a far better presenter than you'll ever be.'

Kitty was gulping in air, her nerves fraught at this exchange and judging by the lack of response, she seemed to have hit a nerve. They listened to Maddison hang up.

'I can't believe I just did that. He's used to getting his own way. I think we may have to brace ourselves for a bit of a shitstorm. He's always been jealous of you.'

'Don't worry,' said Adam firmly. 'We're in this together.'

'We've got your back. Haven't we, Wilf?' Shiraz said, with steely determination. 'Where does that prick get off insulting us all like that?'

'Thanks guys. I really appreciate it,' Kitty said, feeling an unexpected rush of loyalty and belonging. 'We make a great team. I'll find a way to get us through this. Trust me. There'll be no more drama. Not on my watch.'

'Famous last words, Kitty. Famous last words.' Adam said, his smile filling her with warmth and reassurance.

Nothing could have prepared Kitty for what happened next. When they walked back into the church the priest was sat opposite the couple. They were talking in hushed whispers.

Ben was the first to speak. 'Change of plans,' he announced, beaming. They listened as he proudly outlined the proposal to an open-mouthed Kitty. Once again, life was punching her in the gut. 'What do you think?'

Shitting, shitting hell is what I think.

Chapter 27

Sitting in the pew beside Ben and Jess with the priest looking at them all with a kindly, beatific expression, Kitty was stunned.

Ben repeated his question. 'So, Kitty, what do you think?'

What do I think? Kitty asked herself. *What do I think? I think that's the worst idea I've ever heard! I don't need any reminders of being jilted at the altar, thank you very much.*

She kept a smile frozen to her face as she mentally ticked off a multitude of reasons to nip this marital tangent, in the bud. Fine for other people to get married, as long as it did not involve her in any way, shape or form.

'I can't believe we'll be filming a wedding!' marvelled Shiraz. 'What an episode this will be.'

'I know,' agreed Wilf, very excited. 'It's so romantic, isn't it?'

Stop assuming things! Kitty could barely get her head round it. She needed to take charge immediately. Where were her words? She needed to shut this down.

She listened to Ben passionately rush to explain that he desperately wanted to give Jess a sense of family and belonging and he wanted to marry her so much, because he loved her so deeply.

Her stomach dropped at their hushed voices echoing around the church. She felt a light sweat forming on her brow, the scene swimming in front of her. She was finding the air incredibly thin. Out of the corner of her eye she could see Adam staring intently at her. She held on to the pew for support, her cheeks aching from the forced happiness.

Every fibre of her being wanted to reject the proposal but seeing the couple, madly in love and full of hope for their future, she felt trapped. She couldn't refuse.

Kitty gulped. 'Of course. We'll redo the schedule. We'll make this the wedding episode.'

The couple erupted into a frenzy of making plans. The wedding would take place in 48 hours. They would fly in their immediate family the following day. They asked Kitty and Adam to help them source a cheap hotel, a wedding venue for a small celebration afterwards and to assist with the paperwork with Father Alvarez who was looking at the couple fondly.

Anticipating an epic panic attack, Kitty, made an excuse to leave. 'I'll be outside making some calls.'

'Are you okay with all this wedding stuff?' Adam said, breaking into her thoughts as he strode towards her. 'I guess you're a little... apprehensive? Especially after, you know, what happened to us. I mean, what I did to you. For which, again, I am truly, truly sorry.

But there are things that happened that I need to explain properly. And I just never seem to get the chance.'

Kitty threw Adam a side-eye, feeling now was not the time to detail specifically just how crazy weddings tended to make her go. She felt less comfortable at a wedding than a nun at a wife-swapping party. Flashbacks of panic attacks, bitter rants, flutes of champagne tossed in faces and the throwing of several wedding cakes sprang involuntarily to her mind. She was never her best self at any type of matrimonial ceremony.

'A little apprehensive but I'll be fine,' she lied.

'I want you to know you can count on me, Kitty. I'm here for you.'

She studied him for a moment before realising what was different about him. Depth. He had depth. Like the Adam of old. He was no longer thin on the surface. No longer just a pretty face with a rocking hot bod and a head full of messy hair. Adam Johnson was a deep well, ready to be plunged into with a bucket. Her bucket. Her huge, dry, empty bucket. Kitty brought her train of thought to an abrupt halt, unsure such an analogy was entirely appropriate in this holy place.

'You're sure you're okay?' he asked. 'You look pale.'

He was trying to earn her trust. She liked that. It gave her comfort. She'd never wanted to kiss him more.

·♥·♥·♥·♥·♥·

The house hunt took on a new vibrancy. The house hunter couple's enthusiasm and excitement over the wedding infected everyone in the crew. They rattled through the first property before lunch, in record time. There wasn't a leaf blower, lawn mower or neighbour chain sawing the hedge in sight. It was as though luck was smiling down on them.

'We'll squeeze another two properties in this afternoon, then tomorrow we'll help Jess look for a wedding dress once we've done the final two properties. And then it's the wedding and millionaire's mansion the day after that. If we can find one that is,' Kitty was saying, handing out the newly scribbled over schedules to the crew. 'Wilf and Adam, you help sort Ben out. Adam, here's the list of suppliers, if you could kindly ask them to heavily discount *everything* we need in exchange for lots of TV and social media exposure, please? I appreciate it's extremely short notice but we have virtually no budget. Do your best.'

'Freebies? You want me to blag some freebies?'

She ignored the superior stare Adam was giving her. He was lucky she wasn't ripping his top off with her teeth. He looked unbelievably sexy lounging in front of her in his shorts and tight-fitting T-shirt. The sexual attraction between her and Adam was growing more tense by the minute, and Kitty wasn't at all sure whether she would be able to resist the animal magnetism that was currently billowing out from him.

'Shiraz, you're in charge of shooting the behind-the-scenes footage to document the planning and preparation. It'll make an excellent wedding present for the couple, as well as something to hook the Network in with. This couple have a story to tell of happiness, heartbreak, courage and hope and I want to capture it all.'

·♥·♥·♥·♥·♥·

'Are you saying yes to the dress?' Shiraz giggled to Jess the following day. They were in a tiny boutique shop that Kitty had found online and even though this was only the third one that she'd tried on, it looked stunning and was a perfect fit.

'I think so,' said Jess. 'I'm a bit stuck between this one and the last one.'

'Kitty,' boomed Shiraz. 'You try the other one on and we'll compare them side by side. I'll take some photos and, Jess, that'll help you decide.'

Icy fear caused Kitty's heart to stop. 'Sorry but no, I can't. Shiraz why don't you try the dress on instead?'

'But you're both virtually the same size and I'm doing the photos. What's the problem?'

Kitty broke out into a prickle of sweat. Jess was pleading with her. Kitty didn't want to ruin this lovely moment by going into detail of how when her own fiancé had called off their wedding, she'd never been able to so much as look at a bride or hear about weddings without wanting to hurl herself off the nearest cliff.

Before she could protest, with a delighted Jess squealing her appreciation, Kitty found herself being manhandled into a wedding dress.

'That looks stunning on you!' gasped Jess as Shiraz clicked away on her camera. Kitty reluctantly swirled around, fanning the dress out.

'It absolutely doesn't but thank you anyway. Now, let's stand side by side so you can choose. And don't forget, I'll be claiming the money back from the Network so get whichever one feels right.'

Kitty and Jess shuffled over to the mirror as the assistant plonked veils on their heads and ushered them into sparkling, low-heeled, fairytale slippers. When Kitty looked at herself in the mirror it was as though she'd been transported back in time. This dress was nothing like the meringue she had chosen to marry Adam in. It did not have the princess feel of the dress that now lay in her parent's attic, boxed up, pristine. She'd never had the heart to sell it. Kitty's mind flew to the engagement ring that lay in the box with the dress. She'd never been able to face getting rid of that either. Before her mind became overwhelmed with depressing thoughts of the past, Kitty rallied.

'You look incredible.'

Jess gave Kitty a grateful smile back through the mirror, smoothing the outline of the dress. 'They are both so pretty, but I think this is the one for me.'

She watched as Jess swayed this way and that, showing off the back of the dress and it's many, many tiny pearl-shaped buttons running almost the length of it. Shiraz was clicking away, telling her to shift her hip slightly, to lift her arm towards her, to tilt her chin. Kitty found she was absent-mindedly doing the same before coming to her senses.

'Okay, the dress and shoes are done. Next stop, cakes and flowers?' Kitty asked.

Jess waved her phone. 'The boys have sorted their suits and are coming to meet us, so I better get out of this dress. Kitty, would you mind?'

Kitty got to work unfastening the many buttons for Jess as Shiraz continued filming. The last thing she wanted was to be caught wearing a wedding dress by Adam. 'Surely, we don't need *everything* filmed?' asked Kitty, knowing full well Shiraz would ignore her.

'Wait. I forgot to ring Perrie to okay the change in schedule and budget,' Kitty suddenly remembered, bustling over to her bag and whipping out her phone. She had not had a chance to call her the previous day due to squeezing all the property viewings into a single day. She felt sure Perrie would understand the change of plan considering the couple's circumstances, and it should definitely be a ratings winner.

Shiraz tutted. 'You have to learn to live in the moment, Kitty. Life's not all about schedules. Adam says that we should learn to listen with our eyes and look with our hearts.'

Kitty shrugged apologetically, it all sounded like complete bollocks, and stood on the podium in front of the mirror to wave her phone up high in search of a signal.

'Perfect timing! It's Alma, she has some news. Why is the signal so bad?' asked Perrie, appearing on screen.

'I'm in a... in a wedding shop,' Kitty said.

'KITTY!' Perrie suddenly gasped. 'How are you not having some sort of seizure? You need to get out of there immediately. IMMEDIATELY.'

Perrie stuttered, her mouth opening and closing. 'What... how... WAIT! Are you getting married? Without telling us?'

'No!'

'Are you sure? Because you look like a woman trying on her wedding dress!' Perrie's face dropped as she gasped loudly. 'Kitty, are you pregnant? YOU'RE PREGNANT! Oh my god, is this a shotgun wedding? Is it Adam's or, please God, no, no, no, it's not Maddison's, is it? Please tell me that slimey bugger didn't put his...'

Kitty spun round to catch Shiraz filming her.

'Shiraz, please put the camera down. And try not to listen in. This is a very private call. And Jess, please disregard anything you have just heard,' Kitty yelled through the curtain to her house hunter.

'Or do you not know who the baby-daddy is?' Perrie stage whispered.

Kitty stared at Perrie holding up Alma to the screen. She peered closely at Alma. Alma was wearing a dress. Alma was wearing a wedding dress!

'IS ALMA GETTING MARRIED? WITHOUT TELLING *ME*? Why is my fur-baby wearing a wedding dress?'

'Not until you tell me why you are wearing one first. What's going on?'

Perrie listened to Kitty explain about episode four and gushed excitedly. 'It must be fate. Marital vibes are in the air. Alma and Ned have become obsessed with '*Say Yes to the Dress*' so I ordered a wedding dress, veil and shoes for her to wear while she watches it,' explained Perrie. 'They both circle round and round in the basket then rub noses before they plonk themselves down like an old married couple.'

'But she's only known him five minutes,' said Kitty quite shocked. 'Tell them to slow down. She should try a few fiancés on for size first,' she said, shooing away Shiraz who still had a camera stuck to her face. 'And besides, it's always the second wife that gets everything. All these house hunters are usually on their second marriage before they will part with any cash to buy a holiday home.'

Perrie made a sympathetic noise. 'I feel you're projecting your own miserable experience on –'

'Shiraz. Please put the camera down. Perrie, tell Alma she must hold out to be the second wife, never the first. The first wife sacrifices everything and ends up with nothing in return.'

303

Jess stuck her head out of the changing room curtain.

'Except you Jess. You'll be the exception to the rule. But for Alma, she needs to understand that men can't be trusted. They will always let you down.' Kitty's voice was rising unattractively. A wave of panic rose through her. 'Shiraz, I won't ask you again.'

Shiraz, however, was pointing the camera elsewhere.

Kitty turned towards the new object of focus. Adam was standing at the door looking as though he'd seen a ghost. A really upsetting ghost. One who had perhaps tormented his family for generations, and this might be the last straw.

'Is that so?' said Adam. 'I do hope that doesn't make it into the bridesmaid speech.'

Chapter 28

Kitty waited for Adam to stride through the shop, as he came to a halt, towering above her. He glanced at the screen on her phone. His eyes swivelling between her and the image on the screen.

'Are you aware that you and your dog are wearing matching wedding dresses and veils?'

'I'm aware. Yes.'

Kitty blushed, unsure Adam would believe the extraordinary coincidence.

Turning back to Perrie on screen, she continued her conversation. 'I mean she's too young to get tied down just yet. She hasn't seen anything of the world. How would she know Ned's the one? She barely knows herself so, how can she possibly love another person and know that they'll make her happy for the rest of her life?'

Kitty stopped talking. Not only because of the ridiculous nature of it but because she was, more or less, repeating word for word Adam's speech from three years ago.

A discreet silence hung in the air.

Adam lowered his voice. 'You were only twenty-two when we got together, Kitty. You'd never even had another boyfriend.'

This was the truth. Did he doubt that she was sure? It had certainly been much easier to blame him, and spend the years afterwards hating him. It had all been such a mess since that day.

'Can you please focus for five effing minutes, you two?' Perrie roared at them before Kitty could respond to Adam. 'This is about episode four. An adorable young couple in love who simply want to pledge themselves to each other in front of three million viewers. Please don't make it about yourselves.'

As Perrie clicked off the call, Jess emerged from behind the curtain. Kitty took in Ben, Wilf, Adam, Shiraz and Jess all now staring at her expectantly. Technically, from her position in charge, she felt the need to unpack a few things.

'Jess, I didn't mean that *your* marriage would end in divorce, of course it won't.'

'It might,' Shiraz said as she carried on filming the conversation. *Not helping,* thought Kitty, flicking her a look of annoyance.

'My parents divorced when I was three. I'm not sure I've ever really gotten over it,' said Wilf, a sad look in his eyes. 'They used to tell me that they wished they'd never set eyes on each other. But then of course, they'd never have had me. Unless that's what they meant.'

Kitty stared at him. *Why would he say that in a bridal shop?*

Jess grinned at Ben who walked over to plant a kiss on her lips. 'I'm going to be the best husband you'll ever have, you'll ever want, you'll ever need. I'm going to husband the shit out of this marriage.'

'And we've been together since we were sixteen, so I know he means what he says,' Jess said to Kitty matter-of-factly. 'So, my advice to Alma would be that if it feels right, she should trust her instincts and not worry about the statistics or what might never happen.'

'And never stop talking to each other. We tell each other everything, don't we? Alma should always share what's bothering her and they won't go far wrong. Wait, who is Alma?' Ben asked Jess.

'Kitty's dog.'

They all stood looking at one another for a few uncomfortable seconds as Shiraz swivelled the camera to take it all in. *Christ Almighty,* thought Kitty, humiliated to her core as she flew past Adam into the changing room. It was all so embarrassing. Even Alma had a better chance of success than she did. She could hear Shiraz bossing the couple about into poses for the camera, as huge tidal waves of sadness swept through her.

'You lot go ahead without me,' Kitty yelled from behind the curtain, trying to keep the shaking from her voice. 'I'll catch you up at the bakery. I'll pay for the dress and shoes, just leave them at the desk.'

Grateful to hear them all leave, Kitty sank down onto the stool in the tiny changing room, her head in her hands. Her emotions were all over the place. Hers was your typical love story. Boy meets girl. Boy dumps girl at the altar. Girl meets someone even worse and repeats the same mistakes over and over. Her heart felt like it was breaking at the realisation that years of hurt could have been so easily avoided had she and Adam simply been honest with one another, and not acted on impulse.

On reflection, she'd made more mistakes than she'd previously thought. She'd never given Adam a chance to fully explain, once he'd called the wedding off. She'd been so devastated at the cruel rejection, that she'd vowed never to speak to him again. He'd taken her at her word and had never even given her a chance to cool down. Within days, the whole wedding had been cancelled, her humiliation common knowledge and she'd packed her bags in temper and flown to the other side of the country to begin a new life, a new business and a new tradition of choosing unsuitable men.

And Adam had embarked on his quest to replace her with a stellar career. Like he said, too busy making a living, he forgot to make a life. Neither of them ending up happy.

She felt the weight of the situation crushing down on her shoulders, seeping over her bones like tentacles, squeezing the life from her. She slid to the floor and gave herself a few minutes to weep over what a fool she'd been. An utter fool. Her life could have been so different if only she'd made better decisions at that time. Why had she not faced him? Asked him why he wanted to call off the wedding instead of running away without any answers. As the hot tears rolled liberally down her cheeks, she wept for the years she'd wasted.

When her tears finally subsided, Kitty wiped at her cheeks, mascara coming away on the backs of her hands. It was a bit late to start feeling sorry for herself now. She had a wedding to organise, an episode to film and a PR disaster waiting to be avoided. She checked herself in the mirror. Her eyes looked red and puffy, mascara streaked her cheeks. She'd need to pull herself together before she met up with the house hunters. This was a happy occasion, and she was not going to be the one to spoil it. Nor was she going to spoil this dress with makeup stains. She could barely afford Jess's dress never mind this one. She needed tissues and some assistance. She sniffed up the remaining tears and pulled back the curtain.

Adam was standing there with a ruined expression. Kitty's glimmering eyes ballooned. She was mortified. This pity-party was for one person only. They stood staring at one another.

'We need to talk,' he said, reaching for her hand. 'You need to know the truth of what really happened so you can find a way to forgive me. We need to rid you of all this bitterness and anger that I caused.'

She nodded dumbly.

'I just need a few minutes to get changed and freshen up.'

'I'll come back in ten minutes for you.'

As she watched Adam leave the shop, Kitty stood, unable to move, his words echoing round her mind. She felt transported back to that day, that awful day that Adam had rung to say, 'We need to talk.' She'd been trying on her wedding dress for the final fitting. She'd known in an instant that she'd never be wearing it to walk down the aisle. Painful memories flooded her mind - her mother asking what was wrong, the phone falling to the floor, followed by Kitty as she'd promptly fainted.

An assistant, worried for the three-thousand-euro wedding dress, scuttled towards her holding out a box of tissues.

'Gracias,' said Kitty blowing her nose. She took a moment to gather her thoughts. It was time to pull herself together.

'KITTY-CAT. WHAT THE HELL'S GOING ON?'

Kitty nearly jumped out of her skin with fright. Maddison O'Reilly was charging towards her with a concerned look on his face.

'It's that prick Johnson, isn't it? I thought I saw him coming out of here. He's done it again, hasn't he?'

Bewildered, Kitty stared at him. 'What are you doing here?'

'Saving you from making the biggest mistake of your life Kitty-cat.' And as if she was undergoing some awful out-of-body experience, Maddison looked dramatically around at the staff standing open-mouthed nearby, before grabbing her hand and falling onto one knee.

Kitty flinched, trying to slide her fingers from his vice-like grip. Maddison was sweating with the heat, his lavender eyes were bulging from their sockets and his hand wet and slippery. If she didn't know any better, she'd say he was coked off his tits. Before she could react, he slapped his other hand over his heart.

'MARRY ME, KITTY-CAT. MARRY ME!'

Kitty was stunned.

'No! Absolutely not!'

'Don't marry that gym-obsessed, puffed up, egotistical wanker!'

Kitty was at a loss for words. A few months ago, this would have been her ideal scenario minus the sweating and the coke eyes, now it was her worst nightmare.

'He had his chance, and he blew it. He lied to you Kitty-cat. He lied. He was sleeping with Rebecca the whole time. She told me herself!'

Kitty felt the room spin. 'What are you saying?' Suddenly, the flimsy ceiling fan was not cooling the room enough. The air was thin.

'He's playing you for a fool.' Maddison was using his signature hypnotic tone.

'You're the fool if you think she'll fall for any of that crap, O'Reilly,' Adam barked, striding furiously towards them. Maddison scrambled to his feet. Proposal over. She took in their profiles, nostrils flaring, chests bumping, fists clenched, both as tall as the other.

'What do you know, Johnson? Why would she choose you? The very model of failure and downward professional mobility, when she can have me?'

'Because you're a shrivelled-up pervert, that's why.'

As she watched her two ex-lovers squaring childishly up to one another, Kitty realised this whole scenario wasn't even about her. It was very much about *them*.

'I've always been able to satisfy her in bed. Haven't I, Kitty-cat?'

Kitty blinked slowly. *Rise above it. Simply rise the fuck above it.*

'You haven't got the balls,' Maddison was goading Adam.

'Neither have you. I've seen them and they're not a pretty sight.'

'When? When did you see my balls?'

'They slipped out of that ridiculous leopard print thong when you dived in the pool to show off.'

'That is a Versace thong. Hardly ridiculous. It cost eight-hundred pounds. It has a raw silk lining, and the pendants are 24 carat gold.'

Adam scoffed. 'Made in China by some poverty-stricken children. You must be very proud.'

'Versace is exclusively handcrafted in Italy. You're thinking of Dolce & Gabbana or is it Valentino?'

Kitty felt that the two men were somewhat veering off course and when they began clumsily grappling with each other, while trying not to upend mannequins wearing expensive wedding gowns, half-heartedly pussyfooting around glass cabinets displaying tiaras and bejewelled wedding slippers, and occasionally, stopping to allow one another to bend down to pick up elaborately feathered fascinators, she decided to put an end to it.

'If she's going to marry anyone, it should be me. I gave her a puppy,' Maddison yelled as he threw a satin glove at Adam's face.

'Well, that's very nice but I gave her wings!' Adam said, dodging it easily.

'Wings?' Maddison asked, aggressively taking hold of a box of confetti. As he aimed it at Adam, it split, showering him with paper petals.

She opened and closed her mouth several times, but Kitty was too weary to argue with either of them. The wedding dress was becoming very heavy and uncomfortable, the staff were capturing the unfolding drama on their phones and Kitty would rather be sitting gazing peacefully out to sea, drinking a smooth merlot from the bottle while eating a giant slab of cheesecake. Two giant slabs.

She suddenly felt fed up of people pleasing. Pandering to *people's* whims before her own, backing down from confrontation for fear *they* might be uncomfortable, bending over backwards so that *their* lives were easier.

She'd made them both household names and never once had they appreciated it. She'd wasted years pining over these two buffoons. It was time for her to change her ways. And while she was at it, she would shed this heavy overcoat of bitterness for a past life that had never happened. A life that was never meant to happen no matter how much she had wanted it. Standing in a shop, wearing a wedding dress that wasn't hers, listening to her two ex-lovers bicker over the ethics of cutting-edge, designer haute couture practices and the depressing realisation that her dog was in a healthier relationship than she'd ever been in, she finally flipped.

'OUT!' she barked at them. 'Get out! I've had quite enough of you both. I'm far, far better off without either of you.'

They stopped the chest-bumping to look at her. She might as well get the rest out.

'What you both did, whether you think you had good intentions or not, was terrible. The consequences of your actions ricocheted out across my entire life, hounding me for years, while neither of you looked back, so don't ever say that you're doing any of this for *my* benefit. GET OUT AND LEAVE ME ALONE!'

Chapter 29

Knowing she would later regret the outburst, not just the mortification of it but the soul-baring vulnerability, Kitty drove through the winding mountain roads thumping the steering wheel in frustration.

She stole a glance at the passenger seat and wondered if she had done the right thing in abandoning Adam outside the wedding shop, miles from anywhere, without any means of transport and, thanks to his wallet, phone and soft, Italian, moleskin manbag lying on the back seat, no means to pay for a taxi. Kitty's phone rang. She decided to ignore it, but it automatically bluetoothed to the car. It was Perrie. She sounded panicked.

'Sorry to drop this bombshell on you so late in the day but the network have finally pushed the budget. They're flying the whole extended family out tonight as a surprise, so we'll need a bigger venue. Apparently, once the hoohah over the Maddison and Adam video feud dies down, they've been wondering if you and Adam would be interested in doing the *'Couples Come Whine With Me'* show. We'd be taking over from Sporadic. Mind, the Network execs have warned there have to be no more viral videos or speculation.'

Kitty tried to clear her mind of Adam, the things she'd shouted at him and the way he'd looked at her with eyes full of hurt and disbelief.

'Kitty? Are you there?'

'Yes, sorry. Just absorbing the information and trying to think of a suitable venue. Things are already as tight as possible, timewise.'

'Can you get the first lot of wedding prep dailies to me asap? I'll help edit them remotely. How is everything going?'

Kitty thought back to the anger on Maddison's face. Those home truths hadn't landed well at all, not on someone with such a puffed-up ego as him. He was bound to cause trouble.

'Yes, fine. It's all fine,' Kitty told Perrie, keen to get her off the phone. *Lies upon lies upon lies*. Would it never end? Kitty feared she'd have a stroke if she told one more fib.

'I hope you and Adam are managing to keep your hands off each other. Honestly Kitty, I think you're making a huge mistake mixing business with pleasure. It never turns out well. Never. Speaking of Adam, where is he? His phone is going straight to voicemail.'

Ah.

She had the brief embarrassment of explaining that she'd accidently driven off from the wedding shop without him, but that she was confident that even though he was without a phone or any means to pay for a taxi, he would turn up safe and sound.

316

'Jesus Christ. Are you insane? He's going to walk out. I know it. He'll walk out and the whole deal will collapse.'

Perrie was spiralling.

'We lose Adam, we lose the show. We lose the show, we lose the contract. We lose the contract,' Perrie was all but screaming now, 'we lose the extra series, the Awards, our homes. EVERYTHING!'

Kitty took a beat to let this land. Perrie was one hundred percent in the right.

'I don't know what came over me. It's like he has this power to reduce me to my lowest human form.'

'Christ Almighty Kitty! As if we're not already up to our necks in shit! Jake has no money to pay for his rehab. We have no money to pay our mortgages because he's gambled it all away. The bank is ready to foreclose on our business loan. What were you thinking?'

'No, no he won't. Leave it with me.' She had some urgent bridge-building and micro-managing to do and not much time to do it. 'It'll be fine. All fine.'

Kitty swung the car round and sped back towards the shop, only to find Adam was nowhere to be seen. It was blistering hot, and the village was deserted. Her heart sank at the prospect of losing yet more precious time on non-related filming issues.

Keep it together Kitty. You can do this. You can absolutely... more or less... most probably do this.

Resting her forehead on the hot steering wheel, she could feel her blood pressure rising and took a few deep breaths. She could do this. She'd been in this situation before. Well, she hadn't. What woman of sound mind would take a job with a hostile ex-fiancé and two crackpot crew members hellbent on making sure things ran anything but smoothly?

She drove slowly along, safe in the knowledge that Adam couldn't hop on the first plane back because she had his passport. She spotted him walking up ahead and pulled over on the dusty roadside. He turned round and without saying a word, calmly strode over to the passenger side, opened the door and got in.

'I'm so sorry. I shouldn't have... *forgotten* you back there.'

Adam stared coolly back. Kitty felt a wave of relief run through her. Maybe Adam would be happy to draw a veil over the encounter. After all, who hasn't wanted to scream angrily at an ex-lover and leave them stranded abroad in the middle of nowhere?

'I was upset at the... at the 'wings'... thing. It's a bit of a red flag for me.'

He nodded, staring straight ahead. He was making it clear that conversation was off the table. Kitty's every nerve ending was acutely aware of him sitting next to her, as they drove in silence to the hotel.

The following day, Kitty called the crew to a last-minute schedule meeting after breakfast. The atmosphere was frosty to say the least and she had a busy day ahead.

'Now don't forget,' she reminded them. 'While we are guests at the wedding we are also still at work. We're filming the wedding at the church for the end segment of the episode and then the wedding reception party straight afterwards. Adam,' Kitty said, trying to rid her mind of his hurt expression when she yelled at him the previous day. She was not the one in the wrong here. 'If you could possibly just do as you're told and stick to this script for once, that would be great.'

Adam blinked slowly in response, his face unreadable. He'd not taken kindly to Kitty saying that she was better off without him and to leave her alone. He was certainly doing a good job of ignoring her so far.

'And if we all keep to the schedule everything should be plain sailing, and we'll have the final episode in the can, ready to sit down and enjoy the wedding reception with the other guests.'

Adam tutted loudly and said in a bored tone, 'Famous last words, Kitty. Famous last words.'

He could be immensely childish but at least he was speaking to her.

'Nothing will go wrong now that I'm fully in control of my senses. I assure you.'

'Meaning?' Adam looked thunderous.

'I think you know exactly what I mean.'

Just do as you're told for once, you impossibly handsome bugger.

'Enlighten me.'

'No. I think you're forgetting who's the boss here.'

Adam's cheeks reddened even more.

'I think you're forgetting who you're talking to. I'm the star of the show and I distinctly remember you promising to show me *maximum* respect. Is this maximum respect? Is it? Is it?'

Wilf and Shiraz shifted uncomfortably in their seats. It was times like these, when faced with the infuriating and insufferable need of TV presenters to be pandered to, that a programme manager needed to show maturity and strong leadership. Kitty suddenly snapped.

'Grow up, Adam.'

'No, you grow up. YOU GROW UP!' he shrieked.

They all watched as he stomped away.

'I guess that's you without a date for the wedding,' giggled Shiraz. 'My plus-one will join us later for the drinks reception as they're not keen on churches or organised religion.'

You're bringing a date? thought Kitty in alarm.

Shiraz caught Kitty raising her eyebrows. 'Don't worry. We'll be on our best behaviour,' she said brightly, a dreamy faraway look in her eye.

'Well, if she's bringing a guest, I want to bring one too,' demanded Wilf.

Cocking hell, thought Kitty, not looking forward to the wedding reception one tiny bit. Nothing about this entire shoot had gone smoothly but at least this was the final day. Once it was over, they could all fly home. Her phone rang.

'Hello?'

The crew watched Kitty's face fall.

'What do you mean, the cake was sent to the wrong hotel?'

'But we need to take it with us right now. We're leaving in ten minutes to go set up'

'Seriously? You're not sure which hotel you've sent it to?'

Kitty clicked off the call and addressed the worried crew. 'Shiraz, we'll set up at the church while we send Wilf to get the cake. It'll be fine. How many hotels are there along this coastline? Let's not panic.'

'That's such a bad omen Kitty. It's because you said it would be plain sailing. And because you told Adam to basically fuck off when he was just trying to help.'

'No. No it isn't,' said Kitty remaining upbeat as her phone rang again. It was the wedding planner.

'What do you mean you can't supply the tables and chairs?'

'Or the venue? Why can't we have the venue? We booked it with you.'

'That's outrageous. I know it was a freebie, but you promised.'

'Yes, I do wish I'd signed a bloody contract and paid you up front. Okay, I'll think of something else.'

She put her phone down.

'Oh God. The planner has been offered a last-minute booking for lots of cash, so she's taken it. We've lost the reception venue, the dinner service, tables and chairs.'

'Famous last words Adam said. No offence, but I think it's you. You give off such negative energy, Kitty. You haven't got the wedding vibe at all, have you?'

'No. No, it's got nothing to do with me. All we have to do is think of how to feed thirty guests a meal without tables, chairs, plates, glasses or cutlery.'

Shiraz is one hundred percent right, she thought. *It's absolutely everything to do with me.*

Kitty's phone rang.

Shiraz frowned. 'Trouble always comes in threes.'

'Hello?' said Kitty. 'Hello Father Alvaraz. You've doubled booked the church? You're bringing the wedding forward two hours? Okay, I'll let them know.'

Kitty screeched to a halt outside the hotel that Jess, Ben and all the family guests were staying at. She was frantically trying to source some tables and chairs. Wilf was on route to fetch the cake from one of only four hundred hotels along the Costa de la Luz. Shiraz was at the church to set up the kit. Adam had marched off saying he needed 'some time out'. Kitty's lungs were billowing in her chest. She hesitated before knocking on Jess's door and took a deep breath in. The moment Adam had walked out of her life, everything had gone to shit. Now, here he was doing it again, and everything was tumbling down around her. She wasn't sure if she had the energy to begin picking up the pieces for a second time.

'Come in.'

Kitty took in the sight before her. Everyone was downcast. Jess was being gently rocked back and forth by her mum who had mascara streaks down her cheeks. Various relatives were crowded around all sad-looking and some of them were weeping silently into their hankies.

'Oh no. You've heard about the church mix-up?' Kitty said quietly to Jess who was dabbing at her red, blotchy face.

'No. What mix-up?'

'Ah, it's the cake then. Don't worry. I've sent Wilf to go and find it. Hopefully he'll be back in time to drop it at the reception. At least we know it's still here in Spain somewhere.'

At the mention of reception, Jess burst into a fresh stream of tears.

'How did you know about the reception?' Kitty was stunned. She'd only known herself for half an hour. 'Don't worry about that either. We'll find some tables, chairs, plates, glasses and cutlery in time. It'll be fine. I promise. We've still got a few hours to go. I'll find a way.'

Kitty thought she was going to have a heart attack with the amount of lies she was telling the bride.

'What do you mean?' Jess asked, wiping at her eyes. Suddenly, everyone in the room stopped crying and were now looking aghast

323

at Kitty. 'What mix-up with the church? Where's the cake? What's happened with the tables and chairs?'

Kitty gulped.

'Nothing. It's all under control. Why is everyone crying then?' Kitty asked, fearing the worst. 'Oh no! It's Ben. He's jilted you at the altar, hasn't he?'

No wonder everything's gone to shit. It wasn't meant to be. Some brides weren't destined to be married. I should know, thought Kitty, her heart aching for Jess and the years of bitterness, misery and wrong choices in men that lay ahead for her.

Jess answered with amused, red-rimmed eyes. 'You really hate weddings, don't you?'

Kitty listened as Jess explained that they had all been crying because her dad wasn't with them.

'He should be here with us. We asked him to give us a sign. And then you came in with your news and it's as though he's here. Telling us he's still part of our day.'

Kitty did not have a clue what Jess was talking about. Then suddenly the whole room came alive with memories of catastrophic fuck-ups that had happened whenever Jess's dad was involved. Within minutes they were laughing, giggling and smiling at the fond memories.

'There was never a dull moment when he was around,' said Jess's mum explaining. 'He brought everything to life. Gave everything we did an extra sparkle. He loved nothing more than a good cat-

324

astrophe. I've spent the last thirty-five years laughing, crying and dancing through life with him.'

She leaned towards Jess, kissing her gently on the forehead. 'And you'll do the same with Ben,' she said, wiping the tears from her daughter's face. 'Come on. Let's get you married. Your dad will figure something out to make everything all right, I'm sure of it.'

Kitty answered the call while she marched over to her car. Problems were mounting by the second.

'There's good and bad news I'm afraid,' said Perrie briskly. 'The good news is that Jake called last night. He sounds so much better. They're releasing him tomorrow into the day programme. He's going to come and live with me for a week so that I can keep an eye on him. The clinic said that Alma would be a great distraction for him. A bit like equine therapy but with doggy wigs and walks round the park. He can chaperone her and Ned while I work on the edits.'

'That's such a relief. Tell him not to worry about the money. I'm going to put it all on my credit card and I can remortgage my place again. I'll speak to the bank later today.'

'No need. Adam's paid the bill already. And he's wiped the debt. We are no longer in danger of getting beaten up by loan sharks or being made homeless. Jake's going to move in with him as soon as you get back from filming. I thought you knew. Didn't he mention it last night?'

Kitty couldn't believe what she was hearing. Jake was as close to a brother as she had, even if he was the cause of all their financial worries. She felt an immediate lightness that he was going to be okay.

'Oh my God Perrie, that's great. That's so great.'

'I know honey. It blew me away too. Maybe Adam isn't so bad after all. And yeah, I almost forgot. I'm sending you a thing to do. It's from the clinic. They said that me, you and Adam have to follow these steps to forgiveness before we see Jake. He's doing it too. Something about us needing to work out how we forgive him for what he's done to us and him needing to forgive himself, so that we're all in a place where we can move past what happened, together.'

It was like a penny dropping. 'Makes sense. How many steps are there?'

'Not many, I'll send it through now. But listen, don't get too comfy, there's a shitstorm brewing over this Maddison feud and the Network are not happy about it one bit. Somehow there are pictures of you all fighting at the wedding shop.'

Kitty listened, scanning the internet, as Perrie outlined the latest catastrophe. Pictures of Adam looking moody, Adam scowling at Maddison, Adam and Maddison squaring up to each other with a mascara-streaked Kitty, looking tragic in a wedding dress in the background, but as Kitty scanned the text, she was relieved to read there was no substance to the articles.

'It's so unfair. Why drag *me* into it? I'm a behind-the-scenes no one.'

'I know, but it's just clickbait. Nothing more. We need to take control of the narrative. Any ideas? Could you confirm you and Adam are about to tie the knot again, perhaps?'

'Very funny. I'll never marry. Not after everything that's happened.'

Perrie thought for a moment.

'You need proper closure. Maybe it's time for you to come to terms with being jilted at the altar and allow yourself to fall in love with him again.'

'No. Absolutely not.' Kitty placed a hand to her chest. It physically ached to say the words. 'I can't go through all of that again.'

'Okay, I understand. So, what are we going to do about spinning this story? We need to get in there before Maddison.'

Kitty's mind was a blank as to how to get out of this latest predicament. Just when she thought the standards of integrity for this whole series couldn't slip any further, there seemed to always be a new low on the horizon.

'Leave it with me. It's the least of my worries. I've got to get the entire family of house hunters ready two hours earlier than expected, a missing wedding cake to find, an alternative venue to shoot the final segment, legs to shave and a millionaire's mansion to find.' As she was rattling through the list, an idea sprang to mind. 'I'll call you back. Kisses to Alma.'

'Wait! What do you mean a missing –'

Kitty clicked off the call intending to ring Adam. She had no idea whether he'd be speaking to her or not, but she wanted to thank him. What he'd done to help them out was huge. She checked his Instagram to find that he was taking a break from Instagram, hashtag me time hashtag soul searching hashtag shattered dreams, against a video of some pebbles balanced on top of each other on the sand. She watched as the tide came in, causing them to come tumbling down.

Why did TV presenters have to be so melodramatic and over-the-top?

She would deal with Adam later. Her phone beeped. Kitty checked the message. It was Jake. He needed to speak with her urgently. It was about Adam.

Chapter 30

With the wedding party on their way to the church, miraculously, Wilf rang to say he'd found the cake and was on his way back with it.

'I found it! I found it, Kitty! Tell Adam, I found it!'

Good Lord.

There was only the matter of the furniture and party to sort out but Kitty's feeling of foreboding was getting lighter by the minute. Kitty was suddenly struck by a thought. She scrolled through her work contacts. Nobody did over-the-top quite like Britain's number one TV presenter, Grant Govey. Why hadn't she thought to ask him for help? Kitty whipped him off a text.

Within minutes his PA was on the phone. 'Mr Govey received your text and is very happy you are filming at his house. He keeps his own collection of tables and chairs, and he has tableware for private entertaining. He can seat thirty guests no problem. He asks when the cameras are coming and what else do you need from him? He says you are a good friend of his.'

Kitty could have cried with joy at the news and raced over to the church to let Ben know that finally everything was back on track. She rushed through the doors to see it half packed with guests. Shiraz had the camera kit set up. Adam was chatting calmly to Ben at the front. Kitty felt grateful for the music playing softly. The door banged shut behind her causing a multitude of heads to swivel round.

Why hadn't she gone round the side? Why?

She walked self-consciously down the aisle as everyone watched. Every step torture.

And why was she walking stiff and in a straight line? Like a bride? Realising she was also holding the clipboard like an imaginary bouquet, Kitty clamped her arms by her sides.

She could feel everyone's eyes on her as she reached Ben and they all fell silent. She whispered into his ear that the cake had turned up, the venue was sorted and watched him whip out his phone.

It seemed as though all the guests were holding their breath.

'You got your miracle, babe. Now come and make me the happiest man on Earth.' Joy was radiating from his face as the guests burst into applause.

Kitty wiped a tear from the corner of her eye before she caught sight of Adam hovering nearby. Neither of them made a move. There was so much she wanted to say to him as their eyes locked.

Breaking contact first, Kitty swivelled round to find Shiraz. 'You're in charge of the ceremony. I'll dash over to the mansion to help set up ready for the wedding guests. I'll send Wilf over as soon as he drops off the cake.'

Adam folded his arms, tilting his head. 'You're not staying for the wedding ceremony?'

Panic setting in, she hesitated, wondering whether to apologise for her outburst, or whether to mention the whole Jake thing, but looking at the time, decided it was better left until later.

'No,' she whispered, avoiding Adam's glare. 'I can't face it.'

'No worries. Off you go,' said Shiraz, taking charge. 'I have a similar phobia about babies. Do me a favour, babes. Can you put a few bottle of bubbles on ice for me and my hot date, yeah?'

Oh my God.

'Please try to behave, Shiraz.'

Some hours later, Kitty had gathered the crew together on the terrace of the millionaire's mansion to go over the final schedule of the whole trip. It felt like a monumental moment.

'So, quick update. We're scrapping the millionaire segment in favour of the happy ending wedding party scene. Adam, I wrote a new script. We'll film it over there on the balcony with the guests down below eating at the tables round the pool, with the sea glistening as the backdrop. Then the final shot is you clinking champagne flutes and wishing Jess and Ben a long and successful marriage and asking them if they've decided on a house and whether they want to put in a cheeky offer. Can you mention something about it being the icing on the cake and then Shiraz we'll cut to a shot of the actual cake. Okay?'

Kitty knew that she sounded brusque, but her nerves were on end. There'd been no sign of either Maddison or Rebecca or Antonia, but she wouldn't trust any of them as far as she could throw them. Instead, Kitty had been greeted by the housekeeper and a team of staff to help set everything up. The caterers had arrived and within seconds she had been caught up organising the wedding, the lights, the music and the food.

'The guests should be here in about twenty minutes. They are having a drink at that café in the square while the photos are being taken. Everything here looks great. How have you managed it, Kitty? You're a genius,' Shiraz said, setting up the tripod.

Kitty gave Shiraz a thankful smile.

'And I've put the cake in the walk-in fridge,' announced Wilf. 'It only took me seven hotels before I tracked it down.'

Wilf looked like he was waiting for some applause. 'Thanks Wilf, you're a superstar. You've saved the day.'

'I was the one who managed to do both the sound and the filming at the church, that allowed him to swan off to find it in the first place so, you know,' Shiraz cut in, looking a little put out. 'If anyone saved the day, it was me.'

'Yes, quite. You are amazing too. Honestly, you're both...'

Needy children, thought Kitty.

'... superstars. Now let's get this over with. Adam, are you ready?'

He nodded sternly. Kitty's heart sank. A bittersweet quiet hung between them. This would be the final shoot of the trip. The last leg of their journey. The end of the road. The top of the summit. The final curtain. She might not see him again for months. Or at all if he walked away from the deal. She couldn't blame him. She was the one who asked him to leave her alone. And after everything he'd done for her. She wished she could turn back time. A lump formed in her throat.

'Thank you. All of you. This has been quite some journey, despite the ups and downs. Now, let's film this final episode and please try to stay out of trouble until we get everything we need.'

The tables had all been cleared. The speeches had all been made and toasts to absent loved ones had been drunk. The music was playing and the whole garden was lit up with twinkling lights and people dancing. They'd packed all of the kit back up into the cars and now, the evening ahead was their own. It was officially a wrap. Adam walked over to Kitty. She was standing on the balcony of the patio area, overlooking the wedding.

'It's all gone unnervingly to plan, Kitty. Aren't you worried?'

Relief flooded through her. Adam was attempting to make peace. She smiled back at him.

'No,' Kitty said, 'I'm as surprised as anyone that there hasn't been a fight, the bride hasn't been pushed in the pool, the wedding cake is still intact, and nobody has caught fire. You know, the usual sort of thing that happens at weddings I attend.'

Adam's eyes crinkled softly. 'Listen, I'm sorry for yelling at you. I don't know what came over me. I act crazy when I'm around you.'

Kitty nodded. It was true. They brought out the worst in each other.

'I'm the one who should be sorry. I guess we still know how to press each other's buttons. Even after all this time.' She gave him an understanding look. 'Speaking of crazy, have you seen the crew?'

'They disappeared as soon as we finished filming,' Adam said, making light conversation, as darkness set in. 'I feel a bit like a parent with empty nest syndrome.'

'They sure are a handful.'

'I think I'm going to miss them. All that bickering.'

'Well, we've done it. It's done. It's over,' said Kitty staring into space. 'They can do what they like. I am no longer officially in charge.'

'You did an expert job with the show. Despite me being a world class dick. You deserve a medal. We should be celebrating.'

'I spoke to Perrie. She told me what you did for us. For Jake. I wanted to say thank you.'

'You don't have to thank me.'

'Well, we really appreciate it.'

Adam tilted his head to study her face.

'Why do you look so melancholy?' Adam stepped closer. 'Tell me what's wrong.'

'I'm just relieved that everything went okay, that's all,' Kitty looked up at him through blurry eyes.

He wasn't buying it.

'Please tell me.'

'I'm sorry to have to do this now but,' she fiddled with her dress, unable to look at him. 'There's something I need to tell you. You're not going to like it. Jake called me earlier.'

Feeling self-conscious, her cheeks burned when Adam leaned in to brush a stray hair away from her face. In a heartbeat, this small gesture suddenly felt very intimate. Yet at the same time, she felt an emerging distance between them. A newness, as though they were strangers, meeting for the first time.

'I wish I'd never done it. I wish we could turn back the clock and do it all differently,' he said, running his fingers lightly down her cheek.

Kitty's whole body jolted as though he'd poked her with a cattle prod. That strong chemistry that had got her into trouble before, was now pulling her towards him. He had such a dizzying effect on her.

Her timing could have been better, but she needed to get it off her chest before they went any further. Kitty took in a deep breath, knowing her next words were going to hurt Adam more than he could ever know.

'Jake said that a week before the wedding he told you that he was in love with me. That he...' Kitty could barely get the words out. She was shaking. She had been in a state of shock all night. '... that he lied to you and said that I felt the same way. And that's why you left me. You thought Jake and I were in love with each other.'

Adam dropped his hand from her face and stepped back from her. A heaviness hung in the air.

'You know already, don't you?' said Kitty, studying him. 'How long have you known?'

Adam lowered his head. 'He rang me yesterday. But I'd already figured it out that night at the snow hotel. I think that's why I drank so much.'

'And yet you still helped him. Still bailed him out.'

Adam was looking at her, his eyes glassy with tears. 'I still shouldn't have done it, Kitty. I should have had more faith in you. I'll never forgive myself for believing him, and not giving you a chance to explain.'

Kitty's heart was pounding in her chest. 'I feel like he robbed us of our chance to be happy. And it makes me so sad.'

Adam looked instantly relieved. 'Same.'

'I've been so wrapped up in the wrong that I thought you did me, that I haven't been able to enjoy the present. I didn't realise how little joy or emotion I've been feeling, until now. Until you.'

Adam nodded slowly. 'But at least we know the truth. It might be three years too late, but it's still a relief.'

'You're right. Perhaps now we can truly move on.'

Adam stepped towards her. 'I'd like that. No more being angry at the world. Anger begins with madness and...'

'Oh God. You're not going to quote at me, are you? Is this going to end in me staring at a leaf, in order to heal?'

She saw his face light up. 'Anger begins with madness and ends with regret as they say.'

'Nobody says that.'

'They do. It's written on pebbles. On Pinterest. So it must be true.'

'You can't even agree to disagree, can you?' Kitty was pleased that the mood was quickly shifting to a flirty one.

After a beat, Kitty pointed down to the house hunters slow dancing. Sparkles were literally sprinkling out of their eyes as they gazed adoringly at one another. 'They're starting out full of hope and excitement, the best version of themselves for each other. It reminds me of us. How we were.'

Adam took a moment to digest what she was saying. 'You're right. But you know,' he said nodding in Ben's direction. 'Nobody's perfect. He can't promise her that he won't let her down. But he knows that whatever happens, they'll forgive each other, and it'll make them better people.'

Adam entwined his fingers with hers.

'I see. There's no such thing as the perfect partner, the perfect marriage. But they can be perfect enough for each other because they will forgive each other. Is that what you're saying?'

Adam was looking at her in a very strange way as though he was having an epiphany, and nothing was going to get in the way of it.

'Yes, Kitty. Yes. If they're willing to make compromises, they'll be happy enough.'

Was he expecting her to read between the lines?

'So, what you're saying is that if a person marries *you*, for example, there's a good chance that they'll be, on balance, moderately happy?'

'Yes.'

Kitty blinked slowly.

What was he saying? What does he mean? Surely, clarity is key when it comes to discussions of this ilk?

'Nobody's perfect. They'll always disappoint one another eventually. It's the conceptual juxtapose of marriage if you will. Bringing the best *and* the worst out of each other. The blind leading the blind.'

Christ he's exasperating, thought Kitty, unsure she was hearing him correctly. *Was he suggesting they get back together? Give things another go?*

'It sounds as though you're asking someone to tolerate you. You want them to tolerate you for the rest of your life without knowing what to expect.'

'Yes. Yes, I am.' Adam was drilling holes into her with his intense gaze.

Was this a proposal? Was this the second worse proposal that she'd received in as many days?

It was just one of the many downsides to being in the company of a professional talker. They had an awful tendency to use a dozen words when really, only one would do.

Kitty suddenly felt the urge to giggle. Adam looked as uncomfortable as she'd ever seen him. He looked spooked. He looked like a man out of control. A man who hadn't thought this through and was beginning to panic at his own attempt to deconstruct the meaning of true love within the confines of marriage. But more importantly, he looked like a man desperate to bear his soul.

Deep down in her bones, that great weight she'd been carrying around had been lifted. And that hole in her heart that had kept her from being whole, was filling with emotions that were telling her she was in love with him. Deeply, passionately, wildly in love.

Right on cue, fireworks burst into the sky causing them to jump. The secluded balcony lighting up in the darkness with each fizzle, pop and explosion of colour was all terribly romantic. Adam leaned towards her. She felt the soft caress of his mouth covering hers as he pulled her to him. She melted against him, giving herself up to the intoxicating moment.

She would have been happy to kiss him forever, but Adam suddenly pulled away from her and dropped to one knee.

'MARRY ME!!' he bellowed awkwardly over the music pumping out and the fireworks exploding around them.

Kitty took a beat to consider it. It was incredibly corny and unimaginative and if she was honest, she'd have preferred him to have put much more thought into it considering it was the second time round and they were at someone else's wedding, but he was out of his comfort zone, acting on impulse. A man very much in love.

If she'd learned anything at all from this whole trip, then surely it was that she should hashtag speak her truth.

'We need time to get to know each other again. Especially if I'm going to have to tolerate you for the rest of my life.'

Adam gulped, staring up at her. 'But I'm in love with you. I want to marry you.'

Kitty watched a myriad expressions glide over his face, love ballooning from her core.

'Okay, if it means you'll stop talking, I'll think about it. But to be clear, this isn't *the* proposal. You can call it a practice run.'

Relief flooded over his face as he leapt up and swung her round. 'I love that you don't pander to me.'

'OH MY GOD, THEY'RE GETTING MARRIED!!' Wilf bellowed, standing nearby. The commotion seemed to set off a chain of events. Click clack, click clack.

'WHO'S GETTING MARRIED?' Rebecca demanded, her long toes poking from some peep-toed skyscrapers, her spray-on dress and heavy jewellery clanking as she rushed towards them with an equally glamourous Shiraz coming up behind.

Kitty braced herself.

'Why are you here? What's going on? Shiraz are you okay?' Kitty blurted, making a beeline for her, arms outstretched. Kitty scowled at Rebecca. 'Haven't you caused enough upset?'

Shiraz was beaming at Rebecca. Kitty noticed that they were holding hands.

'We're together,' Shiraz said excitedly. 'And... Rebecca has sorted out the social media hoo-hah for us, because not only is she a great dancer but she's a brilliant social media genius and up-and-coming influencer, aren't you, babes?'

The situation felt surreal, yet they seemed genuinely happy so who was Kitty to judge?

'I basically just posted this.' Rebecca flashed her phone at them. Kitty recognised the orgy scene immediately. Maddison was identifying as a lesbian and coming out with some very uncomplimentary terminology.

'He's upset the whole LGBTQ plus community,' she said triumphantly. 'That'll keep him busy and off our backs for a long while. There's no way he'll get the TV Lifestyle Award now.'

Kitty felt pretty sure this was not the way to get the situation under control, but there was no denying they did have the moral upper hand. One glance at Adam's conflicted expression confirmed he felt the same.

'Champagne, anyone?'

They all turned to see Britain's number one TV presenter strolling casually towards them with a tray laden with champagne flutes.

Wilf let out a loud gasp. 'I don't believe it!'

'How are you enjoying my house?' Grant stooped to kiss Kitty on both cheeks. 'Kitty, darling, I hope you didn't invite that wanker O'Reilly. Lives up the road you know. He's an awful pervert.'

Putting the tray down, Grant grasped Adam's hand and shook it vigorously. 'Congratulations, Adam. I'm a huge fan of yours by the way. You're a lucky guy. If it wasn't for Kitty, I'd never have made it this far.'

Kitty blushed. 'We're not engaged. It was only a practice. Everyone, I think you all know Grant Govey, Britain's number one TV presenter.'

'For fuck's sake, Kitty. You've definitely gorra type, haven't you love?' giggled Shiraz, winking at Grant. 'I'm Shiraz. I'm silky and smooth and sometimes a little fruity. And this is Rebecca. We've recently become lovers.'

Grant's eyes popped wide. He didn't seem put off in any way.

'Mr Govey, I'm a huge fan of your work,' gushed Wilf, his eyes out on stalks.

Oh my god. Please don't.

'Well, it looks like we have some celebrating to do! A reality TV wedding, some gorgeous new lesbians, a lovely new fan and an *almost* engagement! And of course, we could include my BAFTA nomination, but I'd hate to steal the limelight.'

Kitty giggled. She felt light, carefree and excited for the future. She raised her glass. 'Congratulations all round. It's officially a wrap. Now let's try and have a night without any drama, shall we?'

Adam pulled her close, staring adoringly at her before he shook his head playfully. 'Famous last words, Kitty. Famous last words.'

The End

Afterword

"Jo Lyons has written a book and it's hilarious!"
Jenny Colgan, The Summer Skies
"Couldn't put it down!"
"I stayed up half the night to finish it."
"So warm-hearted and uplifting. I loved this book so much."
"Best debut I've read in a long time."

If you have enjoyed reading this novel, please leave me a review on Amazon or on your social media. I love to hear your thoughts and it helps new readers discover my books.

Happy Reading!

Acknowledgments

So many writer and reader friends helped me get this book to publication. Huge thanks to all of them. I started writing this novel while on the 'How to Write a Romance Novel' course run by Jenny Colgan. She was brilliant, the course was fantastic and six weeks later I had a first draft completed! I'd like to thank my editor, Nira Begum, for her brilliant support and all the lovely women at CWIP and my fellow waiting-to-be-published long/shortlisters who have been excellent cheerleaders. All at Curtis Brown Creative for their support and encouragement during the many, many writing courses that I have become addicted to. When I started out, I had no idea about three-act structures, POVs or how to save a cat.

Last but not least, my awesome and talented writing tribe and beta readers: Jayne, Jess, Julia, Farrah, Cristal, Amanda, Sid, Wendy, Margie, Liz, Alice, Nicky, Nichelle, Kim, Keith, Claire, Cara, Joanna, John, Wez, Helen, Deb, Genize, Shauna, Mrs B, Mags, Paula, Shelley and my sister Philippa and my lovely aunties who read all the terrible first drafts and encourage me to keep going.

And a special thanks to all my fabulous, funny friends who inspire me with their stories over many a night out. I could not do any of this without them. I have enormous respect for anyone who sets out to write a book and gets to the end without wanting to hurl themselves off the nearest cliff. Be nice to writers – we are ALL in varying states of emotional collapse.

About the Author

Jo Lyons spent years working in Turkey as a holiday rep, in the Alpes at a ski resort, in the south of France at a vineyard trying not to put them out of business before eventually ending up in Spain as a teacher. She thought she'd put her fairly adequate skills of 'getting on with people' to good use, but on her way to The Hague, she became terribly distracted by a DJ and motherhood. Twenty of her best, frozen-foreheaded years flew by before she suddenly remembered her previous ambition for world peace and politics... oh yes, and to write a book.

You can sign up to her newsletter and visit her website at

www.jolyonsauthor.com
Twitter: @J0Lyons
Instagram: @Hinnywhowrites

Benidorm, actually

"Ladies and Gentlemen, we will shortly be arriving in Alicante. Please ensure your big lips and heavy eyebrows are securely fastened, your eyelashes are stowed in the upright position and your leg tattoos are clearly visible for landing."

Connie Cooper's classical music career is at a dead-end. She's singing cheap covers to a sea of bald heads and the nearest she has been to a romantic relationship in years is watching the Bridgerton buttocks scene on a continuous loop.

The last thing she needs is to be on a flight to Benidorm with strict instructions to impress the boss of Jezebel Music. But as she tries to keep up with support band, The Dollz, and the constant flashmob dancing, the going out in less than you'd wear on the beach and their obsession with the promiscuous bearded-Nuns in the villa next door, the boss seems less and less impressed. The clock is ticking. She's meant to be finding her voice, not finding his brooding good-looks irresistibly attractive...

Coming soon...The Coach Trip

Nell Weston is living her second best life; she lost the first one to some prick at work. Workaholic Nell has always thought that an important job title and high-flying career brings success, admiration and plenty of friends. After her sister makes her redundant, and she suspects her boyfriend of cheating, in desperation Nell tells a few white lies to get a new job as a Life Coach in Spain, far away from her meddling sister and controlling mother. But when the handsome stranger at the hippy retreat overhears, he tries to warn her against spinning a web of lies. But will she listen? No, of course not. She's far too angry and bitter to take advice from a tall, beefy, know-it-all with biceps like giant tennis balls... unless she can persuade him to pose as a client and fool her new boss into thinking she's good at her job. The more she avoids facing the truth, the more Nell's new life and new romance begin to unravel...